SEVEN DAYS

A POST-APOCALYPTIC NOVEL

G. MICHAEL HOPF

DOOMSDAY
PRESS

ISBN: 978-1-953462-01-5

Doomsday Press
San Diego, CA

TO SAVANNAH

"TO UNDERSTAND YOUR PARENTS' LOVE, YOU MUST RAISE CHILDREN YOURSELF."
– CHINESE PROVERB

BOOKS BY G. MICHAEL HOPF

DETOUR (Apocalyptic Horror)

<u>SCIENCE FICTION</u>

BINARY (USA Today Bestselling novella)

<u>PARANORMAL NONFICTION</u>

BEYOND THE FRAY: BIGFOOT (with Shannon LeGro)

BEYOND THE FRAY: PARAMALGAMATION (with Shannon LeGro)

<u>CHILDREN'S ILLUSTRATED BOOKS</u>

DOGGIEVILLE

HUDSON WHAT'S YOUR TAIL NUMBER (with Andrew Drykerman)

PROLOGUE

Present Day
Deliverance, Oklahoma

WHEN THE PAIN CAME, it rushed through Evelyn's body like an electrical surge, causing her muscles to tense and become rigid. She cried out; bloody tears streamed down her face. Glancing at Reid, her husband, she begged, "Promise me."

Holding her hand tightly, the rubber gloves of his protective suit creating a barrier to the physical touch he desired, Reid asked, "What? What can I promise you?" Seeing her like this was almost too much to bear. However, if there ever was a time for him to be strong and show it, it was now. Evelyn had been going in and out of consciousness, and when awake, she often mumbled or spoke incoherently.

"Hannah," Evelyn wailed as another surge of pain spread through her body.

1

"What about Hannah?" Reid inquired, trying his hardest to mask his emotions.

Through gritted teeth and with considerable effort, Evelyn managed to say, "Protect her."

"Of course, I'll do anything…"

Drawing him close with a surprising strength, she reiterated, "Do anything. Do you hear me?"

He stared into her blood-soaked eyes, a chilling symptom of the H5N7 virus—or the dog flu, as it was commonly known due to its origin in canines.

The dog flu had first appeared nine months prior in Mexico and spread across the globe rapidly. Initially resembling the swine flu, it soon proved more lethal to its hosts, killing eighty-seven percent of those infected within a week of showing the first signs. The severity of the virus initially brought world powers together. However, this cooperation soon evaporated, leading to a war breaking out between China and the United States. Dealing with the virus was already a challenge; now, a world war sent a chaotic world spiraling further into turmoil.

Reid wanted nothing more than to touch her skin and embrace her, but the protective suit he wore created a thick barrier. Evelyn fell back onto the bed, eyes rolling into her head, body beginning to shudder.

"Evelyn?" Reid called out. With horror, he watched as her shuddering turned into violent convulsions. "Help, please, someone help me!" he cried, but the infirmary remained silent. "Someone, please!" Her hand in his went limp. He looked back to find her lying peacefully, the subtle rise and fall of her chest the only indication she was still alive. "Eve?"

A woman in a soiled white protective suit, bearing the Red Cross emblem, entered the room. "Mr. Flynn, it's time."

"No, I was just talking to her," he replied, voice cracking with emotion.

Two men, also in protective suits, appeared in the doorway with a gurney.

"I'm sorry, Mr. Flynn, but you know the rules. It's time to take her away," the nurse said firmly.

"Please, maybe she'll wake up. I just want a bit more time with her," Reid begged.

Approaching him, the nurse responded, "You know the rules. This is what's best for her—and for everyone in Deliverance."

Without acknowledging Reid, the men positioned themselves at the head and foot of the bed.

"You can take her," the nurse ordered.

Gently, they transferred Evelyn's limp body onto the gurney and wheeled her out of the room.

"What will happen now?" Reid asked, choked with grief.

"She will be taken below. First, we'll administer a sedative, then—"

Interrupting her, he said, "I don't need the details, just tell me it will be humane."

"I assure you, she won't feel any more pain," the nurse said. "Excuse me, I have other patients to attend to."

"But are you sure she won't recover? I did," he said,

reminding her that he too had contracted the dog flu and lived.

"Mr. Flynn, your symptoms never progressed this far," the nurse replied.

"When can I retrieve her remains?" he asked.

"Tomorrow, late in the day. We're backed up right now," she replied, leaving Reid with haunting images of stacked bodies waiting to be processed. "Can I go now?" he asked.

"Of course. You know the procedures for decontamination. Please adhere to them strictly," she instructed before leaving the room. Before she left completely, she turned back and added, "Mr. Flynn, consider yourself lucky— you're immune."

He thought of snapping at her but decided to remain professional. How could anyone think he was fortunate at this moment? He'd just lost his wife, the mother of his only child. What kind of future awaited Hannah in this world, especially now without her mother?

Reid walked down the chaotic hallway of the infirmary towards the decontamination room, where he underwent the rigorous cleansing process. Emerging on the other side, wet and naked but clean and virus-free, he dressed and exited the facility to find the midday sun high in the sky.

Looking up, he found it odd that on any other day he'd appreciate the beauty of the cloudless blue sky, but today, words of beauty seemed impossible to muster. With heavy steps, he walked down the street towards the daycare center where his six-month-old daughter, Hannah, was. Passing a café, he caught a glimpse of patrons huddled around a television. Intrigued, he stepped inside to see what had captivated their attention.

A frantic reporter on the screen was announcing:

"...Washington, D.C., and New York have been struck. We're not receiving word about other cities, but we can confirm—"

Then, the screen went black.

"What happened?" a woman screamed in fear.

Reid didn't need to see more; he understood the gravity of what had just transpired. Turning on his heel, he walked out of the café, feeling the weight of not only personal but global loss. He quickened his pace down the street, passing distraught townspeople now receiving the word of the calamity unfolding in the East.

Reaching the daycare, he entered the lobby, pausing at a locked glass door. Usually, a smiling attendant behind a glass window would buzz him in, but today, no one was at the post. The staff was gathered in the office, anxiously trying to find another television signal. Tapping on the glass window, Reid announced, "I'm here to get Hannah."

A young woman with tears streaming down her face turned towards him and pressed a button. A buzzer sounded, releasing the magnetic lock on the door. Reid opened it and immediately the sounds of crying children filled the air. He made his way to the infants' room and looked inside, expecting to see the attendant but finding no one. "Hello?" he called, stepping into the room. Seven bassinets stood along the far wall. Reid walked over to

Hannah's bassinet and found her sleeping peacefully, seemingly oblivious to the pain and chaos around her.

He picked her up and cradled her in his arms. "How's my baby girl?" he whispered softly.

Hannah cooed and squirmed in response. "Daddy loves you," he said softly.

Opening her blue eyes, she looked at him and reached out to touch his chin with her tiny hand.

"How's my little girl today, huh? I just saw Mama, and she loves you very much," Reid told her.

Hannah opened her mouth and let out a squeal of excitement, followed by more cooing.

"That's right, your mama loves you and will miss you terribly," he said, tears welling up in his eyes.

"Mama," Hannah uttered, saying her first word.

Reid's mouth dropped open in shock. Tears streamed down his cheeks.

"Mama," she said again.

"I love you so much, Hannah. I'll keep you safe, I promise. Nothing bad is going to happen to you, understand?" Reid whispered to her.

Hannah simply stared at him in response.

"Now, let's take you home," Reid said, determination filling his voice.

CHAPTER 1

Nine Years Later
Deliverance, Oklahoma

THE MAN APPROACHED THE GATE, his arms held above his head with palms out. Upon seeing the walls of the town in the distance, he thought it was a mirage at first, but as he drew closer, his hopes grew as high as his arms now were. "Help me, please!" he cried out to the guard posted in the tower, an AR-platform rifle in his hands. "I mean no harm. I'm looking for food."

"Turn around. We don't offer quarter here," the guard ordered, his right eye peering through the red dot sight.

"Please, I need help. My wife, she's back that way, about a day's walk. I ran out of food. Please spare some and I'll go away," the man begged.

The guard, a middle-aged man by the name of Ed, hadn't encountered a wanderer in many months, but something about this man told him he wasn't lying. "What do you offer in exchange for the food?"

The man removed his backpack, opened it, and began to rummage. "Um, I have… let's see, I can give you—"

"I don't need anything from your pack, old man," Ed said.

"Oh, um, I can offer you… ah, I have information if you want, news of the world and what's happening," the man said.

"What sort of information?" Ed shouted down from his perch.

The man fumbled through his tattered jacket and produced a folded envelope, its edges worn and frayed. "I've been collecting information and taking notes since I left Bend, Oregon, six years ago. I can offer news of what's happening. You must want to know," he cried out, waving the envelope with his hands.

Ed was curious about what was happening in the outside world, as were most of the townspeople in Deliverance. They were safe, secure, but ignorant of anything outside their walls minus rumors, and for good reason: no one was ever allowed to enter, and the few who left never returned. But who would change those strict rules? They were thriving, and no one wanted to be blamed for introducing the one thing or person who could destroy their peaceful hamlet.

Before the Great Plague and the war that followed, Deliverance had been an ordinary small town, like many in the Midwest. A single main street ran through the center of town, with blinking lights at either end warning travelers to slow down. Small retail shops, bars, restaurants, and cafés populated the street frontage, with colorful signs and American flags posted along the streetlight posts. There was always some debate concerning why Deliverance had fared so well. Some said it was its size. It was small enough to wall off and manage access, and they'd be correct. Walling off a smaller town didn't require a tremendous amount of resources, but that alone wasn't the reason, as many towns similar to Deliverance had failed and collapsed. No, the real reason for its success was due to one man and the culture of survival he created, and his name was Darren Kincaid.

Kincaid had been the mayor of Deliverance at the time the Great Plague began to spread. He saw the potential for societal collapse and took it upon himself to move aggressively to shield the town from the outside world. At first, he encountered some resistance from those who thought his approach was too much. Those voices soon faded after the bombs dropped. Now, nine years since the last piece of the wall went into place, many in town were thankful for Kincaid and his vision.

The wall, though, was only the first step in Kincaid's plan for survival. He quickly assembled the town into zones and gave every able-bodied person a job. From security, healthcare, education, infrastructure, to food— everyone was given a task. It took some time for people to adjust, but soon everyone did their part and the town thrived. Even after the bombs were dropped and the threat of radioactive contamination spread, Kincaid had a plan. There wasn't anything he didn't think through and prepare the town to handle. It was as if he was built for the job.

While life behind the walls was safe, it was strict. Kincaid, with the help of the city council, implemented tough rules and laws, with the toughest and most enforced being access and how any infected would be handled. While some might describe his rules as mean, they were able to do so because he provided them the blanket of security from which to complain. He ignored those few and enforced his rules and laws with effectiveness and fairness.

Travelers who came to their walls at first told of a world destroyed and unrecognizable from its previous incarnation. The major cities on the coasts had been decimated by nuclear weapons, with the interior cities and states suffering rampant starvation, civil unrest, and disease—not to mention the virus that started it all was still around.

The mayor sanctioned reconnaissance patrols to go out at first, but none ever returned. The last patrol had departed the gates four years ago; they were never seen again.

As more months and years ticked away, fewer and fewer travelers came to the gates requesting aid. The last group before the man now standing in front of Ed had been six months before. Like the others, they had been refused entry for fear of them being carriers or, worse, infected with the dog flu. The town of Deliverance wasn't without mercy though; in exchange for any information, which they were hungry for, they'd give food and fresh water.

What the last group six months before had told them struck fear in the hearts and minds of the people of Deliverance. They told tales of wandering bands of cannibals to the east and warlords to the west. They mentioned only small pockets of survivors, like Deliverance, who also refused access to protect what limited resources they had. One man in the last group told of an island off the coast of California where the government had developed a cure for the virus and had begun to rebuild. When pressed, he said he hadn't seen it, but had heard rumors of its existence. The people of Deliverance found hope in that rumor but quickly dismissed it, with the mayor refusing to send anyone to find it.

"You're willing to give us your notes in exchange for food and water?" Ed asked.

"Yes and no, is it possible for you to copy it? Giving it away leaves me with nothing of value," the man replied.

Ed lowered his rifle, keyed a radio handset fastened to the top of his buttoned shirt, and said, "Base, this is gate two. I have a traveler; he has information that might be useful. Request assistance in accordance with protocol three." Protocol three covered the rules for access, including giving aid in exchange for valuable information.

"This is base; we copy. We'll send a team to perform protocol three," the dispatch replied.

———

THE MIDDAY SUN felt good on Reid's skin. He'd been awake since dawn, working in the garden, and for good reason: with winter coming in a short few months, he knew the importance of having enough food for those long, cold, and dreary months ahead.

He dug his hand into the freshly tilled dirt and came out with a long, squiggly worm on his finger. He sat back and admired the creature and the benefits it provided. With care, he dug a small hole, set the worm down, and covered it. Life was something to be appreciated. No one in the small community of Deliverance took it for granted, especially those who had lived through the Great Plague and the war that followed.

"Dad, tell me again about the ocean," asked Hannah, now nine years old.

He removed his hat, wiped his brow, and took notice of the fast-moving clouds above him. He hadn't heard her question; his thoughts focused on the beauty surrounding them.

"Hello, Earth to Dad," Hannah quipped as she pulled weeds from around the green bean plants.

"Oh, sorry, I was just admiring the picture-perfect sky," he said. "Did you ask a question?"

"The ocean, tell me about it," Hannah said.

"The Pacific Ocean, the only one I've been to, is immense. It's the largest ocean in the world. When you sit on the beach, the ocean roars as the waves come crashing in. The air around smells salty, like brine. Seagulls soar above, many coasting on the ocean breezes. When you look out, you can see nothing for as far as the eye can see."

"Is it like looking out on the plains to the north, but it's just water instead?" she asked.

"Sort of," he replied. "You've seen the pictures in books."

"I know, but I like hearing you talk about it...it reminds me of when you and Mom met."

"Ah, yes, your mother and I," he said, smiling. His thoughts transported him back to a time and place long gone. "On our first date, we walked on the beach in Del Mar. We watched the sunset; it was so nice."

"How did you meet?" she asked, even though she had already been told the story numerous times.

"I've told you this story a thousand times," he said, giving her a smirk.

She wiped her hands on her jeans and sat back on her heels. "I like hearing it."

"If you want," he said.

"I feel closer to Mom when I hear it," she said.

That was all Reid needed to hear. "We met at a bookstore. I was there to find a gift for a friend. I literally bumped into her in an aisle. We instantly began talking, and it led from there."

"What book were you looking for?" Hannah asked, a question she'd never asked before.

Reid searched his thoughts and said, "I picked up a classic by Michael Crichton. It was called Eaters of the Dead."

"Is it a good book?" she asked, genuinely curious, her blue eyes staring at him with anticipation.

"It is a good book. I haven't read it in a long time, but I recall enjoying it," Reid answered.

"Hmm, I'll ask Ms. Pettigrew at the library if they have a copy," Hannah said, putting her gloves back on and beginning to pull weeds again.

"Your mom and I talked so much in the aisle that we took our conversation to a café nearby and then to a restaurant on the beach. Afterwards, we walked and watched the sunset," Reid said.

"Sounds like a fairy tale," she mused.

He gazed at her small frame. Her dirty-blond hair and doe eyes reminded him so much of Evelyn. She was her mother's daughter for sure, although Evelyn's hair had been a light brown. What she did have was his striking jaw; yes, it wasn't a trait you'd normally want for a girl, but it did fit her face and gave her a unique and beautiful look. "It was a fairy tale."

Hannah sat up and wiped the sweat from her face with a rag, then smiled. "Sounds wonderful. I want to see the ocean one day."

"One day you just might," Reid said, although he doubted that would ever occur.

"I hope so. I'm jealous that so many people got to experience all these wonderful things and I didn't," Hannah groaned.

He glanced in her direction and frowned. He felt for her situation. She had never known life outside the walls of Deliverance. And though he sometimes desired for her to see more, he knew that the world he wanted to show her was gone, replaced by a harsh landscape of death and disease. It was easy to forget how lucky they were living behind the twenty-foot walls made mostly of corrugated sheet metal and dotted with watchtowers every few hundred feet. They didn't know the realities of the world, leaving some to take their life for granted and complain.

Then a wanderer would appear at the gates and remind them of how fortunate everyone was inside Deliverance.

"Did you hear they're airing a movie tonight in the park?" Hannah asked.

Reid shook off his dark thoughts and replied, "No, I hadn't heard." He marveled at Hannah's vocabulary and manner of speaking. If he didn't know her and only heard her voice, he'd assume she was six years older. He chalked that up to the education she received at school. Even with the responsibilities every person had in town, a classical education, such as reading, writing, math and science, was taught to the children. This was on top of the practical skills they learned, from agriculture, mechanics, and animal husbandry to advanced first aid and even self-defense.

"They're showing a movie called Shrek; it's animated, Ms. Brown says it's a funny movie for all ages," Hannah said.

"I've seen it, and she's right," Reid said, recalling the first time he'd seen the movie.

"I'm excited. Can we make cookies to share?" Hannah asked.

Reid reached for a tool and felt a muscle tug in his lower back. He grunted and said, "I don't know how, but I tweaked my back."

"You should stretch more. Ms. Brown tells us that flexibility is key; we not only need mindset and fitness, but flexibility is a key element to survival," Hannah said, repeating a lesson she'd recently learned.

He rubbed the spot and said, "Ms. Brown is right."

"Dad, what did you do before?" Hannah asked.

"I told you."

"Can you tell me again?"

He chuckled and said, "You, my sweet girl, are full of endless questions. How about we just pull these weeds and get the garden looking good?"

Hannah shook her head and said, "You know I like to talk. You said I got that from Mom."

"You did, and I normally enjoy our chats and all your questions, but at the moment I just want to think."

A look of concern spread across her face. "Is something wrong?"

"Nothing, now please put your focus on the garden," he stressed.

"Okay." She sighed.

A tall man approached, his shadow casting long. He removed a ball cap, scratched the bald spot on his head, and said, "Reid Flynn?"

Reid looked over his shoulder. He'd seen the man before but couldn't say he knew him. In fact, he didn't even know his name. It was an odd thing to live in the same town for nine-plus years without ever leaving and still not know everyone. "Yeah."

"My name is Lance. Dr. Stone sent me. She is requesting to see you later today. She's currently in a meeting, but sometime around five would be perfect for her," the man said.

Hearing that Dr. Stone wanted to see him, he suddenly realized where he'd seen the man before, and that was alongside Kincaid and the other council members. His name was Lance Weld, and he worked for the council. "What's this about?"

"She'll explain that to you in person," Weld replied.

Reid gave Hannah a funny look and said, "Will you be okay finishing up here alone? I need to get cleaned up."

"I'll be fine, but when I get done, can I go play with Allister and Olivia?"

"Sure, just be back by dark, and don't go near the fence or the culverts," he warned. The culverts he referenced had been placed a short time after the walls were erected. When the first heavy rain came, it was discovered that the town needed additional drainage. Besides their obvious use, the culverts became an area for children to gather and play. Reid didn't like the area and forbade Hannah from going there. The ends of the culverts were grated off with rebar, preventing anyone from climbing through, yet Reid didn't like them and considered it an unsafe place.

"I promise we won't go there," Hannah said.

"Good, then go play with your friends. I'll see you for dinner later," he said, getting to his feet and wiping off his hands. "Mr. Weld, tell Dr. Stone I'll be there."

Weld looked at his watch and said, "Very good and, Mr. Flynn, please don't be late."

Reid turned to go into his house, stopped and asked, "You can't tell me anything about what I'm being summoned for?"

"I can tell you this, if it wasn't important, she wouldn't ask to see you," Weld replied.

KINCAID SKIMMED through a copy of the man's journal. "What am I looking at?" he asked Kaitlyn Stone, a member of the city council and a molecular physicist by trade.

Kaitlyn Stone stood at the end of the long rectangular table, her lean arms folded. Her dark brown hair was pulled back in a ponytail, with the end draping over her left shoulder. Her tall slender frame made it difficult to dress given the limited supply of women's clothes in her size. She pointed to the sketches the traveler had made and said, "These are what I have found interesting."

Kincaid held the sketches and looked at them intently. "It looks like a shoreline, a beach. I don't understand."

Kaitlyn leaned close and said, "There, that's a helicopter."

"Yeah, so what?" Kincaid said.

"Look at the date. It's from five years ago," Kaitlyn said.

"I still don't get the significance. The man sketches well; it almost looks like a picture. He's a talent, that's for sure," Kincaid said, looking up from the sketch at Kaitlyn then to the other council members gathered in the conference room.

"That's military. That tells us they were operational five years ago, and it ties in with the report we got from the last group about a government facility on an island off of California," Kaitlyn said.

"And you're sure this is California?" Kincaid asked, his eyes carefully scanning the sketch.

"According to the man, he said he saw the helicopter in the air heading east, and he was on the coast next to Camp Pendleton, a Marine Corps base," Kaitlyn said.

"So what? There could have been Marines or other military operational then; doesn't say anything about there being a government facility where they developed a cure or that the government is up and running this day," Kincaid said. He put down the material and leaned back in his chair, the metal squeaking under his weight. Kincaid was a large man. He towered over six feet three inches and had a lean muscular build, which he kept fit by daily exercise. He folded his arms and said, "Dr. Stone, the last time we heard these rumors, the people of Deliverance thought there was hope that they'd be saved or that the old world would come back; it won't. Why do people, after nine years, still grasp for some glimmer of yesterday? That world is gone, vaporized by the nuclear warheads or wiped out from the dog flu. Whoever made it past that is trying to do what we're doing, survive."

"I say we send a reconnaissance patrol to the California coast," Kaitlyn said, walking to a whiteboard mounted on the wall. She took a marker in her hands and hastily drew the southern California coast. "Before I came in here, I found a map. There are islands off the coast. They're called the Channel Islands. Many of you have heard of Catalina Island; it's a tourist destination, or was. There are other major islands that could be suitable for a government facility, and before the war, two were used as military training sites. Those were San Clemente Island and San Nicholas Island. Those are viable locations, and we should go find out if that rumor is true."

The room erupted in crosstalk as everyone began to openly challenge or agree with Kaitlyn's proposal and theory.

"Everyone, please quiet down," Kincaid said, waving his arms.

The room grew quiet, with Kaitlyn standing silent in front of the whiteboard, her arms folded again.

"Why?" Kincaid asked.

"Why should we go?" she replied with her own question.

"Exactly. Why? We're doing well here. Because of all our hard work and the cooperation of the people of Deliverance, we aren't just making it, we're flourishing."

Kaitlyn furrowed her brow and replied, "Because we should see what's going on out there. See if—"

"See if what? We know the world is shit, that many have died, and that the government or help isn't coming, ever. And what exactly would they help us with? We have everything we need. We have food, water, safety, and energy, thanks to Joe," Kincaid said, giving a nod to Joe Donaldson, who was sitting across from him and was also a member of the council.

"But—" Kaitlyn said before she was interrupted by Kincaid again.

"But what? Why? We've sent numerous recon patrols over the years. None have returned, not one, and what did we gain? Nothing. What did we lose? A lot. We lost good men for nothing. We used the last of our good fuel back then, and even if we used the degraded fuel we have now, we don't have that many vehicles that will operate well on it. It's not like we have an endless motor pool of pre-1974 vehicles. You and I both know that old gas won't run any of the modern vehicles lying around. Hell, even when we got them started, and that was tough, they ran poorly and stopped. All they're good for now is to be looked upon as monuments to the past. And is the person going on patrol going to clean the carburetors each time he fuels up? So if we don't let them use one of our older trucks, how would this patrol even get there? On foot?" He cleared his throat and continued, "Those earlier patrols proved one thing to me, and that was that the world is probably worse than we imagine."

"Mayor, we need to try. If there's a cure, we should go get it," Kaitlyn said.

"We haven't had a case of the dog flu in eight years. Our protocols have worked, and the only way we risk bringing a case of the flu inside these gates is by letting people in or by having our people leave and return. Why go look for something we don't need? And tell me, who would we send?"

"I have someone in mind who has been to those islands," she replied. "I'm meeting with him later today. But let's all be honest here, we've had many people up until recently who have showed up at the gates sick or talked about the virus still being around."

"But if we keep our protocols, we should be fine," Kincaid shot back. "By the way, who is this man?"

"I'd rather not say just yet," Kaitlyn replied.

"Fair enough," Kincaid said. "Let me say, though, that I believe this is foolhardy and could be inviting trouble more than helping us. You'll need to give me a truly compelling reason besides finding a mystical cure for the dog flu."

Frustrated, Kaitlyn opened her mouth to rebut Kincaid but decided against it.

Seeing that she had something to say, Kincaid said, "Go ahead, Dr. Stone. Please tell us what's on your mind."

"Mayor, I understand what you're saying, but we should at least try. What if there is a cure? What if parts of our infrastructure have been reestablished? And just because we haven't had a case doesn't mean one won't occur. For all we know, it might have mutated, and birds could carry it."

"Birds?" Kincaid laughed. "Listen, I'm not laughing that it might not one day mutate, but if it did, whatever cure is out there probably won't do a thing against the mutated version. I was elected then reelected by the good people of Deliverance because I have kept them safe. We need to also think of what happens if our recon patrol encounters people who don't know we exist. What if, after finding out we're here, they come and try to take what we have? Have you ever considered that?"

She shook her head.

Several others in the room blurted out, "He's right," and others commented, agreeing with Kincaid.

"Dr. Stone, don't get me wrong, I would love to know what's happening out there. It's why we created protocol three, but I don't want to send any more patrols and risk their lives or ours if they result in others finding out we exist," Kincaid said.

"Can you at least consider it?" Kaitlyn asked.

Kincaid relaxed further into his chair and rubbed his chin. He thought more about the potential of having a cure on hand just in case something were to happen in Deliverance. "I'll tell you what, Dr. Stone, if you can provide more information that proves making the trip would be worth it, I'll give it serious consideration, but I won't make any promises."

"I'll take that," Kaitlyn said.

Vince Pardo, a council member and the town's mortician, said, "What else did the traveler's journal say? We've been talking about that sketch but nothing else."

Kaitlyn frowned and said, "Ruins, death, disease, starvation, and cannibals—everything we've heard before."

"Cannibals? Do you really believe people would resort to such things even after all these years?" Vince asked, his face showing his disgust for such an act.

"People are capable of all sorts of despicable acts when separated from morality," Kincaid replied.

"I can understand a person or two being desperate, but roving bands of them purposely hunting fellow humans?" Vince asked. He wanted confirmation for himself that such an idea was not merely a rumor without validation.

"Well, Vince, I don't know that answer, but his journal does reference them to the west, and we've heard about them to the east, so we have to assume that, yes, people have resorted to their baser selves," Kincaid answered. "And that's why I'm skeptical about allowing another recon patrol to leave."

"Vile, to think people would conduct themselves that way as a way of life," Vince groaned.

Outskirts of Dalhart, Texas

The first thing that hit Brienne's senses was the stench. She fully opened her eyes to find she had been taken, something she'd tried her hardest to prevent.

In the dimly lit space she saw others, many of whom huddled by themselves in the corner farthest away from the door.

She stretched the neck of her shirt so it covered her nose, giving her a slight reprieve from the odor, which she now identified as feces, urine and rotting flesh. Gathering her wits, she scanned the space, to find the only access in and out of the room was through the door. She touched the wall to find it was made of sheet metal framed with large steel columns all bolted together. Slivers of daylight slithered through slim cracks in the door frame and along the seams of the siding. This told her two things: one, it was daytime, and two, the building was a stand-alone structure. If she could exit it, she had a chance of escaping.

Looking to the people huddled in the far corner, she asked, "Where are we?"

Her fellow prisoners, their skin gaunt and eyes sunken, gazed at her but didn't reply.

She got up and walked towards them. She tried to avoid the piles of feces that covered much of the concrete floor, but found it impossible. Stopping a few feet away, she asked, "Where are we?"

Still no one answered.

She saw a child, who she estimated was no more than ten. She knelt and asked, "Can you tell me where we are?"

The child, a boy, naked and boney, pulled his legs close

to his chest and shook his head. He looked away from her and tucked his face into his knees.

She reached out to him but was stopped when a woman spat on her. "Leave the boy alone!"

"So you do talk," she said, wiping the spit from her arm. "Where are we?"

"In hell," the woman replied.

Still holding her shirt over her nose, she quipped, "That's obvious, but where specifically?"

"I don't know. We were taken a while ago outside Woodruff. I told my damn fool husband not to travel the old freeways, but he insisted," the woman growled.

Brienne stared at the woman. Her greasy hair hung long and heavy on her bare shoulders. Her soiled skin was covered in sores and bruises. "Why is everyone naked?"

"Don't you worry, they'll soon come to strip you. They do it when he rapes you," the woman said.

Another woman, whose condition was similar, grabbed the other woman's arm and shook her head. "Ssh."

Curious, Brienne asked, "Who is he?"

"I've said enough. They'll be here soon to take you or…"

"Or who?" Brienne asked.

"The boy, they'll take him next," the woman said bluntly, knowing the boy could overhear her.

Brienne thought for a moment, looked around the space, and as she became aware of who was holding them, her expression shifted from concern to terror. "They're cannibals, aren't they?"

The woman nodded.

Brienne quickly shifted her mindset into survival. It was that coupled with her perseverance that had kept her alive all these years so far. She stood tall and looked for anything she could fashion into a weapon; it didn't matter how small, she needed something and fast. Disregarding the feces, she marched around the space looking. She found the skeletal remains of an earlier victim and spotted the one thing she could use. She knelt down, grabbed a rib and pulled until it snapped off. Holding it in her hand, she admired the jagged edge on the broken end. "This will do."

Heavy footfalls sounded outside the door. She sprinted to the door and planted her back against the wall next to it. She didn't know who or how many were coming through the door, but she knew her only advantage was the element of surprise.

The distinct sound of a key inserting and turning in the lock resonated through the room.

Her heart raced and sweat began to form on her brow. She firmly held the rib and waited.

The door opened and with it came the bright light of day. In walked a man, his clothes tattered and soiled, a bolt-action rifle slung over his shoulder. The man looked around the room but didn't see Brienne. "Where's the new girl?" he asked the huddled group.

The woman Brienne had been talking to raised her scrawny arm and pointed directly at Brienne.

The man shrugged and said, "Why are you pointing at—"

Before he could get the last word out, Brienne sprang on

him. She thrust the rib into the side of his neck, pulled it out, and quickly slammed it in again.

He gasped and clawed at the two puncture wounds as blood pumped from them.

Seeing she had the advantage, she continued her assault. She pushed him against the open door and came down hard with the rib, this time stabbing him in the chest. She repeated this strike several times.

Weakened from blood loss, the man slid down the door and fell onto the floor. He gagged a couple of times, blood spewing from his mouth, and gasped one last breath of air before dying with his eyes wide open.

Brienne, covered in the man's blood, smiled at her victory over her larger and armed opponent. She removed his rifle and opened the bolt to confirm it was loaded. She turned to leave but paused. Turning back to the others, she waved for them to follow her, but none did. She couldn't understand why some people simply gave up. Were they actually thinking that maybe, just maybe, their lives would be spared? Were they so accustomed to being prisoners that the fear of dying while escaping was more dreadful than being killed then consumed? She'd never understand and gave it only a second's thought.

Outside the building, she soon discovered that she'd have to do more than just kill one guard in order to escape; she'd need to fight her way out past what now seemed to be a small army that was headed her way. She raised the rifle, took aim at the first person she saw coming, and squeezed the trigger.

The thirty-aught-six round struck the man squarely in

the chest and sent him tumbling to the ground. She cycled the bolt, swung the rifle to the next man she spotted, and began to apply pressure, but before she could fire, she was struck in the head by the woman whom she'd just seconds ago offered freedom to.

Brienne felt her legs give out. She fell to the ground and tried to shake off the hit, but the woman wasn't done; she came down a second time. The blow did the job and knocked Brienne out.

Deliverance, Okalahoma

Reid had met Kaitlyn Stone twice before but only in passing. She always seemed busy and unconcerned for anyone she didn't know. Why he was being asked to meet with her came as a bit of a shock. He had never been summoned to talk to anyone in the council before.

Weld had waited for him to get ready and escorted him to her residence. Stopping at the end of a long walkway, Weld said, "Go ahead inside. She's waiting for you."

"Just walk in?" Reid asked.

"Yes, just go in," Weld said.

"Okay," Reid said, walking to the front door. Nervously, he combed his thick black hair with his fingers, straightened his wrinkled clothes as best he could, and entered the house. The smell of lavender greeted him, emanating from a candle located on a small table in the foyer. "Hello," he called out after closing the door behind him.

"I'm in the kitchen, Mr. Flynn," Kaitlyn said.

He stepped farther into the house, the lavender odor

giving way to the aroma of something savory. He navigated through the large house until he found the kitchen. There, he saw Kaitlyn standing in front of the oven with a large serving platter in her mitt-covered hands.

"Do you like eggplant lasagna?" she asked.

"Ah, sure," he said, standing awkwardly in the doorway, staring at her.

"I have to admit it doesn't taste as good with goat cheese, but I've come to enjoy it. It's been so long since I've had cheese made from cow's milk that I've almost forgotten what it tastes like," she said. "I hope you like strawberry vodka. I had them make this specifically. The strawberries are technically infused; they're added during the distilling process, giving it a great strawberry taste, versus having them added afterward."

Finding the entire scene odd, he asked, "Why am I here? I don't know you, yet I'm here, and you're offering me dinner and drinks."

She picked up two glasses, both filled halfway, and walked over to him. She handed him one and said, "This is odd, isn't it?"

He took the glass but instead of taking a drink, he again asked, "Why am I here?"

"I need your help."

"My help, with what?"

She walked back to the island kitchen counter and said, "Today we gathered more information about a potential cure for the dog flu."

"That's good news."

"I understand your wife died from it," she said.

"She did, and I contracted it myself but was fortunate enough not to die."

"You're the lucky ten percent," she quipped.

"I would never consider myself lucky," he fired back.

"Mr. Flynn—"

Interrupting her, he said, "Call me Reid, unless we should be keeping up the pretense of being formal."

She smiled. "And you can call me Kaitlyn." She took a drink and continued, "I believe the government found a cure but, because of the situation on the ground, hasn't distributed it."

"I suppose there really isn't anyone to distribute it to. I hear there's not much left."

"That's not true. In Deliverance alone, there are three hundred and thirteen souls, all worth saving. And if the dog flu managed to get in here, it could cause the deaths of many."

"But there hasn't been a case in years," he said, almost quoting Kincaid word for word.

She sighed and said, "Don't you want to know what's happening out there? Don't you think it's important for us to find other survivors and possibly a cure or vaccine if there is one?"

"I suppose so," he answered. He sniffed the vodka and found it smelled delicious. Curious about the taste, he took a sip. "That's nice."

She smiled. "I have it infused with strawberries."

"It's fantastic, better than the rot gut I normally consume."

"I applaud everything the mayor has done. His vision

helped us survive the turbulent years following the war; however, we cannot continue to think we won't encounter the flu again."

"But the protocols are strict. If someone does have it, we quarantine them right away; we have a way to limit the spread."

"But what if there are other communities? What if we could reestablish commerce? What if the government is up and running, and all we need to do is go find them? There has to be more than just death outside these walls," Kaitlyn declared.

"Have you thought, though, that might be all there really is?"

Seeing that her vision wasn't resonating with him, she said, "I reviewed your file and found you served in the Navy before the war. I also saw that you worked in the special operations command on the West Coast."

"I have a file?"

"Yes, you filled in that information. Don't you recall doing that?"

It had been so long that he had forgotten about Kincaid's requirement early on. "That's right." Now fully confused, he bluntly asked, "What can I help you with?"

"I never imagined I'd find someone, but lo and behold, out of all the people here, you actually have been to the place I believe the cure is located," Kaitlyn said.

"And where's that?"

"San Nicholas and San Clemente Islands."

"You think a cure is on one of those islands?" he asked.

"Yes."

He took another sip of vodka and said, "I have no idea if there's a cure there. I haven't stepped foot on either of those islands in fifteen years. And you need to remember, while it says I was in the special operations command, I was in a support function as a radar tech, nothing more. I wasn't a SEAL or anything high speed, low drag."

"But you know where they are; you know the layout of the islands, correct?"

"It's been a long time," Reid said.

"But you've been to both islands, right?"

"I have, and if I were to venture a guess, I'd say it would have to be San Clemente Island. The Department of Homeland Security did have a scientific operation out there. I recall seeing many Homeland Security people, and they were setting up a secure site on the southwest side of the island away from the DOD's sites," he said. "I can give you somewhat of a layout. I know where the runways were, barracks, etcetera, but I couldn't tell you anything beyond that, if the labs themselves exist on San Clemente Island."

She gritted her teeth and asked, "Would you be willing to drive there and find out?"

He took a step back and said, "Drive there, in what?"

"Let's not discuss the means of transport until you agree," she said. "You're the only person who's been there. You know the islands better than anyone and could verify if I'm correct."

"Wait, hold on, you didn't ask me to come because you want me to draft you a map of the islands; you want me to risk my life. Not one person who has ever left the town has ever returned, no one," he exclaimed.

"We'd equip you with as much firepower and weapons as you would need. We'd even get you a vehicle."

"One of those half-broken-down trucks that we use for the harvest? I bet those things could barely get to forty miles an hour, and most would break down before I even reached the Texas border," Reid mocked.

"I may have something else in mind."

"You're asking me to risk my life, and for what? To confirm a rumor?"

"You would, but you'd be doing it for the greater good, for your daughter's future," Kaitlyn said.

"You don't even know if the disease is even prevalent anymore. You'd risk my life to confirm a rumor about a cure for a disease that may not even exist anymore."

"I need to bring you up to speed, but it's confidential."

"And that is?"

"We've had people come to our gates seeking refuge. One recently had the disease and was asking for a cure. Of course, we turned them away. Others who have come still talk about people catching it and dying. It appears to have gone dormant but is still prevalent and can be caught. This might be why some of our patrols have never returned," she said, clearing her throat. "With you being immune, you wouldn't have to worry about the disease."

"Then you should go," he said bluntly. "You're immune too, aren't you?"

"Actually, I've never had it, hence why I'm concerned."

She set her glass down, picked up the spatula, scooped out a piece of lasagna for him, and put it on a plate. "Are you hungry?"

"I don't feel right eating your food after turning you down."

"It's fine. I'm asking a lot and have nothing to offer you but a vision. I know it's tough for people to want to give up the luxuries of life here for the harshness of what's outside the gates. I'm a fool to think anyone would go," she said, holding up the plate.

He walked up to the island and set his glass down. "I'm sorry. I lost my wife, leaving my daughter with only one parent. If I died, who would take care of her? I can't risk that."

"You're right. Will you forgive me for being pushy?"

"There's nothing to forgive. I too desire to know what the world has become, but that desire is not greater than that of taking care of my daughter."

She scooped herself a piece, dug her fork into it, and took a bite. "Not bad."

"It's really good, thank you," he said. "Tell me, where's Mr. Stone?"

"I don't know. I have to presume he's dead. He was in New York when the bombs dropped. I happened along here while driving from Oklahoma City. The mayor gave me a place to stay, and here I've been since," she explained.

He didn't know her story and impressed that Kincaid wasn't such a hard-ass. He'd forgotten that in the beginning some strangers were allowed to stay. "I'm sorry about your husband."

"Me too," she said, taking another bite. "Keeping busy with the town has helped me though."

"Do you also stay busy cooking?" he quipped, scooping up a forkful of lasagna.

"And that too." She laughed.

The two enjoyed the rest of their food while chatting about life until Reid noticed the time. "I have to go. My daughter is expecting me to be home."

"Want to take some of this home with you?"

"If you don't mind, she'd love it."

She prepared him a plate and said, "It was nice chatting, and please excuse my bullish behavior. I have these ideas and they get stuck in my head."

"I can appreciate your vision, but I have to look out for Hannah. I made her mother a promise, and I intend on keeping it," Reid said. He looked at the plate and continued, "And thank you for the delicious food. I'll be sure to drop off the plate another time."

She walked him to the door and opened it. "I'll see you around, Reid."

"Good night," he said, and exited.

———

REID ARRIVED at his house to find it dark. He turned on several lights and called out, "Hannah, are you here?"

From the back of the house, he heard whimpering.

Fear gripped him. "Hannah, is that you?" he asked as he sped in the direction of the crying. He ended up at her bedroom door and opened it. "Hannah?"

"I'm sorry, Daddy," she cried. She was curled up in a ball on her twin-sized bed. Her room was decorated in everything pink and ponies, with posters of the ocean and beaches on the walls.

Reid immediately went to her bedside and sat. Touching her shoulder, he asked, "Why are you crying?"

"I'm scared," she whimpered.

"Scared? Oh, honey, I know I'm late. I apologize, but I do have some amazing lasagna for you. I think you'll—"

"I got hurt," she blurted out between sobs.

"Hurt, how?" he asked, a look of concern on his face.

"I'm sorry, but I thought it was nice. I'm so sorry," she groaned. Her back was to him, and he couldn't see any part of her.

"What are you talking about, Hannah? What do you mean?"

She craned her head towards him and said, "I'm so sorry. I don't want to die."

"Die? Hannah, tell me this instant what happened," Reid insisted.

She lifted her right arm. On it was a white bandage with spots of blood soaking through.

"What happened? Is it broken?" he asked, examining it closely.

Rolling onto her back, she wiped tears from her eyes and cheeks and replied, "No, it's not broken."

"Did you fall down? Do you need to see a doctor? This skin is broken; I can tell that from the bandage," Reid said as he began to unwrap it.

"I don't want to die, Daddy," she cried, her body trembling.

"You're not going to die, honey, you just hurt your arm.

The hospital has stocks of antibiotics still, and I think we can get you a shot for tetanus if they still have some, which I believe they do," he said in a reassuring tone.

Tears flowed from her eyes. "I'm scared."

"Oh, honey, there's nothing to be..." he said, then paused when he saw the wound with his own eyes. "It's a bite."

"It looked nice. I didn't know. I've never seen—"

"Hannah, did a dog bite you?" he asked, his tone now showing a tinge of anger and fear. Anger because she knew better, and he had drilled into her head to stay away from any strange animal, especially dogs.

"Yes," she whimpered.

"How did a dog come to bite you?" he asked, his voice raised.

"It was hurt, so I—I walked over to it."

"Hurt, how?"

"The dog was doing the funky chicken," she answered.

This was a term he'd taught her. When they wrestled around, and he acted like he was hurt, he'd flop around on the floor. "The dog was doing the funky chicken?"

"Yes, so I walked up to see if I could help. I reached out, and it bit my arm."

"Where's the dog now?"

"I don't know."

"Where did you last see the dog?" he asked, his voice growing louder.

She sobbed and said, "Don't be mad at me."

"I'm disappointed, Hannah. How many times have I told you not to go near any wild or unfamiliar animals, and dogs are completely off-limits. There's not a single dog in Deliverance. Were you playing near the culverts even though I told you not to?"

She nodded.

He gritted his teeth to stop from cursing. "The dog was at the culverts?"

She nodded again.

"Who else knows about this?"

"Allister does."

"What about Olivia?" he asked.

"She wasn't there. She couldn't come out to play," Hannah answered.

Reid went to the medicine cabinet and got his first aid kit. He began to clean the wound and asked, "Who bandaged it up?"

"I did."

"You did a nice job. It looks as if you cleaned it too, smart. Did you use any antibiotic gel?"

Hannah nodded.

He bandaged the wound with fresh gauze and said, "This will work. I have to go look for that dog."

"Am I going to die?" she asked, her small face flush and her eyes red and swollen from crying.

He was unsure if she'd been infected. There hadn't been a case of the dog flu in Deliverance in years, so maybe the dog wasn't a carrier, but he needed to find out and had to do so without anyone else knowing. If the authorities heard that she might be infected, they'd quarantine her, and that was the last thing he wanted, even though he knew it was the right thing to do for the community. "I need you to get some rest. I'll return as soon as I can."

"Daddy, I'm scared," she whimpered.

He went to her side and kissed her forehead. "I promise I'll do anything to keep you safe. Now get some rest. I'll be back shortly."

———

THE CULVERTS WERE TOO small for humans to climb through, but animals had no problem. And as far as the mysterious dog, it had to be the way it got in.

Armed with a flashlight and a knife, Reid began his search. He shot the beam down the mouth of the culvert but found nothing. By now, the dog could be anywhere, but if it was, wouldn't an alarm have been sounded? He imagined it would, but then again, maybe those in charge wouldn't want to worry the town.

He marched along the fence line, his light streaming ahead of him. He knew he risked having a guard challenge him, and if one did, he had created an excuse, though he hadn't mentioned it to Hannah upon leaving.

His mind began to ponder exactly what he'd do if he found the dog. Would he kill it? Or should he attempt to capture it and have his old and dear friend, Thomas McNamara, examine it? Knowing Thomas all these years, he never thought that he might have to call on his expertise as a veterinarian.

A spotlight cast down on Reid from a watchtower fifty yards away. "Who goes there?" the guard asked.

Shielding his eyes, Reid replied, "I'm Reid Flynn. I'm looking for my daughter, Hannah!"

"Approach the tower!" the guard bellowed.

Nervous, Reid did as the guard said.

"How old is your daughter?" the guard asked.

"She's nine."

"Was she playing with anyone?"

"She was," Reid replied.

"Have you talked to them?"

Reid shook his head and said, "You know, I haven't. The culverts were on my way there; I planned on doing so after looking here."

"Best be on your way. If I see her, I'll bring her in. What did you say your name was again?"

"Reid Flynn, I live on Sooner Drive, 531 Sooner Drive," Reid said, giving his actual address as a way to make his story sound believable.

"Do me a favor, once you find your daughter, keep her away from the culverts. It's not safe."

"I've told her that numerous times," Reid said with a smile.

"We're sealing off the area around them."

Hearing this bit of news gave Reid a sense of relief. "That's good news. It's just not safe; anything could crawl through there."

"Something did."

Reid clenched his jaw. He gulped and asked, "Oh yeah? Like what?"

"We found a dog today."

Reid sighed.

"I'll call your daughter in if you want, see if any other post has found her," the guard offered.

"That's okay, I'll just head to her friend's house now. I'm sure she's there," Reid said, wanting nothing more than to move on. He feared the guard might see the worried look on his face and somehow guess that Hannah had been bitten.

"Are you sure?"

"I'm positive, thank you. Have a good night," Reid said and hurried away.

"Good night," the guard said. He turned off the spotlight.

A question popped in Reid's head. "Where did they take the dog?"

"To quarantine, that's all I know; I imagine they'll destroy it soon though. It's kinda sad. I hear it's a cute pup."

"Good night," Reid said and walked off, not giving the guard another look. He hit the street and turned right. His next stop would be Thomas' house. If they had found the dog, it would make sense that Thomas would know about it.

Five Miles West of Logan, New Mexico

Michael hated the smell of his grandmother's bedroom. He dreaded having to take Nana her meals, a chore he had been given by his father and one he'd been doing since she'd gotten sick recently.

He stood outside her door, a tray in his hands. Steam

rose from the freshly cooked oatmeal. He balanced the tray on his hand and knocked.

"Yes, dear," Nana called out in her weakened voice.

"It's Michael with your dinner."

"Come on in," Nana barked.

Michael turned the knob and pushed the door open, instantly hit by the pungent odor, which he'd described to his older brother, Chase, as a cross between mothballs, stale perfume and feces. He quickly went to her bedside and set the tray down. "Hi, Nana."

"Oatmeal again? Can't your mother make anything else?" she groaned.

Michael hovered above the bed, looking down on Nana's frail body. He felt bad that she had to sit in her room, but with her cough growing worse, it was the best place for her to rest.

"Can you please tell your mother to make me something different for breakfast," Nana seethed. She took the bowl and placed it on her lap.

"We ran out of brown sugar," Michael said, knowing her response would be negative.

Nana grunted and tossed the spoon aside. "No brown sugar? What's in it, then, to make it taste good?"

"Mom found some of those artificial sweetener packets and put one in it for you," Michael replied.

"I hate that stuff," Nana complained.

Michael felt bad for her, but when she acted like this, all he wanted to do was tell her to be quiet and be grateful. Food was scarce, and if it hadn't been for his mother, they wouldn't have the fresh vegetables they had. "Can I get you anything else?" he offered.

"Real food," she whined.

He leaned down and adjusted her pillow. "Now, Nana, you know that we don't have a lot of food. This is the best we can do right now." He swore she was getting leaner each day, but couldn't understand why. He'd pick up her plate and she would have eaten the food. Her silver gray hair was thinning badly on top, exposing her scalp.

"Your father should be going out and finding some, then," she hissed.

Fluffing the pillow, Michael replied, "Dad was almost killed last time, don't you remember?"

She furrowed her brow and thought. "He was?"

"Yes, Nana, he was. Now please enjoy your oatmeal. I'll be back later to get the tray," Michael said as he turned away and headed for the door.

"Michael?" she called out.

He stopped at the door and faced her. "Yes."

"How old are you again?"

"Seventeen."

"You're my favorite, I hope you know that," she said. She gave him a wink and smiled.

"I know, you tell me every meal, but thank you."

Nana gazed back at her bowl and seethed, "Damn Chinamen, they caused all this trouble. Now I have to eat oatmeal for breakfast, lunch and dinner."

No longer able to stand the smell, Michael walked out and closed the door behind him. He rushed to the kitchen, picked up a pitcher of water, and poured some into his hand. He splashed it on his face and with a towel dried it.

"What are you doing?" his mother, Tanya, asked.

"Cleaning off the smell," Michael complained.

"Oh, it's not that bad," Tanya said, a knife in her hand. She cut a cucumber and set it on a plate next to her.

"Then you deliver her meals," Michael groaned.

"I do more than that. I bathe her, change the sheets, and empty the pot, so I don't want to hear it from you," Tanya quipped.

Michael stepped up to her and asked, "Is Nana going to die?"

"She just has a bad cough is all. Your Nana is a tough cookie; she'll be fine," Tanya answered. She finished slicing the cucumber and asked, "Grab me another one."

Michael brought her a basket full of cucumbers and set it next to her. "She complained about the oatmeal again."

"Didn't you tell her that was the last of it? I made a big pot and we don't throw good food away around here. Now stop asking me questions and go out to help your father," Tanya said.

"She's getting worse, her memory, I mean," Michael said.

"I know."

"She keeps asking me how old I am. I feel bad for her."

"I do too," Tanya replied. She set the knife down and with her sleeve wiped her face. "It's hot in here." She picked the knife back up and continued to slice.

"It's not hot. You're just having a hot flash," he said. Michael watched her carefully. He often feared losing her.

Each time he allowed the dark thought to enter his mind, he'd get very emotional. She was the bedrock of the family, and even though she stood at just five feet four inches, she was as powerful as any man he knew, regardless of height. He'd noticed the years had been creeping up, as strands of gray were now showing up along the sides of her head, and deep wrinkles were forming along and below her eyes. "If I get like that, just put me down," Michael said.

Tanya stopped cutting and shot him a hard stare. "Don't talk like that. We take care of family regardless of their condition."

"But we know she won't make it for too long. Why do we waste—"

"Michael Everett Long, you stop that kind of talk. Your nana is family. She's your father's mother, and we Longs care for each other. We're not like the rest of the heathens out there. We will take care of her and provide until she passes away."

He looked down sheepishly.

"Go and help your dad," she ordered.

Michael nodded and exited the house into the twilight. The sun had just melted into the horizon, and soon darkness would be upon them. He found his father, Will, and Chase near the west fence line of the farm. "Dad, do you need help?"

Will lifted his head and shot Michael a smile. "All good, we're just finishing up."

Michael walked up and asked, "What are you doing?"

"How was the smell?" Chase laughed.

Michael punched Chase on the arm and said, "Shut up."

Will laid the last branch over a pit and said, "Second-to-last one done." He patted Chase on the back.

Curious, Michael tried to look through the gaps in the branches. "Is there something in the bottom of the pits?"

"Sticks," Chase said.

"Sticks?" Michael asked.

"These pits all along the perimeter will provide a layer of protection. I secured the gate by laying down nail strips in case anyone comes driving down, and if they decide to scale the fence, well, they'll end up in one of these pits and—"

"Be impaled on a stick," Chase said excitedly.

Michael gave Chase a funny look and asked, "You like that, don't you?"

"Of course I do," Chase answered. He smoothed out his long black hair, put his hat back on, and gave Michael a wink. "Maybe instead of playing wet nurse, you could come help us."

"Leave your brother alone. Your mother needs the help, and we're doing what we need out here," Will snapped. "We're a family, a team; each of us have our parts and they're equal."

"It does sound cool," Michael said. "Can I help make one?"

"Sure, maybe I'll get Chase to help Mom," Will said. He gave Michael a wink and tousled his hair. "The idea of the pits sounds gruesome, but we can't take chances. This is something I should've done long ago, but failed to," Will said, his hands wrapped around the handle of the shovel. Will was a short man, only standing around five feet seven, but he had a wide muscular build, which he'd leveraged in his youth as a football player. His skills on the field were good enough that he'd secured a scholarship to the University of New Mexico to play, but in his second season a bad injury ended football for him.

"So we've got pits all around the fence line?" Michael asked as he spun around, looking at the vast perimeter.

"If you ever came outside, you'd know that," Chase teased.

"Leave your brother alone," Will barked at Chase. Turning back to Michael, he asked, "How's Nana?"

"Grumpy as usual," Michael replied.

"Mike says she smells." Chase chuckled.

Michael again punched Chase's arm and said, "I didn't say that."

"Nana smells?" Will asked as he gave Michael a puzzled look.

"Her room does," Michael answered. He shot Chase a hard look. "I never said *she* did."

"Same thing." Chase laughed.

"Boys, Nana isn't doing well, and she's had some issues lately, not just with her cough but the other things," Will explained.

"She keeps forgetting how old I am," Michael said.

"Not that, it's probably why her room smells," Will said, referring to the feces odor. Another issue Nana had been having was with bouts of severe diarrhea. Will believed it was a flare-up of her Crohn's disease. "She's run out of her medicine that helps with that, and I just haven't gone farther to look for it, much less made a second run into town since my incident."

"Gross, can we talk about something else? I don't want to hear about Nana's poop," Chase groaned.

Michael nodded his agreement. "I worry about her."

Will draped his arm over Michael's shoulder and said, "Me too, buddy."

"What's Mom making for dinner?" Chase asked. "I'm starving."

"I saw her cutting up cucumbers, but didn't see anything else," Michael replied.

"God, I hope it's not oatmeal," Chase groaned.

"You sound like Nana," Michael quipped.

"Yeah, but you smell like her," Chase shot back.

Will smacked Chase in the back of the head lightly and barked, "No more jokes about Nana. Show respect."

"Ok, Dad," Chase groveled.

"Run along. Go get cleaned up," Will ordered Chase.

Chase sprinted off towards the house.

"You boys are something else," Will said with a broad smile as he watched Chase race towards the one-story ranch-style farmhouse. "I haven't thanked you for being so attentive to Nana. It means a lot to me and Mom. Poor Nana isn't doing well, and you jumping in to help has really given Mom an opportunity to get her chores done. Running the house now is so much more work than it used to be."

Michael smiled.

"You're a good kid," Will said.

"Thanks, Dad."

"You're different than your brother; you've got a big heart."

"Does that make me weak?"

Will leaned back and gave Michael a concerned look. "Do you think you're weak?"

"No...but Chase has made fun of me because I tend to care more about things."

"You are not weak, you're just different. Meaning you view the world differently. Chase has his talents, and you have yours. We have to rebuild this world, and it needs all sorts of people to do so."

"Do you really think the world will ever get rebuilt?"

"One day, sure. It can't be like it is now forever, that's just impossible. But when will it happen? That I don't know."

"When you go back out, can I go with you?" Michael asked.

"How about we cross that bridge when we need to."

The creak of the screen door echoed across the field. Tanya stepped out, a towel in her hand. "Dinner is ready."

"You didn't see anything being cooked?" Will asked.

"No, just saw her cutting cucumbers."

"Then I suppose it's oatmeal again."

"Are you complaining too?" Michael asked.

"Not complaining, just...let's just say I'm grateful for the food and will be grateful when there's something other than oatmeal too," Will joked. "Now let's get inside and get cleaned up."

The two walked across the field.

Michael's mind wandered as they walked. He'd been a

boy when the world as he knew it ended. Unlike others, they hadn't suffered, and for that he was appreciative, but he often thought that their luck would one day run out.

Outskirts of Dalhart, Texas

The clang of the door shutting jolted Brienne awake. She opened her eyes to find a strange woman standing in the shadows. The dim light from a single low-wattage bulb gave her the ability to just make out some features. She tried to move her arms but found them bound behind her. Her eyes darted around. She wasn't in the steel building like before. Instead they had her somewhere else, and by the looks of it, her new accommodations weren't as bad as the other. "Who are you?" she asked the woman.

"Is it true you came all this way from Europe?" the woman asked.

Brienne furrowed her brow and shifted as best she could in the chair she was bound to.

The woman stepped closer to Brienne and out of the shadows.

With the woman in full view, Brienne noticed she was holding her diary. "I see you don't honor someone's privacy," Brienne snarked.

Holding the book up, the woman asked, "Is it true?"

"I'll answer your question if you answer mine," Brienne said.

The woman thought as she circled Brienne. Stopping back in front of her, she replied, "Deal."

"Yes, I left Germany over eight years ago," Brienne answered. "My turn, where am I?"

"You're being held by my brother in a compound in Woodruff," the woman replied. "Is Europe as bad as the States?"

"It is," Brienne said.

"Where are you going?" the woman asked.

"My turn," Brienne said. She cleared her throat and asked, "What does your brother have planned for me?"

The woman answered, "He plans on raping you first. Then he'll see if he can sell you, and if that doesn't happen, he'll just continue to rape you until he decides you're no good. Then he'll have you killed and you'll be eaten at a feast," the woman said bluntly.

"I forgot, you're cannibals," Brienne said with disgust.

"Is that a question?" the woman asked.

"No, it's a statement," Brienne said. She'd heard about groups of cannibals but had never encountered them in her long journey until now.

"Now answer my question. Where were you going?" the woman asked.

"To find my husband and son," Brienne replied.

"Where specifically?"

"Yuma, they were in Yuma."

"How do you know they're alive?" the woman asked.

"Nope, my question again."

The woman smiled. "Go ahead."

Brienne stared at the woman's pale skin, not a wrinkle appeared on her face. She was either very young or never saw the sun. It was hard to guess how old she was, but she was curious not only about that but about something else. "Why are you here asking me questions?"

"Because I want you to take me with you," the woman replied bluntly.

Stunned by the answer, Brienne asked, "Is this a trick? Huh?"

"No, it's not. I saw how capable you were in handling those guards; plus you've survived on the road for almost nine years. I want to leave, I want to get out of here, and you're the best chance I've had in years."

"Where do you want to go?" Brienne asked.

The woman approached. She opened another book similar to Brienne's diary and said, "There are rumors of other places, safe places. My brother captured someone a few months ago; he said that there's a small town in the Baja Peninsula called Loreto that is still safe, free of the virus, and untouched by the war. It's unscathed. I want to go there. If I let you go, I want you to take me there."

Brienne's first reaction was to laugh at the preposterous idea of a town in Baja being a safe zone, but relented. If the woman was telling the truth about letting her escape, this could be her way out of this place. "Isn't Mexico where the dog flu started?"

"Not in Baja, it started in the deep interior of the main part of Mexico. I've looked at Baja on a map; it's isolated. I suppose I could be wrong, but it sounds hopeful. A small fishing village still thriving."

"There's rumors of a town in Oklahoma like that too. Why not go there?" Brienne asked, referring to Deliverance, which itself had become a rumor that people talked about.

"I've heard solid info about that place more than any town in Mexico."

"I don't believe it."

"But you believe a rumor about some magical place in Mexico?"

"Will you take me with you if I help you escape?" the woman asked urgently. Voices sounded in the hall.

"Is someone coming? Is that your brother?" Brienne asked.

"No, that's just their voices carrying down the hall."

"Why do you want to leave? Done being part of a cannibal colony?" Brienne quipped.

"I have my reasons. Let's just say I've wanted to leave almost since arriving here many years ago," the woman explained.

"You tell me why and I'll consider it," Brienne said with a tone of bravado.

"I think you're confused. You're the one tied up and about to get raped by my brother. I don't think you have any leverage here," the woman declared.

"Fine, I'll take you, but I need to go find my husband and son first." This was a lot to ask of Brienne. She had survived by herself for years and had now become accustomed to traveling solo, but if the woman could set her free, why not agree?

"I can do that," the woman said. "Yuma is on the way to Loreto."

"I have to ask, and don't get me wrong, I want to leave, but exactly how far are we going to get on foot?"

"We have old motorcycles, but we recently got a car."

"You have a vehicle and good gas?" Brienne asked.

"The man my brother captured, he had a car, a newer car."

"What?" Brienne asked, her tone showing her shock. "Where did he say he came from?"

"The license plates on it say he's from here in Texas, and he said he was from Corpus Christi, wherever that is."

"That's in Texas too," Brienne said flippantly. She thought it could make sense; if any of the many refineries were running again in east Texas, someone could be refining oil again.

"I don't know anything else. The man is dead, but the car works," the woman said. "My brother was driving it around the lot outside earlier today."

"He's dead? Let me guess, you ate him," Brienne mocked.

The woman shot Brienne a look that said she wasn't amused by her mocking humor.

"Aren't you going to untie me?" Brienne asked.

"I will, but I need to go arrange everything. It won't take me more than an hour."

"An hour? Do I have an hour?"

"You do. My brother and his friends are drinking. He's nowhere close to coming for you," the woman said. She turned away from Brienne and disappeared into the shadows.

"And if you're wrong?" Brienne asked, her tongue sharp.

"Then I'm wrong and let me apologize now," the woman said, giving Brienne a snappy reply.

"How do I know you're not like your brother or the others? How do I know you won't get desperate when we're on the road, that you won't kill and eat me?" she quipped.

"I'm not like my brother. I've only done what I've done to survive. This life isn't me," she replied.

"What's your name?" Brienne asked.

"Emily," she said, opening the door. More light poured in, as did laughter and other festive sounds.

"Hurry back."

"I will." Emily stepped out and closed the door.

Brienne sighed loudly. If Emily was telling her the truth, then the good luck she'd had over the years hadn't left her just yet.

Deliverance, Oklahoma

Reid rapped his knuckles against the heavy wooden door. Inside he could hear movement. "Open up, c'mon, hurry."

"Who's there?" Thomas asked.

"It's Reid."

Thomas unlocked the door and cracked it just a bit. He peered out and said, "What are you doing here at this hour?"

"Do you know about the dog found today?"

"How do you know about that?" Thomas asked, opening the door a bit wider to show he was wearing a robe.

"Just tell me," Reid insisted.

"Who's at the door?" a female voice asked from the back of the house.

Thomas craned his head back and hollered, "No one. I'll be right back." He looked back to Reid and said, "This isn't a good time."

"What do you know about the dog that was found today?" Reid asked, his face showing the stress of the situation. "I need to know."

Thomas stepped out onto the front step and closed the door behind him. "Why do you need to know?"

"We've known each other for years; I consider you a friend. I haven't asked for anything from you until now," Reid replied.

"You're putting me in a situation, you do know that?" Thomas said, his thin gray hair blowing in the evening breeze.

"Is the dog a carrier?"

"Has someone been bitten?" Thomas asked, as he sensed that was the reason for Reid's unannounced visit.

"Is the dog a carrier?" Reid asked again.

Thomas reached out and touched Reid's shoulder gently. "Easy, my friend. Tell me what happened."

A wave of emotion washed over Reid as he assumed the answer to his question was yes.

"Is it Hannah?" Thomas asked.

"She saw the dog earlier, said it was whimpering. She's a sweet girl; she only meant to take care of the thing. What am I going to do?"

Seeing Reid in pain, Thomas said, "Oh no."

"So the dog was a carrier?"

"Yes."

Tears welled up in Reid's eyes. "What am I going to do? I lost Evelyn; now I'm going to lose Hannah."

"I need you to bring Hannah to the infirmary."

"No!" Reid barked.

"Reid, you can't keep her at home."

"She's staying at home. No one needs to know."

"But you know that's not the law. She needs to be taken in, you know this," Thomas insisted.

Reid gave Thomas a hard look and asked, "Are you my friend or not?"

"Of course I'm your friend, but you must do what's right for her," Thomas said as he reached out again. "And what's right for the town."

Reid rebuffed Thomas' touch and said, "They can't save her, you know that. They'll just watch her die, nothing more; then when it's too much, they'll put her down like she's some rabid animal."

"It's the humane thing to do, not only for her but for Deliverance. I know you love her, I love her, but you can't risk her contaminating anyone else."

Reid wiped his tears off on his shirtsleeve and said, "I won't take her to the infirmary. If she stays with me, she won't risk contaminating anyone else."

Thomas sighed. He didn't know what to say to Reid if he wouldn't listen.

"Have you heard about a cure, a vaccine of some sort? I heard just today of rumors about one back west on an island off the California coast," Reid asked.

Shaking his head, Thomas replied, "I've heard all the

rumors, but no such cure or vaccine exists. Think about it, we'd know by now if the government was up and running; we'd have soldiers stopping by at our gates, not malnourished stragglers."

"So you won't help me?"

"Help you do what, Reid? What exactly are you asking me to do?"

Reid paused as he thought, out of the corner of his eye, he saw the blinds move. He looked and saw it was a woman, no doubt Thomas' guest. "Your friend is at the window."

With a wide-eyed look, Thomas turned around and opened the door. "Don't be a busybody. I'll be back in soon enough."

The woman disappeared from the window.

Thomas closed the door and said, "Sorry about that. We're just limited for time is all."

Reid thought about asking who she was but refrained. "I'll let you get back to your evening." He gave him a frown and turned away.

Thomas again reached out and this time grabbed Reid by the shoulder. "Don't go, not like this."

"What am I supposed to do if you won't help me?" Reid asked, his back to Thomas. He looked down the street, lights from neighboring houses shining out from closed windows.

"There's no cure, Reid. I wish I could tell you there was one. All I can do is give you advice, and that is to take her in to the infirmary," Thomas said. "She'll get good care."

"She'll be prodded, tested, then killed," Reid snapped.

"I don't have to tell you, but she doesn't have long as it is."

"I'm quite aware of how long she has, Thomas. If you'll remember, my wife died from this too," Reid growled, his back still to Thomas.

"I know you're upset, but she'll need comfort, especially when the symptoms get bad, she'll—"

"I know," Reid said, interrupting him.

"I know this is tough, but she only has—"

Finally facing Thomas, Reid said, "Seven days, I know."

———

BACK AT THE HOUSE, Reid found Hannah asleep, her favorite stuffed animal, a calico cat, curled up underneath her arm. He sat on the edge of the bed and stared at her. He couldn't imagine losing her like he had Evelyn. The thought of watching her waste away while he stood around doing nothing wasn't a solution. There weren't many certainties in life, but it all but seemed certain that Hannah would develop the disease. The one thing that wasn't certain was if she'd die. The fatality rate for the dog flu was high, hovering close to ninety percent, and she might even have a better chance, being that he'd survived. But could he risk those odds? Could he gamble knowing she had maybe a ten percent chance?

In life he never thought of random encounters or chance opportunities as happenstance; he looked upon them as signs. Was his meeting earlier with Kaitlyn Stone one of those signs? Was he being given a way to cure Hannah?

Hannah mumbled under her breath and rolled over.

He touched her cheek and marveled at how smooth it was. He tenderly tucked her hair behind her ear and leaned over to kiss her forehead. "I love you, Hannah."

She turned her head and shifted.

Not wanting to wake her, he left her alone and got up. Before he exited her room, he glanced back at her and whispered, "I promised I'd do anything to protect you, and I'll honor that pledge." He closed the door, leaving a crack, and walked to his office.

He rummaged through his bookshelf and desk until he found what he was looking for, a map. He unfolded it and laid it out, smoothing the creases. He found the Oklahoma panhandle and with a highlighter circled Deliverance. With his finger he traced a route to the southern California coast, marked it with the yellow highlighter, and finished by putting a circle over San Clemente Island, the island he suspected housed the facility. He sat back and stared at the map.

The route had to be over a thousand miles. It was a doable drive before the war, and he could easily have made it in less than two days, but that was then. What were the road conditions? What threats would he encounter? Where would he get a vehicle that could make that long a trip? If he got one, he'd have to find detours and stay clear of the cities he knew had been nuked. Time, he thought, was on his side, but he would have to take her with him, there wasn't enough to go and come back.

Traveling outside the gates was against the law, and if he could leave, even a sanctioned trip with Kaitlyn's approval, there was no guarantee he'd be allowed to return. It appeared that if he could leave, his journey would be a one-way trip. But what were his options? As he sat and pondered, he knew there weren't any but to go with her.

He got up from his desk and made for the door. He opened it and almost jumped out of his skin when he saw Thomas standing there. "Shit, man, you scared the hell out of me."

"I was about to knock, but you beat me to it," Thomas said, now clothed in something other than a robe. In his right hand was a large paper sack.

"What do you want?" Reid asked.

"Can I come in?"

"If you're here to convince me to turn her in, then please go," Reid snapped.

"I'm not. I'm here as a friend and here to help."

Reid grunted and stepped aside. "Come on in, but keep it down. Hannah is sleeping."

Thomas entered the house, and by his body language, Reid could tell he was apprehensive. "Did you see me coming, or were you leaving?" Thomas asked.

With the door closed, Reid answered bluntly, "I was leaving."

"I'm not going to ask where, but know that an investigation concerning the dog's presence here is underway. I need to know if anyone was with Hannah."

"She wasn't alone. Her friend Allister saw it."

Thomas sighed. "I was afraid of that."

"I know I don't have much time to figure something out before they come for her."

"I'm shocked they haven't come yet. That must mean the boy hasn't said a word, but I'm sure it's only a matter of when," Thomas groaned.

"Thomas, why are you here? There really isn't much you can do. You answered the question I needed answered, so how can you help me now?"

"You said she has seven days, that's true when the first symptoms appear, but in reality you have longer. There's a short incubation period of about twenty-four to forty-eight hours. So whatever you've got planned, you'd best start working on it."

"You heard about the rumor today, then?" Reid asked.

"I did. The council likes to pretend what they say behind closed doors stays that way, but not an hour after, I heard about the traveler and his journal. Do you really think the government is around and has a cure?"

"How do I know? But as it looks, I don't have much of a choice but to go find out," Reid said.

"I know you made that promise to Evelyn, and we made promises to help each other, so I'm here offering something that you can use on your trip," Thomas said, holding up the sack.

"What is it?"

"Let me show you." Thomas went to the dining room table and set the sack down. He unfolded the top and reached inside. He pulled out several full IV bags. "I figured you'll have to take her with you, so these will come in handy to keep her hydrated if she gets further along." He dove into the bag and came out with two plastic medicine bottles. He shook them and said, "This is ibuprofen, eight hundred milligrams, for pain management and her fever in the beginning and this…this is Roxanol, essentially morphine sulfate, for when the pain becomes too much." He set them on the table. Holding up a small bottle with a dropper, he said, "This is for her eyes. It will soothe them when they get bloody." He pulled out another plastic container and a small glass bottle with a couple of syringes. Holding up the plastic container, he said, "This one here is Artane. It will help with her tremors in the late stages if she gets that far. Let's pray she doesn't. And this one here." He sighed. "Is pentobarbital, it's for…"

"To kill her," Reid said.

"It will be painless, I swear."

"Painless? How would you know? Have you ever injected it?" Reid snarled.

"I know this is tough. I wish I could offer more, but this will help, and I doubt you'll have access to this or much less find it on your journey."

Reid shook his head. "I'm sorry, I'm just filled with emotions right now. I'm angry, sad, confused. This is all great, thank you. How did you come to get this?"

Thomas cocked his head and smiled. "It helps to have friends in high places."

"You're a retired vet," Reid quipped.

"A retired vet who also works in the infirmary. I still understand biology, Mr. Flynn," Thomas joked.

"Today started out so normal, like any other day, and now I'm faced with losing my baby girl. It all seems surreal," Reid said as he turned away from Thomas and began to pace. "Do you suppose she didn't get infected?"

"You said she had been bitten?"

"Yes."

"And the skin was broken?" Thomas asked.

"Correct," Reid said, fully knowing the answer yet was hoping to hear something that told him she wasn't infected.

"In medicine sometimes things can be…I don't want to use the word *miraculous*, but things sometimes don't go as they should. What I can do is draw a sample of her blood and test it, but that could raise some red flags in the lab."

Reid clenched his fist and felt tempted to punch the wall but stopped short for fear he'd wake Hannah. "No, don't do anything. Who am I fooling? She was bitten by a dog that was infected with the virus; of course she has it. I'm just looking for anything that could mean she'll be fine."

"I'm so sorry," Thomas said. He could feel Reid's pain as if it were his own.

"Why is this happening?"

"Life is suffering, at least that's what Nietzsche said."

"You're damn right it is," Reid quipped.

"When do you leave?"

"Soon, I just need a vehicle, and I might know where to get one. Right now my best chance happened to present itself earlier today. That's where I was going when I found you standing at my door."

Thomas walked up to Reid, placed a hand on his shoulder, and said, "Then go. I'll stay here with Hannah in case she wakes."

"You'll do that? Aren't you worried about getting sick?"

"I'll keep my distance, but if she wakes, she'll know she's not alone."

"You'll do this for me?"

"We're friends, aren't we?" Thomas asked as he gave Reid a wink.

Outskirts of Dalhart, Texas

The click of the deadbolt unlocking tore Brienne away from her thoughts. She looked at the door and prayed it was Emily coming back for her.

The door opened and a figure stepped into the room.

Brienne tried to see who it was but could only make out an outline. "Who is that?" she asked, shifting her head around, hoping to grab a glimpse.

The figure stepped closer. By the sound of a hard-soled shoe grinding into the concrete floor, she knew it wasn't Emily.

Brienne gulped and steeled herself for what would happen next.

A man stepped out of the shadows and into full view. He was tall and lean with long black hair that hung down to his shoulders. His eyes were a piercing blue, with dark circles around them. His skin had numerous blemishes and scars from acne. He approached Brienne and stared down at her. In his right hand he held a chunk of meat. He brought it to his mouth and bit off a piece. As he chewed, the bloody juices clung to the stubble on his chin. He offered her a bite and said, "You hungry?"

"Who are you?" she asked, although she suspected she knew who it was.

"My name is Emile," he replied.

Brienne thought it odd that his name was so close to Emily; then she looked at him more closely and could see the resemblance. They looked about the same age too, making Brienne wonder if they could even be twins.

Emile smiled and took another bite. He paced around her chair, his eyes glaring down at her.

She attempted to track his movements, with an anticipation he'd pounce on her at any given moment.

He stopped behind her and leaned down. He inhaled deeply and said, "You smell good."

"I find that hard to believe. I haven't cleaned up in days," she quipped.

He licked his lips, the sound hitting Brienne's ear sending shivers down her spine. "I'm going to have fun with you later."

The temptation to head-butt him came to Brienne, but she quickly brushed it aside. Any attempt to harm him while bound to the chair would only result in whatever he had in mind for her happening sooner.

He got closer; not an inch separated them. "I wonder what you taste like—" he reached his arm around and grabbed her crotch "—down here?"

She flinched. This time she wasn't able to control her instincts. She swung her head but missed as he quickly stepped out of the way.

He laughed loudly. "You're a feisty one, good. I like them like that. Gives me the opportunity to tame them." He tore off another piece of meat and chewed.

She wanted to yell at him, but again knew anything she did now wouldn't result in anything positive for her.

He came back into view and stood in front of her. "Are you sure you don't want a bite?" he asked as he again offered her a bite of the meat.

"No," she replied with a look of disgust on her face.

"It's thigh meat. I've come to find that the thigh meat of a child, say around seven to ten, is very moist. This is a delicacy around here. Are you sure you won't partake?"

"You're vile," she spat, unable to control herself.

"Vile? No, I'm a survivor," Emile answered.

"Survivor? I've survived just like you, without having to eat people. What you're doing is…"

A smile stretched across his face. "Go ahead, tell me again how I'm vile or revolting. I've heard it all, but you know something; I stand here today only because I was able to do what it took for me and my people to survive. This is the world we live in now."

She shook her head.

"They say in the Bible that the meek will inherit the Earth; that's bullshit. I'll inherit the Earth 'cause I'll hunt down and eat the meek," Emile boasted.

Brienne looked at the chunk of flesh in his left hand and suddenly recalled the boy she'd seen earlier and remembered the woman telling her that they'd come for him soon. Putting a face to what Emile held in his hand made her nauseous.

Laughter could be heard in the hallway outside the door.

Emile looked over his shoulder then back to her. "My friends, they're having such a good time. Best I get back to the feast."

Brienne wanted to look away but decided against it. She wasn't going to be intimidated, although she did feel incredibly uneasy around him.

Emile stepped forward and got inches from her face. "I'm so going to enjoy my time with you." He took the flesh in his hand and stuck it under her nose.

She recoiled, but he pushed it closer.

"Smells good, doesn't it? All it needs is a bit of salt, and this might sound odd, but soy sauce helps too." He smiled, showing his blackened teeth, small chunks of flesh stuck in between.

Brienne gagged at the smell.

Emile chuckled, stuffed that last bit of meat into his mouth, and stood straight up. He chewed, smacking his lips as he did, and gave her a big smile. With his mouth full, he said, "I'll see you soon, darlin'." He spun around and exited the room.

When Brienne heard the clank of the deadbolt closing, she sighed. Emile was everything she imagined a cannibal leader would be. Disgusted and fearful of her fate if Emily didn't return, she pressed her eyes closed and did something she rarely did, pray.

Five Miles West of Logan, New Mexico

"Will, this is a bad idea. Please don't go," Tanya said just above a whisper.

"She needs the drugs, and I have to double-check that old pharmacy. I owe it to her," Will replied.

"But what about what happened last time?"

"I've got Chase with me this time. He's got the rifle."

"And I know how to use it," Chase said with a cocky attitude.

Hearing the voices from the living room, Michael opened his bedroom door and peered into the darkened hallway. The only light was the flickering of a candle coming from the living room as well as a sliver of light pouring out from Nana's door being cracked open slightly.

"I'll return as soon as I've found it," Will said, urgency in his voice.

Curious, Michael stepped out and walked towards the voices. As he passed Nana's room, he could hear her moaning. He stopped and peered in the crack in the doorway to find Nana in the bed, the sheets soiled with what looked like blood and feces. He recoiled from the sight.

"I have a bad feeling about this," Tanya said.

"We'll be fine. We should return in half a day, tops," Will said. He opened the front door, a door rarely used. Chase exited with Will just behind him.

"Hurry back," Tanya said.

Will stopped on the porch, turned and said, "Tell Michael he's in charge of security."

"Love you," Tanya said.

"Love you too," Will said. He turned back and disappeared into the darkness of the late evening.

Michael crept back to his room. As he was about to step inside, an arm reached out and touched his shoulder. He jumped and turned to see his mother there.

"What are you doing?" she asked.

"I heard a commotion. Is everything alright?" he asked.

Tanya pushed him inside his room, closed the door, and asked, "Do you want to help me?"

"Yes," Michael chirped, as he expected his mother to tell him to steel himself, for he was the one who would now protect the women.

"Then go outside. On the line are fresh sheets and towels; go get them. When you're done with that, go get me that plastic bin, fill it with water, and add a drop of soap. Bring it to the room."

His heart melted when he heard he was being tasked with more housework. "What's going on?"

"Nana is having some trouble. We believe she might be having a flare-up of Crohn's."

"What is that, anyway? Dad mentioned it yesterday."

"She has a disease in her guts. Listen, she needs me. Go run and do as I ask," Tanya ordered.

"And Dad?"

"He's going into Snowflake," Tanya replied, her tone signaling her apprehension of the plan.

"Snowflake, he was attacked last time."

"I'm aware of what happened last time. Now hurry, go get what I need."

"But, Mom, it's dangerous out there."

"Chase went with him; they'll be fine. Now go, hurry," Tanya said. She turned and left, closing the door behind her, leaving Michael standing frozen with uncertainty.

Deliverance, Oklahoma

Kaitlyn woke to loud banging at her front door. She rose

and turned on the light. "Hold on, I'll be right there," she said loudly as she stuffed her feet into a pair of slippers. She scuffled out of her room and to the foyer. "Hold on," she cried out, as the banging wouldn't stop. She turned on the outside light and threw open the door to find Reid there, his eyes wide and sweat glistening on his face. "I know the lasagna was good, but I don't have any more," she joked.

"I'll do it," he blurted out.

Tying her robe tighter, Kaitlyn asked, "You're talking about going to the coast?"

"Yes."

She looked past him into the dark but didn't see anyone. A nervous feeling spread across her body. "Why don't you come in."

Reid hesitated.

"What's the matter?" she asked.

"It's not smart for me to come in."

She was taken aback by his statement and again asked, "What's the matter? Why are you being so coy?"

"I, um, I came because I needed to tell you right away."

"What's changed? Something's happened."

"I've just decided to go, that's all. I want to get on the road as soon as I can," he said, rattling off the words in rapid succession.

"What's really going on?"

Sheepishly Reid looked away.

"Tell me. I can help," she offered.

"It's Hannah, she was bitten by a dog."

Kaitlyn's jaw dropped. Shocked by the news, she said, "I heard about the dog that was found."

"That's the one."

"Don't take her to the infirmary," she warned.

"I didn't plan to, but I won't have much time. A friend of hers was there, and soon the word will spread. I need you to put this trip together before they come to take her away."

Knowing the urgency was high, she said softly, "I'll do anything to keep her safe. Just leave it to me. I'll make all the arrangements."

Reid let out a loud sigh. Tears formed in his eyes as, for the first time since he'd found out about Hannah, he heard something that gave him hope.

"Go back home and take care of your daughter. I'll be around as soon as I can," she said and motioned him towards the door.

"You know we only have seven days once she shows symptoms."

"I'm aware of the time-sensitive nature, but it will probably take me a half day or so to get everything arranged. You must understand."

He lowered his head. "I understand."

"Now go home to your little girl."

"Thank you."

"If by chance someone does come knocking, tell them they need to contact me immediately."

"I will," he replied.

"I'll see you later. Goodnight, Reid," Kaitlyn said. After she closed the door, she noticed her right hand was shaking. She could barely contain her excitement at the possibility of a journey to the coast. However, before she could celebrate, she still needed to convince the mayor, but thought that a person infected was just what they needed to get Kincaid to agree to set Reid outside the gates.

Filled with hope, she rushed to her room to get dressed. Time was of the essence and she needed to see Kincaid as quickly as possible.

CHAPTER 2

Outskirts Of Dalhart, Texas

AN HOUR PASSED and no Emily. Soon the hour turned to two, then three and still no rescue, no Emily. Brienne began to wonder if it had all been some sort of game, or had she been caught? What she feared, though, as each passing minute went by, was that the longer it took, the higher the chances Emile would return, and this time he wasn't going to taunt her.

The door clanged.

Brienne snapped her head in the direction of the door and waited.

A figure came into the room and quickly closed the door.

Brienne's stomach tightened as the anticipation of who was there grew.

Emily emerged from the shadows, a backpack slung over her shoulder. "I'm sorry I'm late. Took me longer."

"Your brother came," Brienne barked.

Frozen by the news, Emily asked, "What did he do to you?"

"He did nothing if you don't count offering me human flesh to eat," Brienne answered, her tone angry.

"I'm very sorry. I came as soon as I could get everything set up," Emily said. She briskly walked over to Brienne and loosened the bindings on both her ankles and wrists.

Pulling her arms free, Brienne felt the sudden urge to strike Emily and make a run for it. It was in her nature to be the lone wolf, but doing so now could endanger her escape. She needed Emily at least until she got miles away from her captors.

"We don't have much time. We need to hurry," Emily said. She offered Brienne a hand to get up.

On her feet, Brienne stretched. She shot Emily a hard stare and said, "Give me a weapon."

"A weapon? No, not now."

"What if we encounter anyone? I'll need something to fight back with," Brienne barked.

"No, right now I don't know if you're going to use it against me or not."

A crooked smile stretched across Brienne's lean face. Maybe Emily wasn't as stupid as she thought, she mused to herself.

"I need you to be quiet. If we come up on someone, just act like you're my prisoner," Emily said.

"Fine."

The two swiftly exited the room into a long tiled hallway.

"This way," Emily said and headed to the left. "At the end of the hallway there's a door; it's a stairwell. We'll take that to the ground level then head outside; that's where the car is."

"Lead the way."

They moved down the hall. Lanterns on the wall gave them sufficient light to see. They reached the doorway, Emily opened the door, and there standing in front of them was Emile.

Emile looked at Emily then to Brienne. "What's going on?" he shouted.

Brienne sprang into action. She leapt forward and smashed her clenched fist into Emile's jaw.

He reeled from the hit, falling into the stairs behind him.

Brienne continued the assault, peppering him with several more punches, only stopping when Emily grabbed her hand.

"Enough," Emily said.

"He's a—"

"He's my brother and you're not going to kill him," Emily said firmly.

Wiping blood from a cut on his lip, Emile glared at Emily and asked, "Why? Why are you betraying me?"

"I'm sorry," Emily answered.

"You're leaving…with her?" Emile asked.

"It's not what you think. It's not about you," Emily explained.

His feelings hurt, Emile asked, "You're leaving us, your family, to run off with a stranger? You're abandoning us to go away with…dinner."

Hearing enough, Brienne kicked Emile in the jaw. The impact knocked him out.

Emily gasped. "You didn't have to do that."

"I'm tired of hearing him talk," Brienne said.

With Emile unconscious, Emily knew they didn't have much time to steal the vehicle and get away. "We have to go…now!"

Brienne listened without complaint and followed closely behind Emily as they sprinted up the darkened stairs to the ground level.

Emily opened the heavy door and poked her head out. "Clear."

"Where to now?" Brienne asked.

"That car," Emily replied. She nodded to a white Chevrolet Traverse parked next to a wall.

Brienne looked around as best she could, considering the only light was the half moon. "Where is everyone?"

"Don't worry about that. Let's move," Emily said. She raced across the gravel lot.

The two reached the small SUV.

Emily jumped behind the wheel and motioned for Brienne to ride in the front passenger seat.

"We should buckle up," Brienne said, knowing that the ride out could get rough. She reached and pulled the seat belt across her lap and body and clicked it into the buckle.

Emily hovered her finger over the ignition button.

After a lengthy pause, Brienne asked, "What are you waiting for?"

"I'm wondering if what I'm doing is right," Emily said, her finger trembling.

"You're now wringing your hands over this? How about you get out, 'cause I know for damn sure I'm leaving," Brienne snapped.

"But he's my family, my brother."

"Now you're questioning yourself?" Brienne snapped.

"If we get caught, they'll kill us both."

"They were already going to kill me, so this is clearly better for me, but you need to get going or get out," Brienne barked, her anxiety rising.

Emily sat frozen.

"Start the damn car!" Brienne hollered.

Emily flinched. She hit the ignition, but the only thing that happened was the dash lights turned on. She tried it again, and still the engine didn't turn over. "Oh no."

"Didn't you confirm the damn thing runs?" Brienne asked, her tone filled with anger.

"I know it works. I saw it driven over here and parked," Emily replied, her finger hitting the button.

Suddenly realizing what the issue was, Brienne barked, "Put your foot on the brake pedal."

"Are you sure?"

"Have you ever driven a car?"

Timidly, Emily replied, "No, I've driven motorcycles and watched my brother drive this. I saw him simply hit this button."

"I'm driving. Get out of the seat now," Brienne roared.

Yelling erupted from the far side of the compound.

"How do I know—" Emily asked before being interrupted by Brienne.

"Get out of the fucking driver's seat now," Brienne snapped, her anger welling up into rage.

Feeling Brienne's anger, Emily gulped. She opened the door and ran around to the passenger seat.

Brienne slid behind the steering wheel.

Emily got in, her eyes wide with fear. "They're coming. I hear them."

Confident, Brienne depressed the brake and hit the ignition button. The car roared to life. She put the car into drive and smashed her foot against the accelerator. The car lunged forward.

"You've driven before?" Emily asked.

"Of course. How old are you anyway?"

"Twenty-three."

"Now it all makes sense," Brienne said, turning the wheel hard to the left to avoid several other parked cars. "Where's the exit?"

"Turn that way," Emily said, pointing to the right.

Brienne cranked the wheel to the right, causing the vehicle to skid across the loose gravel. The headlights hit an armed man standing at the chain-link gate.

The guard gave them an odd look then unslung his rifle.

"You're going to want to get down," Brienne warned Emily.

Not hesitating, Emily slouched in the seat.

Brienne pressed the accelerator all the way to the floorboard. The vehicle sped up considerably.

"Stop!" the guard shouted. His name was Jay and his brother, Nate, was good friends with Emile. He raised his rifle and aimed at the windshield.

Brienne wasn't about to stop. She aimed the vehicle directly at Jay.

Seeing that the vehicle wasn't stopping, Jay fired numerous shots from his semiautomatic rifle. The rounds smashed into the windshield and hit the backseat. He managed to get off half a dozen shots before Brienne struck him, tossing his body into the air. He hit the ground dead.

Brienne smashed through the gate, leaving part of the chain-link gate wrapped around the right quarter panel and hood. She knew it would slow her down, but she kept the accelerator to the floor. What she needed was distance between her and the compound. "How far to the main road?"

"Is it safe to sit up?" Emily asked.

"Yeah."

Emily peeked her head above the dash and stared down the long straight dirt road. "Somewhere down there. Just keep going straight; you'll run into a highway."

"What does that mean? Do I go left or right when I get to the highway?"

"Um, I don't know. I can't remember."

"When was the last time you left the compound?" Brienne asked.

"Seven years ago, Emile wouldn't let me leave after…" Emily replied then fell silent.

Picking up on something, Brienne asked, "After what?"

"I ran away seven years ago. He went after me and found me. I got a mile down this road, that's it. He hasn't let me leave since," Emily said, her voice cracking with emotion.

"But you have to remember coming to this place, don't you?"

"We arrived at the compound eight years ago. I was asleep when we made the drive," Emily confessed.

Brienne groaned her disappointment at the news.

"What? It's not my fault," Emily complained, her tone turning whiney.

"You break me out, but you don't know where you are or where we should be going?" Brienne asked.

"But I got you out, didn't I?"

"That's true."

The piece of the gate was beginning to effect the steering.

Brienne slowed the car.

"What are you doing?" Emily asked, her head looking around in all directions.

"I've got to stop and remove the gate or it will cause irreparable damage," Brienne replied as she hit the brakes and brought the vehicle to a full stop. She got out and went to the front end.

Emily watched her through the bullet-ridden windshield, the headlights illuminating Brienne's toned physique.

Struggling with the gate, Brienne called out, "I need help. Get out here."

Emily did as she was asked.

"On the count of three, we'll pull as hard as we can," Brienne said.

Emily nodded.

"One, two, three."

The two pulled with all their strength. The gate broke free. They tossed it aside.

"Let's hit the road," Brienne said.

Back in the vehicle, Emily sighed at what they'd just done, hardly believing they'd escaped.

"How is it you have blondish hair and your brother has black?" Brienne asked.

"He dyes his hair," Emily answered as she dug through her pack, looking for something to eat.

Brienne laughed. "He dyes his hair. Oh my, now I've heard it all."

"Is that funny?"

"Yeah, kinda. Anyway, tell me, why risk your life to leave and travel to some unknown place? You sorta had it good back there, besides the eating-human-beings shit you guys do."

"I was trapped there. My brother, he...let's just say he mistreated me."

"Like sexually abused you?" Brienne asked, as that was what it sounded like Emily was alluding to.

She sheepishly looked away. "He's a bad, evil person. I like to think I'm not."

"Well, that's to be seen."

"There it is," Emily said as she pulled out some dried human flesh. Not thinking, she offered it to Brienne. "Are you hungry?"

Brienne gave the open ziplock bag a look then leered at Emily. "You're offering me human jerky?"

"Oh, I forgot..." Emily said. She recoiled her arm and hid the bag.

Reminded of who her traveling partner was, Brienne stewed on her circumstances and what could lie ahead with Emily at her side. She made a quick decision and got out of the vehicle.

"Where are you going?" Emily cried out. She watched as Brienne walked over to her door and opened it. "What are you doing? Do we need to do something else?"

"Yeah, I need to dump some baggage," Brienne said. She grabbed Emily by the neck and yanked her out of the vehicle. She threw her to the ground and said, "I'll be eternally grateful that you helped me escape, but I'm not traveling with a fucking cannibal."

"We made a deal," Emily howled, her face covered in dirt.

Brienne slammed the door.

Using the only thing she had, Emily pulled out a semi-automatic pistol and pointed it at Brienne. "Let me back in the car or I'll shoot you."

Looking down at the muzzle, Brienne put up her hands and said, "Fine. You can ride, but no more human jerky, human carpaccio, human whatever."

"I forgot. I didn't mean to offend you."

"Your brother taunted me with it, so you sort of triggered me," Brienne said. She stepped forward and offered her hand. "C'mon."

Warily, Emily took her hand.

Brienne pulled her up quickly, smacked the pistol out of her hand, and then came across Emily's face with the back of her hand. "That's for pulling a gun on me." She let go of Emily and shoved her back to the ground.

Emily hit the ground hard, landing on her butt with a thud.

Brienne picked up the pistol, shoved it into her waistband, and said, "Thanks again for helping me escape, but like I said, I don't travel with people who eat other people. Call me old-fashioned, but I'm afraid you might take a bite out of me." She sauntered back to the driver's door and gave Emily one last look. "See you later, cannibal."

"I hate you. I fucking hate you!" Emily shouted before opening the passenger door. She reached in and grabbed her backpack.

Brienne jumped back into the car and aimed the pistol at Emily.

Emily hopped back out of the car. "Don't shoot me."

"I'm tempted, believe me," Brienne said, reaching across the passenger seat and closing the door.

"I'll find you one day, I swear it, and when I do, I'll kill you," Emily spat.

Brienne raised her middle finger.

"I will hunt you down, I swear it," Emily fumed.

Brienne put the vehicle in gear and sped off, leaving Emily in a cloud of dust.

"If it's the last thing I do, I'll find you, and when I do, I'll eat your fucking heart!" Emily screamed.

Deliverance, Oklahoma

Kincaid wiped the sleep from his eyes. He stretched and let out a loud yawn before he turned to Kaitlyn and asked, "You woke me up just so you can try to pitch me again on sending out a recon team to see if this island sanctuary is real or not?"

"It's more than that. I have the perfect candidate, and I guarantee that when I'm done, you'll sign off on this," Kaitlyn said, standing tall in front of his home office desk.

"Can I at least get a cup of tea before we do this?" he asked as he scratched his head. "God, how I miss coffee. Maybe this recon mission, if they return, can find us some coffee. How long has it been since we had coffee, six years?" He stood from his desk, walked past her, and headed towards his kitchen.

She followed right behind him.

He turned on a light. It flickered before becoming fully bright. "I need to get Donaldson to take a look at the batteries. We're having power issues again."

Joe Donaldson was in charge of the solar and wind power arrays located south of town. It was one of the first major accomplishments that Kincaid had set into place once he saw that the town would have to become self-reliant.

"This team can go looking for replacement parts too. We can make its objective more than just finding this facility," Kaitlyn said. She appreciated that he had given her another reason to make the run.

He filled a pot and walked to the stove. With a flip of a switch, the electric coil began to heat up. He set the pot on it and turned to face Kaitlyn. "Will you be wanting some?"

"Sure."

He could tell by her composure that she was nervous. He rarely, if ever, had seen her this way before. "Go ahead. Tell me why this mission needs to happen."

"You were concerned yesterday about losing someone. Well, I have a volunteer, he needs to go, and there's a reason that I know you'll understand, being that you're a father."

He grunted and said, "Kate, just spit it out already. You're really building this up."

"The dog we took in, well, it bit a little girl."

His eyes widened and nostrils flared. "We have someone infected inside Deliverance?"

"We have to assume so. The father—"

Cutting her off, Kincaid stiffened his spine and snapped, "Please tell me this girl is in the infirmary and under quarantine."

Kaitlyn looked away.

"She's not, is she?" Kincaid asked, and by his tone, anger was rising in him. "This is a violation of our protocols, the very ones that have kept us contagion-free for years."

"I'm aware of that; hence why we need to send the father and the girl on this mission."

Kincaid marched from the room and towards his office.

"Where are you going?" she asked, following him.

He didn't answer. He reached his desk, picked up the rotary dial phone, and shot her a hard look. "Who is this man?"

"Tom, please, if you go to the man's house, there will be trouble, and we'll lose our opportunity. The girl is quarantined in his house."

"And the father?"

"He's there too. No one is leaving, I can assure you," Kaitlyn explained.

"We can't have someone with the virus inside the town limits. I'm sorry, Kate, I need to call this in," Kincaid said and went to dial zero.

She rushed to the phone and depressed the hook switch. "Tom, please, let me explain, and if you're not satisfied, you can make the call."

The water in the kitchen began to steam, the sound coming down the hall.

Kincaid put the handset back on the cradle and said, "Explain it all to me over some Earl Grey."

Five Miles West of Logan, New Mexico

Michael thought the smell of Nana's room was bad until he had to haul away the heavily soiled sheets. Nana was unable to make it to the bathroom, resulting in her defecating in the bed, but what was different and alarming to his mother and father was the amount of blood and pus that was present. She had lived with Crohn's for many years and had it under remission for many of those years. However, she had run out of her medication a year ago and thought she'd be fine. She was wrong. Her symptoms now proved that her flare-up wasn't just bad, it was severe. With their only recourse trying to find the same medications she'd taken before, Will and Chase had left to look for them and prayed that the unique medicines might still be on the shelves in the local pharmacy.

Tanya filled a basin with fresh water and, with a bar of soap she'd made, started to wash up from the ordeal that had taken hours to clean.

"Mom, how long will Dad and Chase be gone?" Michael asked. He was sitting at the small dinette table, his weary head in his hands.

"Soon, I'm sure," Tanya replied.

"I don't understand why they think they'll find her medicine in Snowflake. Didn't Dad already go there before?"

"He's double-checking."

"And if there isn't any? What will happen to Nana?"

"Michael, please, can you stop asking me one question after another? You're acting like a child," she snapped.

"I'm just trying to understand," Michael said, defending himself.

Tanya toweled herself off and sighed. She took a seat across from Michael and reached over to take his hand. "I know you're trying to understand. I'm just tired and stressed out. I don't like your father or Chase leaving to go into town, especially after what happened recently, but I'm also fearful for Nana. You saw the sheets; you saw the blood. Her Crohn's is bad, and while I recall it's not fatal, that might have been in a world with available medicine and health care. I don't know what's going to happen. There, you have my answer, I just don't know, but we can never give up."

"I'm sorry."

"You don't have to apologize, but what I do need you to do is think a bit differently."

"Like what?" he asked, his right eyebrow raised.

"You've always been more tender and sweet than your

brother. I need you to find a way not to be if something happens."

"What do you mean, Mom?"

"I mean that while I adore your sweet side, I might need you to be a bit more like your brother, a bit tougher."

"You don't like the way I am?" Michael asked.

"I do, but I'm scared right now. I need to know you'll be there for us if…" She paused and lowered her head.

"If what? If Dad doesn't come back home? Do you think that will happen?"

She lifted her head, and tears had formed in her eyes. "It's a possibility I've had to face every time he has left, but this time Chase went too. Now it's us—you, me and Nana. Can I count on you?"

"Of course, I know I come across as sweet, but I can fight if you need me to. I can do anything that Chase can," Michael said defiantly. "Dad has trained me with a gun. Heck, I shoot better than Chase does."

"But…"

"Do you really think Dad and Chase won't come back?"

Again Tanya paused. "Every time he leaves, I prepare myself mentally that he may not return."

"Mom, you can trust that I will do whatever I can to protect you," Michael declared.

She squeezed his hand firmly and said, "Glad to hear it."

A wave of insecurity washed over him. "Do you really think I'm not capable?"

"I never said that you're not capable. I'm asking you only to start thinking that you might have to be a fighter."

Even though she had hurt his feelings slightly, he wasn't going to show it, only because that would have validated the narrative that he was soft.

She wiped a tear from her cheek and said, "I'm going to go check on Nana. I think you should go get some sleep." She stood and left the room.

Michael remained, his gaze fixed on the lantern at the center of the table. The orange flame flickered and danced. He prayed that his father and brother would return safely, but he also prayed for the opportunity to prove to his mother he was capable and strong.

Deliverance, Oklahoma

Kincaid tapped his fingers on the desk as he pondered what Kaitlyn had told him.

"Well?" Kaitlyn asked. She knew Reid was at home, stressed and waiting to hear from her.

"I'm not convinced," Kincaid said.

"What is the harm in it?"

"How is he even going to make it in time? You give the time frame as if he can drive there. He can't. None of our vehicles can make that trip without having issues, you know this."

"He can," she shot back.

The leather squeaked as he settled in, leaning back in his chair. "You have a vehicle that can make the trip and I'm not aware of this?"

Kaitlyn sat down in a cushioned chair opposite Kincaid. She nervously smoothed out the creases in her pants and said, "I have an operational vehicle. It's not perfect, but it can get him far enough to make it...theoretically."

"Where's this mystery vehicle?"

"In a garage in the north end of town. I've been working with a gentleman who had a Tesla Model S. He's done some work on it, modifications, and he believes he's given it a range of about five hundred miles on a full charge."

"That sounds good, but that doesn't get him far enough. It's twice that distance," Kincaid said.

"As I said, he made some modifications that he feels will enable him to charge the car as he drives."

Kincaid widened his eyes. He was curious to see this vehicle and also disturbed that behind his back Kaitlyn and this man had been working on this Tesla. "How long have you been plotting to leave?"

"Leave? No—"

He raised his hand, motioned for her to stop talking, and said, "Don't lie to me, Kate. You're smarter than that."

"A year plus," she confessed.

"You don't think I would've wanted to know about this vehicle?"

"Why would you? You don't want to leave town; why would an operational vehicle mean anything to you?"

"I like to know what's going on in my town," he stressed.

"I'm sorry we kept it secret, but now you know, and now we have a chance to find out what's happening in the world."

"I'm disappointed in you, Kate. I thought I could trust you."

"You can trust me."

"I want to know more about this vehicle and its capabilities." Kincaid leaned forward, placed his elbows on the desk, and gave her a hard stare.

Kaitlyn thought about how she could describe the vehicle, then decided on a different course of action. "How about you come with me and I'll show you?"

Kincaid stood. "Let's go."

She smiled and said, "Does this mean you're going to allow him to go?"

"I'm not sure yet, but I am putting off placing that call."

Her smile grew.

He stepped around the desk and put his hand on her shoulder. "Don't ever lie to me again."

"Never."

"And, Kate."

"Yes."

"Destroy the house the second he's gone," Kincaid ordered.

Forty Miles Southwest of Dalhart, Texas

"No, no, no!" Brienne howled as her fist slammed against the steering wheel. She pressed the accelerator, but all the SUV did was sputter.

The yellow light telling her the vehicle was running low on fuel had come on not a minute after she kicked Emily out.

The vehicle coasted and came to a stop.

She glanced in the rearview mirror and saw the light of

dawn approaching. Soon it would be morning, and no doubt with that would come people looking for her. She did have the advantage of miles in between her and them, but she wasn't going to assume they couldn't catch up. She rummaged through the vehicle, looking for anything of value, but came up short. She needed food and water and would need it soon. Ahead of her on the road was an abandoned vehicle, a Toyota Camry. If the car had gas in the tank, it had no doubt gone bad, but why abandon a vehicle unless you had run out of gas? Curious, she walked over to the Toyota and opened the door.

The skeletal remains of someone fell out and hit the pavement.

She recoiled. In her haste she hadn't bothered to see if anyone or anything was in the car. She stepped over the remains and poked her head inside to find three other bodies. On the floorboard was a semiautomatic pistol. She picked it up and dropped the magazine to see the fifteen-round magazine was half loaded. She press checked it and discovered a round in the chamber. Looking back to the remains that had fallen out, she saw a large hole in the side of the skull. "Not a survivor, huh?" she smirked.

Not squeamish, she pulled the latch and popped the trunk. She lifted it up and said, "Let's see what we have here." Her eyes widened when she saw a cardboard box full of crackers and an assortment of chips, but the biggest surprise was a semiautomatic rifle and a backpack, something she sorely needed. "Jackpot." She pulled out a bag of tortilla chips, tore it open, and stuffed several in her mouth, only to find that the chips had become stale. She shrugged and kept eating. The one thing she lacked was water, and she was now in the desert. She had enough to last her a day or two, but after that she'd need to find some.

She tore through the backpack to find mostly personal effects of the passengers, including a photo album, underwear she couldn't use, and clothes that were too big for her. She dumped everything she didn't need into the trunk and promptly loaded the backpack with the food she'd found.

In the middle of all the oversized clothes she spotted a small hardbound book. Curious, she picked it up and opened it to find it was once used for taking various notes. She then thought of her own journal. It had been in Emily's backpack, meaning it was gone for good. "Damn," she barked. She'd had the journal since Germany. It contained a detailed account of her life since she'd departed Europe to come back home. She glanced back east. She felt compelled to go find Emily and get her journal back, but knew that was a foolish endeavor.

She completed her search of the Camry and found it had been a success. In her pack she had a few days of food, a little water, a pistol she could use as a backup, and more clothes. She had tried to start the Camry but found the battery had died. By her guess, Yuma was about four hundred miles away, and on foot that would take her about ten days, provided she didn't run into any more trouble. To avoid becoming a prisoner of anyone like had just happened, she planned to walk off the road, keeping it just in sight but staying away from it altogether, and secondly, to stay as far away from people as she could.

She threw on her pack and instantly felt the forty-plus

pounds. She grunted and said, "Maybe it will be more like twelve days." She set out and began the trek across the barren terrain.

Time wasn't really a concern to her. She'd already been traveling for years and what was an extra day or two now. She was close and with each step closer to hopefully knowing what had happened to Jake and her son, Dustin.

Deliverance, Oklahoma

After waking Arthur, the man with the Tesla, Kaitlyn waited with Kincaid at the garage door.

The sun was now cresting the horizon to the east, and soon a new day would be upon them.

"How did you come to meet Arthur?" Kincaid asked, his hands stuffed in his pockets. The early morning was cool, with a slight breeze from the north making it feel colder.

"By accident, it's too long a story, and really, that doesn't matter," she replied.

"How many other people know about this?"

"You, me and him. You should know, Arthur is a bit unusual. He tends to stutter when he's nervous, so expect a lot of that, and he…well, how do I say this? He's just odd, you'll see," Kaitlyn said. "But besides his unusual behavior, he's a genius."

Metal clanging came from behind the closed garage door. "Oh no…dang it!" Arthur bellowed.

"We're waiting, Arthur," Kaitlyn said.

"One second, just give me one second. I..." More bangs. "Darn thing," Arthur barked.

Kaitlyn shot Kincaid an embarrassed look and said, "He really is quite brilliant."

"And clumsy," Kincaid added.

The garage door slowly opened. Bright light shot across the driveway.

Arthur emerged and briskly walked up to Kincaid, his hand extended. "Mayor Kincaid, it's a real pleasure."

Kincaid took his hand and shook. "I hear you've made some interesting modifications to your car."

"Yes, I have, I, uh, I-I," Arthur said. He paused for a moment then continued, the tempo of his speech deliberately slowed. "I have, and it's an honor to show you."

"I'm anxious to see it," Kincaid said.

Arthur ran his stubby fingers through his thinning gray hair in an attempt to brush it to the side, but it didn't help. He shoved his black-framed glasses up onto his face and said, "Please come in." He stepped aside and motioned with his arm for Kincaid to come into the garage.

Kincaid, followed by Kaitlyn, walked into the space.

The first thing Kincaid experienced was the smell of burnt metal. His eyes instantly focused on the silver car. It was the body of a Tesla Model S, but that was as far as it came to looking like the car he had seen before. On the hood and roof were solar panels. Thick black cables came from underneath the panels. The roof's cables ran down along the rear panel and went inside the trunk space. Another thicker black cable came out of the truck via a hole cut into it and went directly into the charging port on the rear left side. The cable from the hood panel ran down the left quarter panel, then alongside the bottom of the frame and into the trunk. All the cables were bolted to the body.

"It uses solar power?" Kincaid asked.

"Yes, yes, it does, so it can recharge as it's parked or driving. I had to do some things to bypass the car's programming that didn't allow it."

"But those panels can't generate that much power."

"Correct, that-that is true; what they do is-is allow it to have a longer range. I'm estimating that based upon the amount of kilowatts they can generate, of course, d-d-depending on if there's sunlight, they will give it a range of about five hundred miles or so if you start out with a fully charged battery. The car's batteries themselves give it a range of three hundred and seventy miles. Now, we do lose about five percent due to the drag caused from the panels being on the car, but I made up for that loss by cutting power to anything electrically nonessential. I diverted that power to get the battery to warm up faster, which helps it from losing about three percent. Of course, range is also determined by outside temperature, airflow and the speed. If the driver is driving fast, he can lose—"

Kincaid held up his hand and said, "I'm not a wonky sort of guy, no need to explain everything you've done. Are you sure it will work?"

Arthur gave Kaitlyn a glance and replied, "Yes."

"Being that I've not heard about your car driving around town, how did you test it?"

Arthur rushed to a corner of the garage. He returned

pushing what could only be described as two long metal frames with rollers in between. "I use these."

"Where did you get them?" Kincaid asked.

"I made them."

"Are you an engineer or something? How did we not see you on the lists we made? We could have been using your expertise long ago," Kincaid said.

"Oh, no, no, I-I-I'm not an engineer or anything. No, no, that's not me," Arthur said sheepishly.

"Then what? Where did you go to school?"

"School, no, no, I didn't go to school."

A look of shock spread across Kincaid's face. "What do you mean you didn't go to school?"

"I didn't go to college. I-I-I'm a janitor," Arthur confessed.

Kincaid gave Kaitlyn an odd and confused glance and said, "You're a janitor now?"

"No, no, I was before," Arthur said, a whimsical smile on his face. He took great joy and telling people what he did before.

"A janitor has retrofitted a Tesla and increased its driving range?" Kincaid said.

"Correct." Arthur chuckled.

"Can we drive it?" Kincaid asked.

Arthur gave Kaitlyn a look of fear and said, "Oh, I don't know. I'm…I-I-I'm not sure about that."

"What do you mean? I'm the mayor. There's no fear about being seen. I want to see what your car can do."

"I won't get in trouble?"

"None. In fact, I'm trying to figure out how I can reward

you for this innovation. I need you on our team," Kincaid said.

"I'll be right back," Arthur said and ran off.

Kaitlyn walked up to Kincaid and asked, "You're impressed, aren't you?"

"Very," Kincaid said. He got close to the car and ran his hand over it. He stopped at the panels on the hood and looked down. "If he can do this, he can help Joe get our batteries back up and the system running more optimally."

Arthur returned, a hat on his head. "I'm ready."

The car only had enough space for two people comfortably, with a third if they squeezed in the backseat alongside the equipment and tools.

Arthur took Kincaid out and drove him up and down the street that fronted his house. He showed him how the car still had the performance from before. He was very proud of what he'd created and wanted nothing more than for Kincaid to be just as happy about his creation as he was.

They pulled back into the driveway.

Kincaid exited the car and smiled at Kaitlyn.

"So?" she asked, barely able to contain herself.

"You can go," Kincaid said.

Arthur got out and asked, "Go? Where?"

Kincaid replied, "Take your car to California."

The joyful expression melted from Arthur's face. "My car isn't going to California. N-n-n-no, it's not going anywhere."

"I'm confused," Kincaid said.

"I haven't had a chance to talk with him yet about the plan," Kaitlyn said.

"What plan? No, no one is taking my car," Arthur said, his body tensed, and he stepped back away from Kaitlyn.

"Arthur, we have an emergency. Someone needs to use your car. They need to take it to California to see if they can find a cure for—"

"No!" Arthur shouted.

"Arthur, please calm down. Let me explain," Kaitlyn said softly.

"No," Arthur again barked.

"Why can't we take it?" Kincaid asked.

"'Cause it's mine. I've been working on it for years…literally."

"We can get you another one," Kincaid said.

"Another one, where?" Arthur roared.

Kincaid stepped closer and said, "What do you do now?"

"Huh?" Arthur asked, confused by the question.

"Your job in the community, what do you do?" Kincaid asked.

"I work in the community garden," Arthur said.

"Not anymore. I need you, Arthur. I need you; the town needs you. I want you to work with Joe Donaldson in our energy department. I need you to work with him on getting the solar and wind arrays working as efficiently as possible," Kincaid offered.

"I can work on that?" Arthur asked.

"Yes, you're brilliant. We need you," Kincaid said.

"But we need your car. We need it desperately," Kaitlyn said.

Arthur paced back and forth in the driveway, mumbling to himself.

The commotion drew the attention of several neighbors, who began to walk by, with some stopping to watch what was happening with curiosity, most notably staring at the car in the driveway.

"Arthur, by letting us use the car, you can be a part of this town's legacy. If we find a cure for the dog flu, it will mean you had a role in that. Don't you want to be known for helping the town, helping mankind, so to speak," Kaitlyn said.

"Yes," Arthur answered. He chewed on a fingernail and spit out a piece. "Can you find me a new car? I want to recreate what I've done here."

"We'll do our best. I think you're probably the only person in town who had an electric car, but we can ask," Kincaid said.

"Could we go looking for one?" Arthur asked.

Kincaid gave Kaitlyn a concerned look. "We'll see. I'm not open to that idea, but I'm willing to discuss it. Is that fair?"

"You'll let me work with Joe Donaldson?" Arthur asked.

"Yes," Kincaid answered.

"When can I start?"

"Immediately, today; if you haven't noticed, we've had some issues," Kincaid said.

"The flickering lights, yes, those are power surges. I think I know how to fix that," Arthur boasted.

"Then today it is for sure," Kincaid said.

Arthur walked up to Kincaid and handed him the key

fob. "I'll need to meet with whoever is taking the car. I'll need to make sure they understand how it works."

Kaitlyn smiled and said, "Not a problem, you stay here, and I'll have them here within the next two hours."

———

REID STOOD AT THE DOOR, shocked by the news Kaitlin had just given him. He could go. He had been given the green light, and it appeared he also had a vehicle. He had a couple of conditions, and one was that he and Hannah had to wear decontamination suits while they were inside the town limits. There was no way Kincaid would allow a sick girl to travel across town, being a carrier of the disease.

Time was of the essence, so he immediately started packing. He needed to get what he thought he could use on the trip and get to a house in the north end of town in the next hour. He tore through his garage and found a large backpack. In it he stuffed a laundry list of items. When he was done, his pack weighed close to seventy pounds. He didn't care because he didn't plan on having to carry it. He reemerged from the garage, to hear Hannah crying.

He raced down the hall with the decon suit in his arms. When he entered her room, he saw her sitting up in bed. "What's wrong?"

"I had a bad dream," she whined.

The morning light had begun to spill into the room through the slits in the blinds, and her lantern was still on.

He went to her bedside and put his arms around her. "It's just a dream, nothing more."

"I'm scared," she cried.

"It was just a dream," he said in a soothing tone.

"I'm not scared about the dream, really, I'm scared about…" She held up her arm and nodded to her wound.

His heart again melted at the sight of the bandaged bite mark. "I've got some good news. Do you want to hear it?"

She nodded.

"We're going somewhere to get you…" he said then paused. He had lied to her and for what? They were about to embark on a long and dangerous trek, one where they might not return or even make it, yet he felt compelled to lie.

"I'm going to die," she said.

He took her hand and squeezed it gently. "No, I will do anything, and I am. We are going to be taking a trip."

"Where?"

"The coast, you will get to see the ocean finally, like I promised."

"Are you taking me there before I die?" she asked.

"Stop talking like that. We're going there because there's a place that might have a…cure."

"Do I have it?"

He hesitated. He wondered how he should reply. Should he lie, or should he tell her the truth? In a split second he decided to be honest, or as honest as he could be without causing her undue stress. "There's a chance that you do, but we're not confident yet until you get tested."

"Did you find the dog?"

"The authorities did," he answered.

"Was the dog sick?"

"Yes."

She looked away and began to cry. "Then I'm going to die."

He pulled her close and said, "Don't say that."

Tears streamed down her face. "It's true. I'm going to die like Mommy."

He took her face in his hands and stared deeply into her eyes.

She looked away.

"Hannah, look at me," he said.

She continued to look away.

"Look at me," he said again.

She locked eyes with him.

"I know this is hard, but I need you to be strong, that includes to think strong, think positive. Can you do that?"

"But I'm...I'm going to die," she cried.

"We're going to the coast, and we will find a cure. The trip will be tough, but we'll make it. I need you to be strong. Tell me you'll be strong."

"I can't."

"Hannah, please, tell me you'll be strong."

"I'll be strong," she whimpered.

With his finger, he wiped a couple of tears away. "I love you, Hannah banana."

"I love you too," she said, her voice just above a whisper.

"How do you feel?"

"My arm hurts."

"Let me look at it," he said.

She pulled away from him.

"I just want to take a quick look. I might need to bandage it again," he said.

She gave in and offered her arm.

Reid untaped one end and pulled it back to reveal the wound looked less swollen than the night before. "It looks good."

"Does that mean I'll be fine?"

He taped the bandage back up and replied, "I need to pack up a few things for you, and then we'll go see the car we're taking to California."

"We're driving in a car?"

"Yes, isn't that exciting?" he said with a smile. "Can I get you to pack up some things? Treat it like a sleepover. Pack several pairs of pants, shirts, underwear, also get your—"

She hopped off the bed and went to her dresser. "I've got this, Dad."

Just like that, her demeanor had changed. He gave her a perplexed look and asked, "Need my help?"

"No," she said as she pulled out the pants and set them on top of the dresser. "What's that you're holding?"

"Oh, this, this is a suit you need to wear. We need to make sure no one else gets sick," Reid explained.

"Can I get people sick?"

"I don't think so, but they're being cautious. You're not contagious until you develop symptoms, but listen, I'm wearing one too, so consider it like a father-daughter costume."

"Okay."

"I'll go get a bag for you to pack your stuff, and don't forget—"

"My toothbrush," she said, cutting him off a second time.

"Yes, your toothbrush." He chuckled. He stepped out of the room and took a few steps down the hall when a wave of emotion crashed over him. He began to cry. Not wanting her to hear him, he shuffled down the hall and went into his bedroom and closed the door. There he started to sob. He had asked her to be strong and there she was doing it. Oh, how he loved her. She was so special, so sweet. He couldn't imagine living his life without her. He had to get her to the coast as fast as possible.

———

"You can't bring all of that stuff, nope, no, not that, no, no room, s-s-s-sorry," Arthur blared as he looked at the bags and gear Reid had before him. He gave Reid and Hannah a puzzled look, then shot a concerned look towards Kaitlin. "Are they sick?"

"No," Kaitlin replied. "She's got the disease, but she's not symptomatic yet."

"Oh, o-o-okay," Arthur said then turned his attention back to Reid. "No, no and no on all that stuff."

"But I'm going to be gone for a long time," Reid complained. The suit was making him sweat already; he hated it with a passion. It also reminded him of when he'd worn it to visit Evelyn during her time in the infirmary.

Kaitlyn walked over and said, "He's the expert and this is his car. Do what he says."

"But—" Reid protested.

Kaitlyn pulled Reid aside, out of earshot of Arthur and Hannah. "I've also packed a rifle, ammunition, food and water. If you're going to make it the entire way in that car, you just don't have the room inside. The backseat is full, the generator helps to convert the power generated from the sun, and the other equipment takes up a lot of space."

"Let me strap it to the doors," Reid offered.

"I heard that! No, you'll create more drag and reduce your range," Arthur chirped from the far end of the garage.

"So what can I take?" Reid asked.

"What I said plus the medicine you were given, and maybe a change of clothes," Kaitlyn replied.

Hannah lifted up her arm and asked, "Can I bring Meow Meow?" In her hand was a stuffed animal that looked like a cat.

"Meow Meow can go," Kaitlyn replied.

Hannah squeezed the stuffed animal and cheered.

"Fine," Reid said. He tossed his bag aside.

"Good, now let's have Arthur go over the details of the car," Kaitlyn said.

He took her arm and stopped her. "This is all approved?"

She nodded.

"The mayor has given this the green light?" he asked.

"Yes, he was just here an hour ago. You can go," she answered.

"And can we return?" he asked.

"If you find a cure, yes, come back and tell us," she replied. "But I can make no guarantees now that you'll be able to return if you can't find anything."

"I can't believe you made this happen," Reid said.

She gave him a slight nod and said, "Time is everything. Let's get you schooled up on the car; then we'll get you loaded and see you off."

Arthur covered with Reid how the car ran, and stressed that he'd need to keep his speed at a reasonable rate to maximize the battery charge. He covered how it recharged and told him the dos and don'ts.

Reid had never driven a Tesla, but for the most part, it ran like any other car.

"Do you have any q-q-q-questions?" Arthur asked.

"No, I'm good to go," Reid said.

Arthur pushed his way past Reid and ran his hand over the car. "I'm going t-t-to miss you, girl." He suddenly turned and jogged over to Reid. "I almost forgot." He reached into his pocket and pulled out a map of the southwest United States. "This is an old map of charging stations. It's from an old brochure. It shows where Tesla had charging stations set up along the route I believe you'll be taking."

"There's charging stations I can stop at?" Reid asked, shocked by the revelation.

"Yes, well, if they're still working. You see, um, um, Tesla had begun to build self-sustainable charging stations along remote routes like th-th-the desert. This was a new development before everything went to-to shit. These were powered by solar and the energy stored in Tesla batteries like the ones they use for their power walls. I-I-I-I'm not sure if you'll run into any, but you should check."

"I'll do that. How will I know where they are?" Reid asked.

"If you're taking the interstate, look for the symbol on signs. It looks like a-a-a gas pump with E-V on it. The sign will be blue," Arthur answered.

"Good to know."

Arthur walked off.

Reid turned around and said, "I'd like to say I'll bring it back in one piece, but..."

"She is not an it," Arthur barked as he whispered to the car.

"He's attached to the car, as you can see," Kaitlyn said as she gave Reid a nudge with her arm.

"I see that," Reid replied.

"When are we leaving?" Hannah asked. She walked up to Reid with Meow Meow cuddled in her arms.

"Soon," Reid answered.

"How do you feel?" Kaitlyn asked. The question triggered everyone and reminded them of why Reid was leaving.

"I feel fine," Hannah replied.

"That's good, dear," Kaitlyn said warmly.

"Hannah, jump in the car," Reid said. His nerves became heightened as the reality of it all began to sink in. "This is so surreal. Just yesterday I was in the garden with Hannah; now we're leaving Deliverance and she's got seven days or so to live."

Kaitlyn touched his arm. "I wish you all the luck in the world."

"When I found out she'd been bitten, I was sure she'd

die. Now I have hope at least, and I have you to thank for that."

"Just come back with Hannah well, a cure, and word that there's more out there than death," she said.

"I'll do my best," Reid said. He got into the car and started it up. He missed the guttural sound of exhaust, but who cared? This electric marvel was his means of getting them across the thousand miles they had to travel. He pulled out of the driveway and drove it down the streets slowly.

Passersby stopped and pointed, with many trotting to keep up. They were curious as to where the car had come from and where it was going.

"Everyone is staring at us," Hannah said. She pointed at the people through the heavily tinted glass.

"They haven't seen a car run in a long time," Reid said. He turned right and pulled up to the main gate.

A guard grabbed his handset and radioed in, "He's arrived."

"Open the gate," the voice crackled on his radio.

Perched in his office and staring down the street at the car, Kincaid watched. He knew without a doubt that would be the last time he'd see the car or its passengers. The hopes and aspirations that Kaitlyn had fed him were, to him, nothing more than fantasies, hence why he was fine with the deal he'd made. In Arthur he'd found a man very capable of handling many of the technical issues in town, in addition to Donaldson. "Goodbye, Mr. Flynn," he said. He turned around and went about his normal duties.

The guard unlocked the gate. The metal creaked as it

swung wide enough for the car to fit. It had been years since it had been open.

From behind the wheel, Reid watched in awe as the gate opened fully. Straight ahead of him lay the road. He hadn't driven on it in over nine years. Weeds, grass and debris lay strewn across it.

The guard waved him on.

Reid didn't move. He kept his gaze fixed on the furthest point on the straight road ahead. Soon he and Hannah would be there, then farther until they lost sight of Deliverance.

"You're clear, now go!" the guard howled.

Reid pressed the accelerator.

The car moved without making the sounds he had grown accustomed to in a normal combustion engine.

They crossed through the gate and were now on the far side. He stopped and looked into the rearview mirror as the gate began to close. He saw the curious faces of the towns-people slowly disappear until the gate shut with a loud clang.

He reached over, took Hannah's hand, and asked, "Are you ready to go see the ocean?"

"I am," she replied.

CHAPTER 3

Five Miles West of Logan, New Mexico

MICHAEL STOOD in the hallway and listened to his mother crying in her room. It had been over a day since his father and brother had left to go into town. The previous times his father had left, it took him twelve hours at the most to make the round trip. With the time passing twenty-four hours, it appeared that something horrible must have happened.

He walked to her door, raised his hand, but stopped short of knocking.

"Psst, just let her cry," Nana said behind him.

Michael turned to find Nana standing in her doorway. "Why are you up? You should be resting."

"How am I supposed to sleep with her crying nonstop?"

Michael went to Nana and said, "How are you feeling?"

"It's gonna take more than shitting blood to keep me down," Nana blurted out.

Repulsed by her choice of words, Michael steered the

conversation to something else. "Can I get you something to eat or drink?"

"I am hungry. Is there any more chicken stock left?"

"Can you have that?" he asked, concerned that she might be asking for something not on her diet.

"Will you get it for me, or do I have to go do it?" she snarled.

He sighed. "I'll go get some, but first you need to go lie down."

"Fine, now hurry up," Nana said. She stepped back into her room and closed the door.

He went to the kitchen but couldn't find the stock they'd had the night before. He rummaged through the pantry, looking for a can he could open, but found none.

"What are you looking for?" Tanya asked.

Michael jumped, startled by his mother's surprise presence in the kitchen. "Oh, um, I'm looking for chicken stock. Nana wants—"

"We're out of canned," Tanya said. "I can make her something else if she's hungry."

Michael didn't reply. Instead he walked up to her and said, "I heard you crying."

She couldn't lie; her swollen eyes were evidence. "I'm worried about your dad and brother."

"Maybe they went farther to look," Michael said.

She poured water into a saucepan and dropped in a chicken-flavored bouillon cube. "Maybe they did."

"I can go and look for them," he offered.

She shot Michael a look and said, "No."

"What if they need help?"

"No."

"You just told me that I needed to be more like them. I'm capable of helping them," Michael declared.

She faced him and said, "I'm sorry I said what I said to you. I was merely saying that things could change, which would change your role in the family."

"I'll be fine. Let me go and find them," Michael said. He was serious, though the idea was frightening, but proving to her that he could be just as useful as Chase drove him to the idea.

"I need you here more than ever," she said.

"But what about Nana?"

"If something bad happened to your father and brother, I can't risk losing you too."

"But what about Nana?"

She faced the counter again, her gaze now cast out towards the field and trees beyond. The morning's light was just peeking over the horizon. "She'll have to make do without her medicine. It's just the way it is."

"So my life is more important than Nana's?"

"Michael, stop with all the questions," Tanya snapped.

He stepped closer to her and said, "I can find them, I can."

"You don't even know where they went or where to look for them. You haven't been to Snowflake in years. Sending you out there would be a mistake."

"So you doubt my abilities?"

Frustrated, with her nerves frazzled, she barked, "I am doubtful, yes. There, I said it. You're a boy. You are a beautiful, wonderful and tender boy who would get destroyed out there. The world is vicious now, it's ruthless, and you, my precious son, are not ruthless."

Shocked by her brutal honesty, he asked, "So we just forget about Dad and Chase?"

"No, we don't forget about them, but your father made his choice. He did it out of devotion to Nana. I told him not to go, but he insisted."

"You said we do everything for family," Michael said.

"And I mean that, but there are times when we have to choose between one over another, and unfortunately, losing your father over Nana wasn't a choice that was fair to the family as a whole."

"But—" Michael said before he was interrupted.

"Your mother is right," Nana said. She shuffled into the kitchen and took a seat at the dinette table.

Startled by Nana's sudden appearance, Tanya asked, "How long have you been eavesdropping?"

"Long enough to hear you say something wise," Nana said. She cocked her head towards Michael and continued, "I would never have okayed your father or brother leaving to get me medicine; never in a million years would I have said go. I wasn't given a voice in the matter. Your father was always like you growing up."

"Me?" Michael asked, stunned by the comparison. He crossed the kitchen and sat down across from Nana.

"Yes, he was. You only know him as the rough-and-tumble man, but growing up, he had a tender heart like yours. He cared for everyone and everything around him. He was also talented physically, hence his ability on the football field. Unfortunately for you, you chose to play video games growing up versus playing outside with balls. I blame your mother for that," she sneered.

Tanya shook her head.

"But you are very much like your father, and I believe you're just as capable. Thing is, you lack confidence and sometimes lead with weakness."

"It's because no one allows me to do anything," Michael complained.

"And right there is some of that weakness," Nana said.

"Huh?"

"You blame others. Doing that is wrong. You must remember that you're ultimately responsible for your life. If you want to be physically strong, go do push-ups, get strong. Don't complain about it as if someone held you down while you got soft. If you want to be strong in the mind, change your mindset, take ownership of your mistakes and failures. Failing isn't a bad thing; hell, it's a good thing. Not a person I know who has succeeded in life didn't know failure. In fact, they failed more than they ever succeeded. Embrace your failures, let them make you a better person."

Michael listened to her words. They stung, but he knew deep down she was right.

"I'm not saying you should go in town to prove yourself. In fact, I think your mother is one hundred percent correct. But if you want to show her you're able, start acting like you are," Nana said.

He turned towards Tanya and found her looking on him with fond eyes.

Nana reached out and touched his hand. "Now where the hell is my chicken stock?"

"I'm making you some right now," Tanya replied as she rolled her eyes.

Nana stood and wobbled to the closest wall.

Michael rushed to her side and offered his arm for her to balance on. "I'll take you back to your room."

The two walked slowly, not saying a word to each other until they reached her door. She looked deep into his eyes and said, "You're stronger than you think, you must know that. Don't do anything foolish though. If your dad and brother don't return, your mother will need that strength of yours in order to survive."

"But shouldn't I go look for them?"

She stopped and growled, "No. They decided to go. If they don't come back, that's that."

"But Dad is your son," Michael said.

"Don't get me wrong, I love him, but his running off on fool's errands is on him. I'm old, sick and probably near death. Risking his life was just stupid." She coughed up phlegm, pulled out a handkerchief, and spit into it. After she wiped her lips, she continued. "You're a sweet boy, and you're able to do what's necessary, but running out to prove something will only get you killed."

"But Mom is really upset."

"I know she is, but you going out and getting killed won't make her happier."

"I know, but—"

"No, don't you dare think about it," Nana barked.

"But—"

"Do you understand me?" she asked sternly.

"Yes, I understand."

"Now, walk me to my bed."

He did as she said, helped her climb in, and covered her up. "I'll be back with your chicken stock shortly." He left the room, and as he walked back to the kitchen, all he could think about was proving to his mother that he could be the savior of the family by finding Dad and Chase.

Texas-New Mexico Border

"I need to go," Hannah whined. She'd been asleep for hours then woke up suddenly with the urge to urinate.

"I'll pull over here. Looks safe enough," Reid said as he slowed the car to a full stop. He carefully scanned the area. With the sun up to the east and the terrain flat with only sagebrush and tall grasses, it was easy for him to see. He pulled the pistol from a holster he had stuck between the console and seat and shoved it into his waistband. He exited the car and was instantly hit by a cool brisk wind from the northwest. A chill ran down his spine, and goose bumps broke out across his body.

Unable to wait, Hannah got out of the car. She looked around and asked, "Where should I go?"

"Just go next to the car."

"But—"

"Hannah, no one is out here. Just go."

As she went, he took the time to relieve himself too and get a good stretch. He'd been driving for twelve hours but had only gone one hundred and forty-five miles. The condition of the road was horrible and restricted his speed greatly. This concerned him, as he still had approximately one thousand miles to drive. He was happy to have a vehicle, but the Tesla's suspension couldn't handle the rough road. At the current rate he was going, he wouldn't be able to make it to the coast in time.

With his mind filled with thoughts, he didn't see Hannah as she walked over to a road sign.

"Welcome to New Mexico, The Land of Enchantment," she read.

"Huh?" He spun his head and saw her standing below the large yellow sign.

"Don't wander off."

"Are we in New Mexico?"

He stepped away from the car and walked over to her. "As soon as we pass the sign, we will be."

"So New Mexico is right there?" she asked, pointing at the ground just beyond the sign.

"Yep."

She took a few steps and said, "Look, I'm in New Mexico."

"You've now officially been to three states."

"Three?"

"I'm standing in Texas."

"When did we get to Texas?" she asked.

"Last night sometime," he replied. "Now we have a long drive across New Mexico, and then we'll be in Arizona, then across that state to California."

"Why is it called the land of enchantment?"

"Good question. I have no idea."

She turned and looked to the west. "I can't wait to see the coast and the waves crashing."

"Me too."

"I hope we get there before..." she said before she paused.

He walked up alongside her and put his arm over her shoulder. "We'll make it, I just know it."

"It's pretty out here," she said, a gentle smile on her face.

He gave her a tender look. Even with the weight of death hovering over her, she could still see the beauty in everything.

She spotted a small flowering bud coming from a weed, bent down and picked it. "Look, Daddy, a flower." She brought it to her nose and sniffed.

"I don't think it's that type of flower."

"Can I keep it?"

"Of course."

"It will remind me of being here. Call it a keepsake," she said.

"C'mon, Hannah, let's get back on the road," he said and took her hand.

The two walked back to the car.

He opened her door and let her climb in. He walked around to the driver's side, but before he opened the door, he inhaled deeply. The crisp cool air smelled good.

Hannah cried out, "Daddy."

He opened his door and got in. "What's wrong?" He saw her staring into the visor mirror, terror all over her face.

"Daddy, no," she cried.

"Honey, what's wrong?"

She faced him and then he saw it: a dark red bloody mark was in the corner of both her eyes. He hadn't noticed when they were outside, but then again he hadn't stared at her face.

"It's the first sign, isn't it?" she moaned.

He couldn't answer her; instead he leaned over and embraced her. "We're going to make it to the island, don't you worry."

She was right, blood-colored eyes was the first symptom of the disease. This was now confirmation that she had it and meant that the clock had officially begun. He had seven days from now to find her a cure or pray that she was among the less than ten percent who would survive.

Outskirts of Dalhart, Texas

Two men threw Emily to the floor. She scurried to run off, but they quickly grabbed her and held her still.

Sitting in a chair adorned like a throne, Emile held a glass in one hand and a long knife in the other. "Sister, sister, sister."

"Emile, please let me explain," Emily cried.

"How do you explain away the fact that you helped that woman get away? How do you explain that you let her beat me, and stole that new car?"

"She made me do it," Emily lied.

Emile shook his head and said, "No, she didn't. You chose to do it, just like you did years ago. You've been wanting to leave since we came here, and I don't know why. How is it that you're my sister yet you don't care about our relationship? I'm not just disappointed that you let that woman beat me, I'm heartbroken."

"I'm sorry. Please forgive me," Emily begged.

"What should I do with you this time? One man is dead because of you."

"Please, Emile, forgive me this one last time. I won't ever do it again, please," she pleaded. Tears ran down her face.

Emile motioned for the two men to leave the room. When the door closed, he stood and walked over to her. He squatted in front of her and lifted her head. He looked deeply into her eyes and said, "What should I do with you?"

"Forgive me."

"You know I can't do that this time, not after you killed Jay. No, there must be a consequence for your actions."

"Just don't kill me, please," she cried.

"What other choice do I have? How do I go tell Jay's brother that I've let you live. You know our rules, an eye for an eye. By those rules you should die for what you did, and he can then consume you."

She reached out to him, but he pulled back.

"Tell me another way and I'll try to make it happen. You're my sister, and I don't want to see you die, but if I do nothing, I risk my own position," Emile urged.

"Let me go," she replied.

"I can't. You should have been smarter and not walked on the road. You should have known we'd come looking for you. Now I'm stuck making a decision that no doubt will result in your death, the death of my own flesh and blood."

"Please, Emile, please," she cried. "It wasn't my fault. That woman made me do it."

He shook his head and stood. "Stop, just stop."

"She took me hostage," Emily lied.

"Have dignity at least, Emily. These lies are beneath you."

She crawled towards him and sobbed at his feet.

"Emily, just stop. It's pathetic," Emile said. He scooted away from her, leaving her moaning on the dirty floor.

"I'm going to hand you over to Jay's brother, Nate. Your fate is in his hands now. If you can convince him to spare your life, then so be it," Emile said, taking a seat.

Emily got to her feet and raced to Emile. She dropped to her knees, clasped her hands together as if in prayer, and pleaded, "No, Emile, no, don't give me over to Nate. You know him, he's brutal. He'll rape me then torture me. I don't deserve this."

"I'm sorry, Emily, you did this to yourself," Emile said, a sadness on his face. "I've done everything in my power to protect you, keep you innocent and pure. No man has ever touched you because I want you to stay the beautiful sister I've always known."

"I'm your sister, your twin sister!" she lashed out.

"This is the most difficult decision I've ever had to make, but I can't let you go. I can't show you mercy, because you had a hand in killing Jay."

She buried her face in her hands and sobbed.

He leaned down and put his hands on her shoulders

and softly said, "Remember when we found Mom and Dad dead?"

She nodded.

"What did I tell you then?"

"To be brave," she answered, tears streaming down her face.

"I need you to be brave again. You're a smart girl, you can survive this, but I can't have a hand in it."

She lifted her head to look at him but saw something else, something she could use to free herself. Not hesitating, she reached out, grabbed Emile's knife by the handle, and pulled it free of its sheath. With it held firmly in her grasp, she cocked back then came forward and plunged the six-inch blade deep into his chest; the only thing stopping it was the hilt. She removed it and plunged it in again.

He grunted in pain. The expression on his face shifted from sadness to shock. He clutched at the two wounds. Blood poured freely, drenching his clothes and leaving his appearance ashen. "Why?"

Fearing that he could cry out, she placed the blade against his throat and slid it across.

His neck split open and blood oozed out.

He let out one last gasp then slumped over dead.

"Sorry, brother," she said. "But I'm tired of being your prisoner."

On a table next to him sat Brienne's journal. She grabbed it and headed for the rear exit.

Twelve Miles Northeast of Logan, New Mexico

Brienne found cover under a desert broom, an evergreen shrub, and relaxed against her pack. Her mind raced about the events of the past twenty-four to thirty-six hours and how lucky she had been to get away from Emile and his pack of cannibals. Her fear that they'd come after her was now gone, as they didn't have the means to travel the distance to find her. But after finally experiencing people like that, she'd be more careful. Her goal was to get to Yuma, and if it took her a few more days or even weeks because she was traveling overland versus roads to avoid people, then so be it.

She pulled out the plastic bottle of water and took a sip. She swallowed and glanced at the half-full bottle. "I need to get some more and soon."

The road she was paralleling was a few hundred feet away, and she knew that before long she'd encounter a town or a house; then she'd have to take the risk to secure more water.

She recalled the notebook she'd found in the Camry and took it out of the pack. She leafed through it to find some random notes, grocery lists and even a couple of pages of tic-tac-toe games. She missed her journal and this would suffice. Writing about her journey had become a habit, and it also served as a form of therapy for her. Having lost it to Emily was upsetting, but she wasn't someone who clung to things like that.

After finding a pen, she went to jot down the date but had to think hard. She remembered the date from the day before she'd been captured and knew that two days had come after that, giving her the current date. She then backdated and wrote about her entire encounter with Emile and Emily back in Woodruff. She described in detail the holding area with the other people and how Emile had come to see her, a piece of freshly cooked human flesh in his hands. She explained how she'd escaped with the help of Emily and how shortly after she'd abandoned her on the road.

She stopped and thought about what she'd done. Had she sentenced Emily to death by leaving her there? Or would Emily carry on alone like she had for all these years? Who knew, but when she thought about regret, she had none. Maybe before the world went to hell she would have reconsidered abandoning someone in a dangerous place. But even after everything that had happened in the world, killing and eating another human being seemed like a bridge too far.

However, there was plenty of evidence from history to show that sort of depravity wasn't rare. She recalled reading about incidents where desperate people had resorted to such things. In college she took world history, and during her studies of pre-World War Two Europe, she read about how the Soviets under Stalin had sent six thousand people to an island in Siberia called Nazino. They were political prisoners and petty criminals. Stalin's plan was to allow them to live off the land and be free of support from the state. Under the watchful eye of soldiers, the settlers, for lack of a better word, were deposited with only twenty tons of flour and nothing else. They were given no tools, shelters, equipment, literally nothing. Quickly chaos erupted, and within weeks the people resorted to violence, murder and cannibalism. So to think that after such a short period of time people back in the 1930s were eating each other, now fast-forward to post World War Three America and it seemed reasonable, but still she just couldn't get her head around it.

She paused and wondered if she could ever find herself capable of such a thing and quickly dismissed the idea. There were some people who could, and some who would never; she put herself in the latter camp.

She finished her thoughts and closed the notebook. Leaning back, she stared into the blue sky and watched as the pillowy white clouds slowly moved, their forms changing. Nature didn't seem to care what had happened. The sun still rose and the moon still appeared in the sky. When looking at the bigger picture of the planet, what humans had done to each other wouldn't matter. This was just a blip, a microsecond in the existence of the world.

Of course, many people had predicted it, with some going as far as preparing for it. She wondered if one could truly prepare. Was it possible to imagine all scenarios or have the requisite mindset to do what is necessary? Of course, when one was sitting in the comfort of the modern world, they could, but to truly experience it was something else. She remembered her father, who was a veteran; he didn't talk much about his time while in service, but she did overhear him now and then talk with friends he'd served with. How they'd joke about armchair tough guys sitting behind the glow of their computer screens, ranting and raving about how they'd do this or that, when they never could cut it, really. They'd talk about how those armchair warriors were always ready to declare war or fight, yet when they were young, they had an excuse for not joining. His father always called them the 'almosts'. They'd meet him, and as soon as it came to his serving in the war, they'd say I almost joined, blah, blah, blah.

Her father, though, had been affected by his time over-seas fighting. She recalled how her mother would joke about his inability to sleep or how he'd wake cursing. Living on the razor's edge between life and death took a toll on someone's mental well-being, so how could someone really prepare? she thought. Yeah, they could get all the fun stuff and so forth, but how could one prepare to see chaos, death, brutality? The truth is you can't. Even the toughest soldiers eventually tap out or get what's called combat fatigue.

It did make sense to prepare, to have the amenities or sustenance to make it in the weeks or even years after a calamity, but the true survivors had a mindset, a hardness to them that no one could prepare for—you know when you know. She often wondered if she'd eventually crack, and quickly came to the conclusion that if she had to deal with the likes of Emile frequently, she probably would. In all her travels she had killed but had only done so to protect herself, and found that justification satisfactory to her mental state, but to murder—she didn't think she could do that and still remain human.

A hummingbird flew past her face and hovered just in front of the desert broom. It darted up, down, left and right before veering away just as fast as it had arrived.

She marveled that life still kept going without regard for what humans had done. It was nice to just sit and feel. Too often her days were spent living on the edge, her senses heightened, but for this brief reprieve she was taking in the moment, living in this small space and time. She watched the hummingbird dart from bush to shrub before it disappeared out of sight. Her thoughts then shifted to her life before and how she rarely had much reflection or appreciation for nature. She had been given a beautiful world, yet her time had often been spent immersed in the devices and things that man had created. Regret quickly consumed her. She wished she could go back and take the time to watch a hummingbird or show her son the beauty of life, but like most people then, she had been consumed by the trappings of modern human existence. She'd given that too much significance to take notice of a colorful bird or a cloud or anything.

In the years that followed, she had questioned how it all came to be. How could a world already struggling with fighting a deadly disease think it prudent to go to war with itself? Not even then could the nations of the world think past their own special interests. It was as if humans were doomed from the start. We had given in to our primal instincts, and even now she found people unwilling to work with each other, with some even consuming the flesh of their fellow humans.

Weary from the preceding days and distraught over again witnessing humans doing what humans do best—kill —she cleared her thoughts and relaxed further into the pack. Her eyes grew heavy. Sleep sounded perfect; sleeping during the day also made more sense. Best to travel at night.

She closed her eyes and fell asleep.

Forty Miles Southwest of Dalhart, Texas

When the headlight of the 1970 Honda CB350 motorcycle hit the back of the Chevy Traverse, Emily spotted the Texas license plate and knew it was the vehicle Brienne had been driving. She coasted the bike and came to a stop. "Well, well," she said, looking at the vehicle. She hopped off the bike and walked up to the open driver's door. With the light from the motorcycle giving her ample light, she glanced in. Seeing the car was empty, she looked around the area. Ahead of her was the Camry, and by its condition she knew Brienne had scavenged it.

Like Brienne before, she walked to the Camry and gave it a once-over but came up short of anything of value except a map of the United States.

She had managed to leave the compound relatively easily. But, of course, it required that she think outside the box. Knowing that the entrance would be guarded like before, she planned a distraction to pull everyone away, and the best way to get people looking another way was to set fire to something, and the bigger the fire, the better.

Even though some of the old gasoline wasn't potent enough for modern vehicles, it still was flammable enough to light on fire. She took a few gallons of old fuel, dumped it all over the motor pool area, and lit it. In no time the flames were licking the top of the twenty-five-foot-tall barn where they held their small fleet of motorcycles. This was all she needed. With everyone focused on addressing the fire, she stole one of the bikes with a sidecar loaded with fuel cans and headed out the now unguarded entrance.

The drive was easy, she took the route she'd gone earlier, but she never expected to find the Traverse. If that vehicle was abandoned, it only meant that Brienne was on foot.

After fueling up her motorcycle, she opened the map and searched on it until she found approximately where she was. Her finger then guided over the roads or highways that would take her to Loreto, stopping when she saw the name Yuma. "Hmm, interesting."

Her thoughts shifted to Brienne and what she'd done to her. She removed the diary she'd taken from her and flipped it open to a page she had dog-eared. She traced down the page until she came to Brienne's address in Yuma. "So this is where you're going. Well, maybe I'll pay you a visit on my way to Loreto. She closed the diary, shoved it back in the backpack, and placed it in the sidecar.

Never in her life had she ever felt a sense of purpose. Life in the compound was a daily routine, one that required not much from her. Emile kept her safe and gave her almost no responsibilities. She hated it. She did despise the fact that they had turned to cannibalism to survive, but after so many years of doing it, it had become second nature. When she'd hear about the rumors of secret bases or cures or safe zones, she'd become intrigued and hungered to go find them. Not until she'd heard about Brienne's abilities and after reading her diary did she believe she'd found the one person who could help her realize her dream of getting to one of these safe zones.

She was free of the compound and her brother, and the world lay before her. She could do anything now, go anywhere, but all she could focus on was Brienne and paying her back for the way she'd treated her. She didn't want to kill anymore, she reckoned herself a changed person since leaving the compound, but when she thought of Brienne, she saw red, and if she had to give herself one excuse to kill, it would be to kill Brienne and her family if they were still alive.

She kick-started the motorcycle and throttled the engine. A smile stretched across her tender face; it was a smile of a woman with a purpose and a destination. That destination was Yuma, and her purpose was finding Brienne.

CHAPTER 4

Five Miles West of Logan, New Mexico

MICHAEL ENTERED the hallway from his room and paused. He listened for any sound that would tell him if his mother was awake. He heard nothing. He moved to her bedroom door and pressed his ear against the door and could hear her breathing heavily, a sign that she was deeply sleeping. Quickly he rushed towards the kitchen, stopped at a coat closet, and opened it. He found what he was looking for, a jacket, and pulled it out. He slipped it on, ensuring to be as quiet as possible. He scurried into the kitchen and jumped when he saw Nana sitting there.

"What are you doing?" he asked.

She gave him a curious look and replied, "I could ask the same of you. It's five in the morning and you're awake and wearing a jacket. Just where are you going?"

"I, um, I'm going outside to do some work on those trenches Dad and Chase were working on."

"Come and sit," she said and motioned to a chair next to her at the table.

He sat down. "I need to get to work."

"Is that what you're doing?" Nana asked.

"You and Mom asked me to change, so I am. I'm going out and continuing the work Dad was doing."

"Is that all?"

"What do you think I'm doing?" he asked.

"You wouldn't be headed into town, would you?"

"Ah, no, of course not," he replied. He cut his gaze from hers and stared down at his fidgeting thumbs.

Nana reached across the table and took his hands into hers. "Look me in the eyes and tell me that."

He swallowed and did as she asked. He stared into her hazel eyes and said, "I'm going outside to work on those pits Dad didn't finish."

"And nothing more?"

"And nothing more. Now can I go, please?"

"It's still dark out. Why would you go out to work on the pits?" Nana asked.

"The sun will be up soon. I'm getting all the stuff together in the barn, then going," Michael said.

"And you're not lying to me?"

He grunted and said, "No, Nana, now can I go?"

She cocked her head, let go of his hands, and said, "Go ahead."

He stood up promptly and headed for the door.

"Michael."

He turned and asked, "Yes?"

"In life people can only ask; no one can make you do

anything. It's up to you whether you do. Those are called choices and you should make them weighing all the available information and calculating as best you can the risks, and if those risks bring something greater than what you could possibly lose."

"Okay," he replied, his tone indicating he wasn't quite sure what she was saying.

"But if you do have something planned that's risky, don't do it because you think you need to prove something, do it because you believe that, one, you can do it, and two, that if you can't, the damage done isn't irreparable."

"Nana, I'd like to get working."

"Go ahead and, Michael, don't ever forget that you're my favorite."

"How would Chase feel if he heard you say that?"

"How do you know I don't say it to him too?" She smiled.

He shook his head and exited the house.

Two Miles East of Santa Rosa, New Mexico

"They're burning," Hannah cried as bloody tears streamed down her cheeks.

"Don't rub them, whatever you do," Reid pleaded with her.

Hannah's eyes had gotten worse. A searing pain and uncontrollable itchiness were now plaguing her. The entire whites of her eyes were now gone, replaced by a blood red.

Reid had pulled the car over so he could attend to her and stop her from rubbing them. The timing of his stop was fortuitous due to the road ahead being blocked by debris. He saw a path around it, but he wanted to scout it out before driving forward.

"Do something!" she moaned.

His stomach turned and his heart melted when he looked at her sitting there, blood covering her cheeks and her beautiful eyes now tortured by the disease. "Let me get the drops," he said. He reached in the back and pulled out the bag of medicines that Thomas had given him. He recalled there was a bottle of eye drops. He dug through until he found it. "Here," he said as he screwed off the top.

"What is it?" she asked.

"They're eye drops. They'll help soothe your eyes."

She didn't hesitate; she scooted close to him and lifted her head so that her head faced up.

He hovered the dropper over her eye and squeezed the bottle. A series of drops fell into her eye

She yelped in pain. "It stings!" She lifted her head and went to rub her eyes with her palm.

"No," he said, grabbing her hand. "You can't do that; it makes it worse. I know that sounds strange, but soon the pain will go away."

"When?"

"Soon, a day or so," he answered.

She sobbed, bringing more bloody tears down her cheeks. The tears dropped from her cheeks and chin and dotted her tan shirt, coloring it red.

"Let me do the other eye. This will help," he said.

"No, it stings. Leave me alone."

"Hannah, this will help them. Thomas wouldn't have given it to me otherwise."

She pulled away from him. "No."

"Hannah, stop. This will help soothe them. I know it stings at first, but it will help."

"NO."

"Hannah Marie, stop."

"Daddy, it hurts," she cried.

"I know it does, sweetheart, but these drops will help even though you might think it won't," he said as he softened his tone.

She sobbed.

"Help!" a scream came from outside the car.

Reid looked up, startled. He scanned all around but saw no one.

"Help!" the scream came again. This time Reid identified it as a woman's voice and pinpointed that it came from down the road in front of him. He looked out the front but saw nothing except a large billboard sign, advertising a Flying J truck stop miles ahead, with thick shrubs all around the base of it.

Hannah slowed her crying and listened. "Is that someone yelling?"

"Yeah," Reid said softly.

"Help me!" the woman yelled.

Hannah wiped her cheeks and said, "Are you going to help her?"

"I don't know."

"But she needs help."

"Please help me!" the woman shouted.

Reid kept his gaze fixed on the road ahead, looking for any movement, but saw nothing. Fear began to grip him. He started the car and put his fingers on the gear shift when Hannah stopped him. "You're not going to help her?"

"Something doesn't feel right," Reid replied.

"But she's in trouble and we're here. Shouldn't we help?"

Various scenarios ran through Reid's thoughts. All of them resulted in something bad happening.

"Daddy, aren't we supposed to help those in need?" she asked, referring to a saying she'd learned in school.

"Yes, we're supposed to help people, but…"

"But what?"

He looked at her and said, "This is different. We're not in Deliverance anymore. Those rules don't apply out here." He couldn't help but think that the road being blocked and the scream had something to do with each other.

"Why not?"

"Please help me, hurry, please!" the woman shrieked. Her voice sounded desperate.

Reid sat frozen. He kept scanning everything out in front of him but saw nothing, no woman, no one. He couldn't explain where the woman was except to think she was behind the thick shrubs.

Hannah opened her door and stepped out.

Startled, Reid gasped, "What are you doing?"

"She needs help," Hannah replied bluntly.

He reached out and grabbed her arm. "No, stay in here."

"Help me, please God, help me!" the woman cried out.

"Daddy, she needs our help. We must help her," Hannah

said, her tone showing a strength and conviction rarely seen in her.

"Fine, I'll go, but you stay here, okay?" Reid said. He was hesitant but also felt a tinge of sympathy for the woman. He realized he could be risking them, but just leaving her could literally be signing her death warrant.

"You'll go?"

"Yes, now get back in the car," Reid ordered.

"Promise."

"I promise, now get back in the car."

Hannah did as he said. "Well?"

He removed the pistol from a holster he had tucked next to the console and opened his door. "You know how to drive this, so hop behind the wheel. If something happens to me, drive, just get out of here."

"And go where?"

"Just do as I say," Reid said. He exited the car and closed the door. "Get behind the wheel."

She climbed over the console and adjusted the seat. She motioned with her hand for him to go.

"I'm going," he said.

"Yes, please come help me," the woman said. By her comment it was apparent she could see him.

"Where are you?"

"Underneath the billboard, I'm tied to a post," she cried out.

"Are you alone?"

"Yes, but hurry, please."

"I'm armed, so this had better not be a trick," Reid said.

"Please hurry," she hollered.

Reid cautiously advanced, his head slowly scanning left then right and back again, looking for anything out of place or anyone else. He cleared the distance between the car and the billboard sign and found an older woman. She was in her late fifties and tied to the far right post, which was covered by bushes. "Who did this to you?"

"Some men, they'll come back for me," she answered, her thin gray hair blew across her gaunt and wrinkled face with each passing breeze.

Again Reid was struck by a deep sense of dread. This didn't make sense, he thought.

"Sir, please help untie me," she begged.

"Why are you tied up here?" he asked and looked around. "There's nothing around here. This is the middle of nowhere." Reid was right, they were surrounded by nothing but flat desert. The only thing around was the billboard sign.

"Are you going to untie me or not?" the woman asked. She struggled with the bindings.

Hannah screamed.

Reid spun around to find a man standing next to the car, a rifle in his hands, with the muzzle pointed at Hannah. Reid raised his pistol and aimed at the man.

"I suggest you put down your gun or whoever's in that car will get shot," the woman said.

"No," Reid barked.

"I'll shoot her!" the man said. His voice sounded like someone with a speech impediment.

"Do as my boy says," the woman ordered. She slipped out of her bindings, grabbed a revolver she had hidden, cocked the hammer, and pointed it at Reid. "Best you drop it."

After he heard the distinct cock of the hammer, Reid realized he'd made a colossal error in judgment. He had two choices: shoot the man and hope he could get the woman, or give up and suffer whatever fate these two had in store for them.

The woman walked up behind Reid and said, "Drop it."

"What do you want? If it's food, we have it. If it's water, we have that too. Just tell me what you want."

"I want you," she said. "And whoever is in that car with ya."

"It's a little girl, Ma, a little girl," the man said excitedly.

Hearing the man speak again, Reid now recognized that the man sounded as if he had special needs, maybe even Down syndrome. "My daughter is sick."

"How old is she?"

"She's nine, but she's sick. You need to let us move on. You don't want to get the dog flu."

The expression on the woman's face shifted to joy. "She's sick with the H5N7? How perfect."

Reid cocked his head back and gave her an odd look just as she struck him in the head with the butt of the revolver.

The blow to the head was enough to knock him out.

Hannah screamed in horror as she watched her father fall to the ground.

The man laughed hysterically.

The woman approached the car, stopped at the driver's side window, and said, "I hear you're sick, sweetheart."

"Daddy, Daddy!" Hannah screamed.

"It'll be okay now, sweetheart," the woman said, motioning for her son to lower his rifle.

"Leave us alone," Hannah screamed.

"Look, Marvin, her eyes. She is sick and only a day or two. This is perfect."

"Ha ha, we did good, didn't we, Ma?" Marvin chuckled.

"Leave us alone!" Hannah screamed again.

"Sweetheart, it's your lucky day 'cause my name is Dr. Hillary Cobb and I can heal you."

One Mile Northeast of Logan, New Mexico

After coming across a fourth building, Brienne knew she was closing in on a town. With a town came people, which translated into possible trouble. She needed to get a better vantage point than what she had, so that required her to find higher ground.

She climbed out of the dry creek bed she'd been traveling down and headed towards a rugged slope to the west. There she hoped to get a view of her surrounding area.

She crossed a road, and it was there she saw a sign that read SNOWFLAKE. "Isn't that quaint," she said to herself with a chuckle. She quickly navigated around small boulders, rocks and brush until she reached the top. She took cover behind a massive boulder and removed her pack. She dug through it and pulled out one of the lucky finds from the Camry, a set of binoculars.

"Let's see what's out there," she said to herself. She put the binoculars to her eyes and adjusted them until she could see clearly. In front of her, which was south, she saw the edge of Snowflake. It was a small town and just before the war had boasted a population of about five thousand people. She carefully scanned the buildings in sight but saw no one; however, she wasn't satisfied. The last thing she needed was to make an assumption the town was vacant only to start heading that way and get caught again, which had happened back in Woodruff.

A scream echoed in the distance and gave her confirmation that the town wasn't a proverbial ghost town.

With her elbows propping her up, she pivoted on the boulder and scanned the area to find the source of the scream.

Another scream bellowed out.

This second scream enabled her to narrow the area where it was coming from. She adjusted the binoculars and scanned, but still came up empty. "Where are you?"

Out from around a building a young man ran. It was Chase.

She saw the movement, turned, and caught him in the binoculars sprinting, and by the look on his face, he was terrified. She guessed him to be late teens. Another group of men appeared from the building, and by the looks of them, they were not happy. She watched as Chase tore around another building and took cover in a shed.

The men in pursuit ran past the shed and continued in the direction they felt Chase had gone.

"Don't look in the shed; please don't look in the shed," she said to herself.

A full minute went by.

Chase stuck his head out and headed back in the direction he'd come, only to be spotted by the men again.

"You'd better run," Brienne said.

Chase raced around a single-level commercial space, stopped when he spotted a pipe lying on the ground, and picked it up. He put his back to the wall and waited.

"Smart, best to fight back," Brienne said, happy to see him finally take a stand even though she felt his luck would probably run out.

The men made the turn.

Chase swung the pipe and hit the closest man in the jaw. He toppled to the ground.

"Ouch." Brienne chuckled.

Chase took a step and swung once more. This time he missed as the man jumped out of the way.

"What are you going to do now?" Brienne asked, referring to Chase's harrowing situation.

Surrounded by three men, Chase kept swinging the pipe but to no effect.

"They're just wearing you down," Brienne said, frustrated.

Movement to the west, about a quarter mile out, caught her attention. She lifted her head from the binoculars and looked to confirm that she'd seen something. She caught sight of the movement again. It was someone ducking and covering as they moved. "Hmm, who are you?"

A scream echoed from below; this time it sounded different.

She peered through the binoculars to see Chase had

been caught, but they weren't taking him prisoner. One of the men had driven a knife into his chest. "Shit."

Chase yelped one last time. He dropped his head and fell to the ground.

The men mumbled something unintelligible and walked off, carrying their colleague who had been struck with the pipe.

She watched them intently until they went back to the building from which they'd come. It was then she spotted something near the far side of the building. She focused on it and realized it was a body. Blood was spattered on the wall behind it and the body was lying on its side. She could tell by the size and build that it was a man, and the only distinguishing item was a dark green military field jacket. Were this person and the young man just killed together? she wondered. "Damn killers," she said. The movement to the west caught her attention again. This time she brought the binoculars into play. It was a younger boy, and by his look she guessed he was anywhere from fifteen to sixteen years old. "Don't do it; don't go into town." What she didn't know was it was Michael, and he was there to find Chase and his dad.

Michael had taken cover behind an abandoned car. He lifted his head, looked left then right, and tucked his head back down.

"Just stay where you are." Brienne gritted her teeth.

Unaware of what had just transpired with Chase, Michael shot out from his hiding space and sprinted across a small gravel lot and took up a hiding place behind a dumpster. He was heading in the direction of the original building Brienne had seen Chase and the other men come from, meaning he was headed into the arms of the very men who had just killed Chase.

In shock and distress, Brienne could see what was about to happen as if it were a slow-motion train crash.

Like he had at the abandoned car, Michael peeked around the dumpster and looked around.

Through the binoculars, Brienne could see he had fear written all over his face. "No, please just stay where you are." She also could see a resemblance. "You're family, aren't you?"

Now less than a thousand feet from the building where the men had retreated to, Michael only had to run to his right at a forty-five-degree angle to be in front of it.

"Don't do it. Just stay where you are," Brienne grumbled.

As if Michael had heard her, he shifted to the left side of the dumpster, looked around the corner, and took off in the opposite direction of the building.

Brienne sighed. The tension for her was riding high. After witnessing the murder of Chase, she did not want to see the boy killed.

Hollering came from the building.

Brienne shifted and looked to see the three men had stepped outside and spotted Michael running. "Oh, c'mon."

The men gave chase and ran towards Michael, who had now spotted them and was racing away.

Brienne had seen enough. She lowered the binoculars, slid down the boulder, and grabbed her rifle. "Time to make this a fair game." She got back up but now had the rifle in her shoulder. Using the boulder to steady her, she peered through the optics. "God, I hope this is sighted in." She placed the reticle of the scope on the first man in the pack. She flipped off the safety with her thumb and placed her index finger on the trigger. She steadied her breathing and began to apply pressure to the trigger.

The rifle fired.

The first man tumbled to the ground; dirt flew up around him. His body lay motionless. She turned her sights on the next man, who was looking around in fear at what had just happened. She fired again and dropped the second man with a well-placed shot to his chest.

The third man stopped, turned around and ran away.

Brienne wasn't done. She put the reticle on his back and squeezed the trigger. Like the other two times, the rifle fired and her aim was true.

The 5.56 mm round struck the third man in the center of his back. He collapsed to the ground face-first, dead.

Satisfied, she mused, "It appears it's sighted in."

Michael, fearful that he could also be a target, disappeared in a drainage ditch.

Brienne looked at the building, anticipating others might emerge, but after a few minutes, no one did. She knew there was another man, the one who had been hit with the pipe, yet he didn't come out. She lowered herself off the boulder, flipped the selector switch to SAFE, and grabbed her pack. She felt good that she'd helped a young kid and chalked it up as her way of getting good karma. "Well, this town is a no go."

Michael sat in the ditch, panting. He looked at his pants

and saw they were wet. At first he didn't know how; then he recalled urinating on himself out of fear. He wasn't sure if he should get up and make a run for it or just stay and pray that no one was coming for him.

With her rifle at the ready, Brienne made her way to the ditch. She stopped twenty feet away and hollered out, "Hey, kid, I'm not here to hurt you, but if you want to live, best you come with me."

Michael sat frozen.

"I won't hurt you, I promise," she said.

"I'm armed," Michael cried out.

"No, you're not. Now c'mon before some others come out."

Michael thought about it and came to the conclusion that she was right. He didn't know what he had been doing in the first place and quickly discovered he wasn't ready to take on anyone. Plus if she was a threat, why hadn't she shot him when she had a chance? "Don't shoot," he said. He slowly stood with his arms raised.

When she saw his youthful face appear, she laughed. "Hurry up."

"Please don't shoot me," he begged.

"I'm not going to shoot you. Now hurry up," she said.

He climbed out of the ditch just in front of her.

She saw that his pants were soaked in his crotch and down his left leg. "Where were you going?"

"To find my father and brother," he said.

"They were in town?"

"Yeah."

She thought of the young man who had been killed and wondered if he had been his brother.

"If they came here, it might not have been such a good idea," she said.

"Hey, you!" a voice boomed in the distance.

"Listen, kid, more of those guys are coming, and now they're going to be pissed. If you want to live, come with me."

"But my father and brother?"

"Like I said, if they came here, it doesn't look good."

A series of gunshots cracked in the distance.

She lowered herself and barked, "You come with me now or stay; but I'm leaving." She faced north and sprinted away.

Michael followed her.

The two ran north for ten minutes. When they had put more than a mile between them and where they had been, she stopped and said, "Let's take a break."

He was out of breath and ready to stop.

They took cover in the dry creek bed, with him on the ground exhaling heavily and she near the rim keeping an eye out.

"Why did you help me?" he asked.

"'Cause you needed it, that's why," she replied.

"Thank you."

"Where are you from?"

"That way a few miles," he replied, his finger pointed west.

"Luckily for you, I'm headed that way," she said. "What's your name?"

"Michael, my name is Michael."

"How long have your father and brother been gone?" she asked, her gaze fixed on the south and her rifle nestled in her shoulder.

"Well over a day," Michael answered as he took deep breaths.

"And you're sure they went to town?"

"Yes."

Feeling confident they weren't being followed, she slid down the embankment and laid her rifle in her lap. "Do you have water at your house?"

"Yes, we have a well with good flow," Michael replied. "Dad set up a manual pump on it after we lost our power years ago."

"How about I escort you back to your house and you repay me by giving me some water and food?" Brienne said.

"But what about my father and brother?" Michael asked.

She weighed telling him what she'd seen.

"Can you help me find them?" he asked.

"I'm not going back there, and I suggest you don't either."

"But I need to find them," Michael stressed.

"You saw those men; if they caught you, they probably would have killed you."

"Why would they do that?"

"Why does anyone do anything? I just escaped from a compound run by cannibals, so trust me, I don't know why people do what they do. But I will say this, if your father and brother went there and haven't returned, there's a good chance those guys got them."

"You think they're dead?" Michael asked.

Brienne chewed on the idea of telling him what she had seen, but doing so might upset him to the point of making it impossible to get him back. "Anyone at home waiting on you?"

Michael looked down shamefully and said, "My mom and Nana."

"I'm sure they're worried sick."

"I'm such a loser."

She could see the sad look on his face. She wasn't sure about the dynamic at home, but for her he was nothing of the sort. He was willing to risk his life to find his family. "I don't know why you'd say that, but going out to find them was a bold move. Although I have to ask, what was your plan if you encountered anyone bad?"

He pulled out a pocketknife and held it in his palm.

"You were going to stab them with that?" she asked in a mocking tone.

"My dad gave it to me," he said. The knife was an old non-locking blade with a fake ivory handle. "It was given to him by his dad."

Knowing the sentiment, she shifted her tone and said, "Looks like a nice knife."

"They're dead, aren't they?"

"I don't know, but if we hang around here too long, we might be. Let's get moving to your house, okay?"

Michael nodded. He got to his feet and brushed off his pants. "Why are you helping me?"

She shrugged her shoulders and said, "Sometimes we have to help each other. And to prove a point that not everyone out here is bad."

One Mile South of Santa Rosa, New Mexico

Reid opened his eyes. Above him was the poster of a kitten dangling from a tree branch with the words *HANG IN THERE* at the bottom. He went to sit up but found his arms and legs were bound and secured to the table he was on. He looked left and right; around him were stainless steel tables and carts. On the walls more posters were hung. These were not adorned with cuddly kittens; instead one was about the importance of vaccinations, and another covered the food pyramid and eating healthy. A stainless steel cart was parked next to him, and on it was a syringe, empty vials, rubber tubing and cotton balls. By the looks of it, he was in a doctor's office.

The only light in the room was a small lamp, which told him wherever he was, they had power.

"Hey!" he called out. "Where's my daughter?"

The only door quickly opened behind him. He swung his head, but he couldn't see who was there. All he could do was hear the heavy breathing. "Untie me and take me to my daughter."

Footfalls approached Reid.

"Just untie me and take me to my daughter, that's all I ask," he said.

Marvin appeared. His face and mouth were smeared with a dark red substance.

Reid instantly thought it was blood. "If you hurt my daughter, I'll kill you."

Marvin brought a piece of bread to his mouth and took a bite. He chomped loudly, smacking his lips as he chewed. Whatever was on his face was smeared on the bread.

Reid looked closer and saw it was jelly. "Who are you?"

"Ma, this one is awake," Marvin called out.

"Tell your mother to untie me and take me to my daughter," Reid snapped as he struggled with the bindings on his arms.

Marvin took another bite of the bread. A clump of jelly fell onto the table next to Reid. Marvin used his finger to scoop it up, then licked his finger clean. "Ma, the man's awake!" Marvin hollered, his mouth full of half-chewed food.

"Let me go," Reid said, staring into Marvin's brown eyes.

Marvin was short, standing around five feet six inches, and he suffered from a rare form of Down syndrome called mosaic Down syndrome, or mosaicism, which left him with fewer symptoms than other forms. He still had many of the physical characteristics—a flat face, small ears, slanted eyes and slurred speech—but his mental acuity was far improved over others with his disorder. "Ma!"

"I heard you. Now stop shouting. The little girl is resting," Hillary said, appearing in the doorway.

"He's awake, Ma," Marvin said, his stubby finger pointed at Reid.

"I want to see my daughter!" Reid barked.

Hillary stepped around and stood opposite Marvin.

"Mr. Flynn, Hannah is resting right now. I can assure you that she's safe."

"What are you doing with us?"

"I know this must seem quite odd, but we're here to help," she said calmly.

"Taking me and my daughter prisoner doesn't feel safe to me," he snapped. He lifted his head and gave her a look up and down.

She was dressed in a white lab coat with a stethoscope around her neck.

"You're a doctor?" he asked.

"I am," she replied, a smile stretched across her face.

"What are you doing with us? What do you want?"

"Mr. Flynn—"

"How do you know my name?"

"I made sure to search your vehicle, very impressive, by the way," she replied. "Once we brought you back to my office, I made sure to see if there was anything in the car of value. It appears that the car is the biggest prize of all."

"What do you want with us?" Reid asked.

"I should introduce myself. My name is Dr. Hillary Cobb."

"I don't care who you are. I want to know what you're going to do to me and Hannah."

Marvin began to chuckle.

She gave Marvin an unpleasant look and said, "Go harvest the eggs from the chickens and prepare something for Mr. Flynn. I'm sure he's hungry."

"Okay, Ma," Marvin said. He turned and exited the room.

Hillary pulled up a stool and sat. "I do apologize for how we met and that bump on the head, but I'm here to help people like your daughter."

"How?"

"I don't want to go into great detail, but eleven years ago I was on a team of scientists and virologists—"

"I don't care. How are you going to help my daughter?"

"Mr. Flynn, yelling at me isn't productive, but I do understand your frustration."

Reid tensed his body and again tried to break free. "I want you to remove these. If you're here to help me and Hannah, then untie me."

"Removing those straps isn't a good idea. If you behave yourself, I might consider it, but as far as your daughter goes, I've begun my treatment."

"Treatment? What are you doing to her?" Reid exclaimed, his eyes bulging with anger.

"Mr. Flynn, I worked on a team years ago. We created the dog flu, and I believe I have the one cure for it with a current vaccine I've developed."

Reid's anger melted away when he heard what she'd said. "Wait, you *created* the dog flu?"

"Yes."

"I don't understand. Why? Why would you do something like that?"

"It's too long a story to go into, but I feel that after all these years, I might have designed the one cure. You could say working on doing this has been my way of redeeming myself for what I helped create."

"The dog flu is manmade?"

"Yes."

"What kind of demented and sick person are you?"

"I was one member of a team, and when I joined them over a decade ago, I had no idea what we were doing. They kept us separate from the other members of the team. I was working on sequencing DNA, nothing more. I thought we were designing a vaccine for Ebola."

"I want to see my daughter," Reid said.

"In a bit," she said then stood. "Mr. Flynn, I'm not here to harm you or your daughter. I know it might seem contrary, but I'm one of the good people. And if I'm right, your daughter will survive this." She exited the room, closing the door behind her.

"No, come back. Hey, come back and take off these bindings. I want to see Hannah. I want to see my daughter!"

Five Miles West of Logan, New Mexico

Michael and Brienne stopped at the gate. His house was off in the distance; several dim lights shone through the windows.

"Why are we stopped here?" Brienne asked.

"My mom is going to be mad," Michael said.

"I suppose she has every right to be. You up and left her alone with your grandmother."

"All I want to do is make them proud of me, and again I've proven to be an idiot, weak, stupid—"

"Enough complaining. I'm hungry for some real food,"

Brienne said. She climbed over the gate and waited on the other side for Michael. "Well, are you coming?"

"I don't want to go back."

She shrugged and started down the driveway.

"Where are you going?"

Not looking back, she replied, "I'm going to go get a hot meal and water. I'll tell your mom you're out here pouting."

He grunted his displeasure, scaled the gate, and ran up to her. "You'd do that?"

"Yeah, I would."

"But what if I just turned around and took off?"

She stopped, grabbed him by the arm, and spun him around so they were facing each other. "Then go, but if your mom comes looking for you and you end up getting her killed, all because you want to have a tantrum, then so be it. Or you can come with me and tell her you tried to find them but were unsuccessful. What you need to get into your head is you're not a failure for not finding them, you just didn't find them; that's it. Stop making it more than what it really is. Your dad and brother could have gone in a million different directions looking for the medicine for your grandma."

"Her name is Nana."

"Whatever. Just stop pouting like a child. It took real grit to go out there. Yeah, you came up short, only because you were going to be hunted down, but that's not your fault. Heck, you might walk in the house and find your dad and brother are home."

He snapped his head in the direction of the house and asked, "Do you suppose they are?"

"They could be," she said, though she didn't believe it to be the case.

He headed down the driveway briskly.

"Now you want to go," she snarked.

"They might be there. Dad might be there," he said, his heart filled with hope.

She rushed up alongside him and once more stopped him. "Don't roll in there with high expectations only to have them dashed, okay?"

"I won't."

"Good," she said with a slight nod.

He continued on to the house.

———

Upon seeing Michael, Tanya raced up to him and wrapped her arms around his body and squeezed tightly. "Where have you been?" She glanced over his shoulder and saw Brienne standing a few feet behind him. "Michael, who's the woman?"

"That's Brienne."

"But who is she? Can we trust her?" Tanya asked.

"Yes, we can trust her," Michael insisted.

Tanya gave Brienne a wary stare for a second then turned her attention back to Michael. She pulled away and glared. "You scared me to death. What were you thinking?" she snapped, her tone angry.

"I went to look for Dad and Chase."

"Why would you do that? Huh?"

"Are they here? Have they returned?" Michael asked, looking into the kitchen from the front room.

"No, they haven't returned, and once I saw you were gone, I feared the worst about you too," Tanya said.

Nana emerged from the hallway, a look of disappointment written on her face. "You're no longer my favorite."

Michael smirked.

"Come inside and warm up," Tanya said. She stepped out of the way so Michael could pass.

Michael entered the kitchen. He removed his jacket and said, "Sorry, Nana."

"Don't apologize," Nana said, lowering herself into a chair.

Tanya stood in the doorway. She gave Brienne another glance and asked, "I suppose I should invite you in?"

"Your son sort of owes me," Brienne said.

"Owes you what?" Tanya bristled.

"My life, Mom; she saved my life," Michael said.

Tanya didn't like strangers, especially attractive women who happened to show up with her son. "Since you saved Michael's life, I should invite you in."

"That's mighty nice of you." Brienne laughed.

Tanya got out of the doorway.

Brienne walked in and looked around the front room. It had been a long time since she'd been in a home that was still being maintained; even the smell reminded her of life before. "You have a nice home."

"Come back to the kitchen. I assume you're hungry," Tanya said.

The two entered the kitchen, with Brienne stopping just

at the arched entryway. She looked around the room and settled her stare on Nana, who, like Tanya, was giving her a once-over. "Aren't you a pretty little lady?"

Brienne unslung her rifle and removed her pack. "Has it been that long since you've seen a woman besides…?" she asked, motioning with her head towards Tanya.

"You're the first stranger this house has seen in nine years," Nana replied.

Tanya returned with a steaming bowl of chicken broth, set it on the table, and said, "I have some bread. Care for a slice?"

The second the aroma of the broth hit Brienne, her stomach churned and hunger pangs came on strong. Her mouth watered as she sat in front of the bowl. She didn't wait for a spoon; she picked up the bowl and began to sip loudly, soup spilling down her chin and onto the table.

Nana and Tanya stared at her.

"Been a while, eh?" Nana asked.

Brienne gulped the rest of the broth and set the bowl back on the table. Using her sleeve, she wiped her chin. "Yes, it's been a long time since I've had hot food like this. Thank you."

"Want some more?" Tanya asked.

"If you don't mind," Brienne replied happily.

Michael took a seat next to Brienne, a hot bowl of broth in front of him, yet he sat staring at her.

Tanya returned with a fresh bowl and gave it to Brienne, who this time used the spoon.

"Tell me about how you two met?" Tanya asked.

"I went into town to find Dad, when—"

"I want to hear it from her," Tanya said, putting a slice of bread next to Brienne.

Given her cue, Brienne explained how she'd been just outside town and was merely scanning the town when she saw Michael coming towards it. She mentioned how the men were pursuing him and she took it upon herself to kill them. Unsure of how they'd act, she left out the incident with the young man, who she now thought could have been Michael's brother.

"You must be a dead shot," Nana said. "We need to keep her around here."

"Did you happen to come across a man, middle-aged, average height, he would have been traveling with a young man?" Tanya asked.

"No," Brienne answered. "I only saw Michael and those men."

"Do you think those men might have something to do with them not returning?" Tanya asked.

Before Brienne could answer, Nana blurted out, "Of course those hooligans could have something to do with them not coming back. He was attacked the last time he went into town; that's why his trip was foolish. He risked his life along with Chase's just to save an old dying woman."

"Mom, please don't talk like that in front of Michael," Tanya snapped. Her nerves were already frayed with Michael missing; having Nana be so coarse just added to her pain.

"The boy should know the truth," Nana fired back.

Tanya slammed a bowl down on the counter, shattering

it into pieces and cutting her finger. "If you believe you're dying, then die already."

The room grew quiet.

Nana's lip quivered. She wanted to say something back but held it. Unable to sit in the room any longer, she got to her feet and shuffled out of the room.

Michael hopped up and went to her. "Let me help you, Nana."

"Leave me be," she said, dismissing his help.

Brienne dismissed it all and kept eating her broth.

When Nana disappeared, Michael swept back into the room and said, "Why did you have to say that to her?"

Tanya spun around and fired back, "Just the other day you were talking about that, now you're defending her?"

"She's old—"

"She's the reason your dad and brother are missing," Tanya replied, her voice cracking with emotion.

Michael went to Tanya and put his arms around her. "I'm sorry, Mom."

"I just want them home. I'm so worried," Tanya cried.

Brienne clenched her jaw tight. She wanted to say something about what she had witnessed, but each time she came close, she relented. Was it better for them to know they were dead or not? People said they liked closure but was that really true? Some people like to have hope and are fine living with the thought that their loved ones are still out there somewhere. She glanced at Michael and Tanya embraced. She felt for them while also feeling a sense of jealousy. They might have lost two family members, but they still had each other.

Tanya wiped the tears from her cheeks, shot Brienne a look, and said, "I'm sure you wish you weren't here to witness all this drama."

Brienne gave her a smile and answered, "Life is hard, I know."

"Where are you from?" Tanya asked.

"Originally from Seattle but was living in Yuma when the shit hit the fan," she replied.

"Do you mind if I ask why you're traveling?" Tanya asked.

"I'm heading home," Brienne said.

"What's it like out there?" Tanya asked. "Will told me stories, but he only went as far as Snowflake."

Brienne sat back and wiped her mouth with her sleeve. "You've never left the farm?"

"No."

"And you?" Brienne asked Michael, who was still standing next to his mother.

"Today was the first time," he answered.

"Hmm, how do I describe it? It's surreal, actually, at least that's how it was right after. I kept thinking it was all a nightmare I would wake up from, but each time I opened my eyes, I saw the same thing—death, decay, chaos, with sprinkles of hope when I'd encounter a kind person. The cities are to be avoided at all costs, especially those that were nuked. What's most shocking is just how vast the destruction is. You just can't fathom that the entire world as we know it has been plunged into this, from Europe all across the US."

"You've been to Europe?" Tanya asked.

"That's where I was when it all happened," Brienne replied. "I knew I shouldn't go, but with the economy in shambles after the outbreak, then the war with China, I took a contracting job at a base in Germany. I wasn't there for a month when the bombs started raining down. That was nine years ago. I've been trying to get home since."

Tanya's expression changed from curiosity to shock. She cleared the distance from the counter to the table and sat next to Brienne. "Oh dear, you've been out there all this time trying to get back home?"

"Yeah."

"Do you have family?" Tanya asked.

"I did when the bombs dropped," Brienne answered.

"Children?"

"A son, he'd be about Michael's age now if he's alive."

Tanya reached out and touched Brienne's hand. "I pray they're alive."

Brienne recoiled. She wasn't accustomed to human touch. Feeling awkward, she said, "Is your plumbing working?"

"No. If you need a bathroom, we have a pit latrine outside around back," Tanya said. "Michael, do you want to show her where it is?"

"Sure," Michael said.

"No, that's fine. Just tell me how to get there," Brienne said.

"I suppose it's easier to just go out how you entered the house, turn right, and follow the porch around. It's in the backyard about fifty yards away," Tanya answered. "Michael, get her a lantern to take with her."

"I've got a flashlight." Brienne got up quickly and rushed out of the kitchen. She followed Tanya's directions and found the latrine, but she didn't have to use it. She just wanted an excuse to take a break from the conversation.

Finding a log, she sat down and thought about Dustin and her husband, Jake. There wasn't a day that she didn't think about them and wonder if they were alive. Her thoughts then shifted to whether she'd want to know before arriving in Yuma. If someone knew, would she also want to know? Would knowing give her closure, and if she did know, then what? Would she still need to go back to Yuma, or could she go somewhere else? What about her parents in Seattle? Maybe she could try to find a new home, some-where safe, somewhere like where she was. They seemed self-sufficient and isolated. This could be a good place to make roots if they invited her to. She did often wonder if they were alive, and part of her journey home was to find them, dead or alive, because she did need to know. She wouldn't have been making this journey if she knew they were dead. And what about Michael? Would he continue to go and try to find them? Or would Tanya eventually make the trip in hopes of finding her husband and son? She knew she would. Filled with purpose, Brienne went back into the house.

"I hope you found it okay," Tanya said. She was back at the counter, cleaning up the debris from the broken bowl.

"They're dead," Brienne blurted out.

Tanya and Michael both snapped their heads in Brienne's direction. "Who's dead, your family?"

"No, I think your husband and son," Brienne said.

CHAPTER 5

One Mile South of Santa Rosa, New Mexico

SLEEPING WAS near impossible for Reid though he did manage to get some. When he woke, he found himself still staring at the kitten poster, and his arms and legs were still bound to the table. The urge to urinate was intense, so much that he feared he would wet himself. "Hey!"

Silence.

"Hey, is anyone there?" he called out. Again he struggled with the bindings but found them impossible to get free from. "Hey, I need to piss."

Footfalls sounded in the hall outside.

He breathed a sigh of relief when he heard them.

The footfalls stopped at the door, but that was it. Whoever it was didn't come into the room.

"Hey, I know you're there. I need to use the bathroom," Reid barked.

The footfalls continued on.

"No, come back and let me use the bathroom. Show some damn humanity," Reid hollered. His anger welled up inside. Using every ounce of strength, he pulled both his arms up. The veins in his neck, arms and forehead popped as he strained to pull loose. "C'mon, damn it," he growled as he pulled.

Pop, ping.

The restraint on his right wrist broke free.

Reid quickly went to work unbuckling his left wrist then his feet. Free of the restraints, he jumped off the table, turned, and found himself face-to-face with the muzzle of a pistol.

"You're not a patient man, are you?" Hillary smirked.

"I need to see my daughter," Reid exclaimed.

The two squared off, neither saying a word for what seemed like an eternity.

She flinched first and lowered the pistol. "I need you to trust that I'm helping your daughter."

"Can I see her?"

She stepped out of the way and motioned with her hand to the doorway. "She's at the end of the hallway."

He pushed past her and raced down the dimly lit hallway. At the end he found a single closed door. He opened it, and there, lying comfortably in a bed, was Hannah.

She opened her eyes, which were still bloody, and said, "Daddy."

He raced to her side and embraced her. "Are you okay?"

"I'm fine. The woman has been nice. She gave me an IV and a pill yesterday and one today," Hannah said.

On a nightstand next to Hannah's bed sat a cup of

water, a syringe, alcohol pads, bandages, and a pair of curved surgical scissors. He snatched them up quickly and placed them in his pocket.

Hillary suddenly appeared in the doorway. "She should start showing signs of improvement soon."

"What did you give her?" Reid asked.

"It's best you let her rest; that will give us time to talk," Hillary said, her pistol tucked in her waistband.

Reid caressed Hannah's arm and asked, "Will you be okay?"

"I'm fine," she replied. "Tired, I feel real tired."

Reid turned to Hillary. "Is she tired from the virus or what you gave her?"

"That is a symptom of the virus. She's also developed the stomach rash," Hillary said.

He pulled back the sheet and lifted her shirt. There on her belly were the signature small red blisters.

"Mr. Flynn, come, it's best we let her go back to sleep," Hillary said.

He got up and said to Hannah, "I'll just be outside."

"I'm going to sleep. I'm tired," Hannah said.

He gave her a smile and exited the room.

Hillary closed the door, but before she did, she gave Hannah a quick wink. Facing Reid, she said, "I'm not here to harm her, but you should know what I gave her is experimental."

"Meaning?"

"The worst case is it kills her."

"Kills her!" Reid exclaimed.

"I don't think it will, but she could have complications

or unintentional side effects," Hillary said. "I've never tested this batch yet."

Reid gave her an odd look and asked, "Is that why you took us?"

"Can we go sit down in my office?" she asked and moved past him to a door on the left. She opened it and went inside. She took a seat on a cushioned chair and put her feet up on a desk.

Reid followed. He passed a door on the right that was cracked open slightly and saw a young woman tied to a table like he had been. He was sure she was a prisoner like he was. He kept on and entered her office. "Tell me, is that why you took me and Hannah, so you can test this drug on us?"

"I'm not proud of what I've done, but I'm doing it to save people, you must understand."

"What if she wasn't sick? And that woman back there, is she being tested too?"

"Mr. Flynn, it doesn't make any sense to talk about this. She's here, she's been infected, and now I've given her a trial drug that might work."

"How long have you been doing this?" he asked as he hovered near the doorway.

"Since I left the team, right before the outbreak," she confessed.

"You've been trying to find a cure since then?"

"Yes."

"And nothing, of course," he said.

"We shall see if this works or not," she said.

A disturbed look spanned his face as something horrific

dawned on him. "You've been doing this all this time, which means you've been testing on people, victims like me, but where are they?"

"They're dead, Mr. Flynn, is that what you wanted to hear so that you can look at me like I'm some kind of monster."

"Maybe you are, have you ever considered that? Kidnapping people and testing on them isn't done by nice people," Reid shot back.

"Have you ever heard of the trolley problem?" Hillary asked.

"What?"

"The trolley problem was first proposed by British moral philosopher Philippa Foot in 1967 to a class at the University of Wisconsin. It goes like this: a runaway trolley is barreling down the tracks. There are five people tied to the tracks in front of it. You are standing next to a lever that controls a switch. If you pull the lever, the trolley is redirected onto a side track. Those five people on the main track will be saved. However, there is a single person lying on the side track. Your decision either dooms five to die...or one. What is your ethical responsibility? I know my answer."

Reid laughed.

"You find this funny?"

"I have heard about the trolley problem now that you describe it, but if you'll recall, the moral dilemma goes further. What if that one person on that track is your child? Like you, I know my answer."

She pursed her lips and glared at him.

"What if you're wrong and this kills her?"

"Then I'm sorry, but your daughter only had a ten percent chance of survival anyway," she replied.

"Not where I'm going," he shot back.

"And where's that?"

He was about to tell her but stopped short. "I hear there's a cure out west in California. I'm heading there."

She chuckled.

"What?"

"You bought into those rumors?"

"I don't have a choice. I need to keep moving, so if you're done testing on my daughter, I need to get back on the road," he said.

She leaned forward, placed her elbows on the table, and said, "I'm sorry, but she needs to stay here so I can see how this works…or not."

"No, 'cause if you're wrong, I need to find them," he said.

"There is not a them anywhere. Just who do you think has created a cure? Huh?"

"The government has a research facility. They're working on it now."

She shook her head. "There is no such place; those are all rumors. Your best shot is staying here with me."

"No, there is a place and I'm going there," Reid snapped.

"Where is this so-called place?" Hillary asked. "Give me the name of a place and I'll tell you if it exists."

"There's a facility on one of the Channel Islands," Reid answered.

"You're talking about the labs run by the Department of

Homeland Security? If there was anyone, they're long since gone."

"You don't know that," Reid shot back.

"I know that you're going to be disappointed. I ran into a gentleman from there a few years back. He said the facility had been overrun."

"You're just saying that to keep me here. I'm going, period," Reid barked.

She pulled the revolver from her waistband and set it on the desk. "Please don't make me force you, again."

Marvin suddenly appeared behind Reid, a bat in his hand. "Hello, mister."

"What you're doing is wrong, you're risking her life for your experiment."

"You should be so lucky that I'm not testing you. I thought I had two to work on, but after taking your blood, I found antibodies. You've had the virus before and lived, didn't you?"

He stepped towards her desk.

She raised the pistol and said, "She stays here."

"Please let me take her. I'll come back and tell you if it worked or not, I swear it," Reid pleaded.

She looked past him towards Marvin and ordered, "Take him to room four. Give him some food then lock him in."

"We have the girl in room four," Marvin replied.

"Then room three, just put him in a room, Marvin!" Hillary barked.

"Don't do this," Reid snapped.

"I don't like this any more than you do, but this is science. I need to see how she reacts to the drug."

He lunged at her.

Hillary scooted back, just missing his grasp.

Marvin raced in, swung his bat, and struck Reid in the lower back.

Reid howled in pain then dropped to his knees.

Marvin pressed his attack. He put Reid in a choke hold and squeezed.

"Don't hurt him too much," Hillary barked.

The two men rolled around on the floor, with Reid kicking and thrashing in a vain attempt to break free from Marvin's grasp.

"Can I put him to sleep, Ma?" Marvin asked.

"Go ahead," Hillary replied.

Marvin wrapped his left arm around the back of Reid's head, in what's called a rear naked choke hold, and squeezed more, his right forearm pressing against Reid's throat.

Using all his might to pry Marvin off, Reid wasn't successful and passed out.

Five Miles West of Logan, New Mexico

The savory smell of eggs cooking wafted down the hall. Brienne picked up on it when she left the spare bedroom to go use the latrine. She passed through the kitchen to find a steaming cup of tea and a plate with two fried eggs sitting upon it but no one around. Her mouth watered when she gazed upon the food. She was tempted to pick up one of the eggs and devour it but decided against being a rude guest. Needing to use the latrine, she made her way outside.

The late morning sun was up, and its rays felt good on her face. Having arrived during the evening, she hadn't gotten a chance to see the farm. Now her eyes scanned the expansive land with its rolling hills and sparse outcroppings of trees. Large fields surrounded the house, but nothing was growing. She imagined at one time it had held crops. The large center pivot irrigation systems sat no doubt where they'd last run years before when the Longs had shuttered the commercial part of the farm.

Down the yard she went. Much of the once green grass was gone, replaced by sporadic patches of dirt and dead grass. It was nice spending the night in a bed; it was something she hadn't done in a long time. She could get used to it again but doubted the hospitality would last much longer considering the information she had divulged last night.

She was reaching for the latrine door when it burst open and out stepped Michael.

He sheepishly smiled and said, "Excuse me and good morning."

"Good morning," she replied.

Michael rushed off towards the house.

Brienne turned and called out, "Were those your eggs I saw on the counter?"

"No, they're yours," he answered.

A smile broke out on her face. Freshly fried eggs would hit the spot, she thought.

After using the latrine, she headed back to the house, her mind obsessed with the eggs. She could hardly wait to dig into the creamy yellow yolks. She prayed there was bread to spare to dip into it.

Reaching the house, she again ran into Michael, who was now sitting on the front step of the porch. She stopped and said, "Where's your mom?"

"Still in her room."

"And your nana?"

"Same."

She could see the melancholy expression on his face and thought it had to do with what she'd confessed last night. "Can I sit next to you?"

"Don't you want to eat your eggs?" he asked, his chin buried in the palms of his hands.

"I'll get them in a bit. You, though, I want to talk to now," she said as she took a seat next to him.

The second her butt hit the step, he scooted away from her a few inches.

"You don't have to be afraid of me," she said.

"I'm not," he snapped.

"Listen, I know what I said probably has you upset, and I can understand why."

"Why didn't you tell me before?" he spat.

His tone was harsh, but she was hard to offend. "I didn't say anything because I didn't think it mattered then. You already seemed upset and that would have made you worse. Plus I didn't want you thinking about going back to seek revenge."

"You could have told me," he said.

"If I was wrong, I apologize," she said. Long strands of

her hair fell out from the thick rubber band she was using to hold it back in a ponytail.

"I know I'm just a kid, but I'm not as weak as people think I am," Michael said.

She could tell by his tone that his so-called weakness was an insecurity and was deep-seated in his psyche. "Going to look for your father and brother wasn't weak, that took courage, but—"

"Here it comes," he snarked.

"But it was foolish. If you're going to do something, be a bit more prepared. I know you were doing your best, but if you're going to ever travel out again, have a weapon, a firearm, not a small knife."

"I don't know how to shoot," Michael confessed.

She raised a brow. "You grew up in the country and on a farm and don't know how to shoot? How is that even possible? I thought everyone in the country shot guns."

"My mom and dad aren't against them; they also aren't for them. My dad has a rifle and a shotgun. Oh, and he has a nice little pistol too. I'm sure he took that with him along with his rifle."

"You're telling me all you have here to protect your family is a shotgun?"

"Unless my dad had other stuff," Michael mused. "Come, let me show you something."

Michael led Brienne down to the barn and pushed open the large heavy door. The late morning sun illuminated the space.

Brienne looked around. On her left was a workstation with tools strewn everywhere. In front of that were wooden horses holding part of what must have been an unfinished project. Straight ahead of her sat something large covered by a tarp, and to her right were stacks and stacks of cardboard boxes of various sizes. It appeared they used that section of the barn for storage.

"Over here," Michael said, walking over to the large item in the barn.

"What's under there?" she asked. "Looks huge."

Michael tossed the front of the tarp up to reveal the prop of a plane. "It's an Air Tractor 502B."

"Air Tractor?"

"Yeah, a crop-dusting plane," Michael confirmed.

Brienne pulled back and looked left and right. "Where are the wings?"

"They're over in the corner," Michael said. "Dad used to be a crop duster; then the war came. He had to take the wings off to put the plane in the barn."

"Does it run?"

"Not anymore, there's no fuel for it. My dad is hoping that one day when the world becomes normal again, he can get back in the cockpit; those are his words."

"Do you remember him flying?" she asked.

"Not really. I kinda think I do, but I don't really. Maybe one day I'll get this plane back together and, if I can get some fuel, fly it to the coast or maybe somewhere…"

"Different?"

"Yeah, someplace that's not here," he said. "What did you do for a job before?"

"I was an executive acquisitions manager for a big

pharma company. I had just taken a new position when everything went bad."

"Is that why you were in Europe?"

"Yeah, I went there for the new position. We were working with the WHO to try to combat the dog flu, and when the war turned nuclear, I got stuck there," she said.

"Why would you go there, be so far away from your family, when all that stuff was happening? Heck, my dad stopped going into town and kept us home from school even though they had lifted the quarantine at school."

She thought about his question. It was a tough one for her to answer because the job she took wasn't necessary, yet she took it knowing she'd have to travel at a time when air travel was greatly restricted and a war was waging with China. "I thought at the time my career mattered more, I suppose." She paused, thought some more, then told him a lie. "It was a calculated risk I was taking for my family. I wanted us to have a bigger house, maybe even move out of Yuma if I could convince Jake. If I'd known I'd be stuck there and would have to travel for almost nine years, I wouldn't have gone."

"But you did, and look what happened," Michael said. He didn't know how deeply his words cut her.

"Thanks for the pep talk, kid. You don't think I regret getting on that plane every day since?" she growled.

"I want to go to Europe one day."

She put her arm over his shoulder and said, "Don't, here is pretty darn special. You don't know how lucky you are to have this secluded haven."

He craned his head to her and asked, "Did you walk the

entire time?"

"Not just walk, I've been on ships, boats, bicycles, cars, trucks, and even a train for a short time; but in between there's been periods of nothing. I got stuck in Bermuda for a period of time, then made it to the east coast. We first landed in Maryland, but we heard that Washington was awash in radiation, so we sailed down to North Carolina. I spent time in the mountains during winter; couldn't do much driving or walking with four feet of snow."

"Dad said the weather's different since the war."

"They call it a nuclear winter. There's a lot of debris and particles in the upper atmosphere; it blocks out some of the sun's rays, something like that."

"Do you really think my dad and brother are dead?" Michael asked, his tone turning somber.

"I don't know if it was them or not, 'cause I've never seen them before, but I saw a young man about eighteen or so running from those men. He was…" She stopped herself from telling him the grisly details.

"He was what?"

"I saw him die, but like I said, I could be wrong, but I have a feeling I'm not."

"I wish I knew," Michael said.

"I do remember what they looked like. If you had…"

Michael took her hand and walked her out of the barn. They marched up the yard and into the house. He walked up to the fireplace in the living room and removed a photograph from the mantel. He handed it to her and said, "Chase is on the left and that's my dad." He pointed at Will on the right.

She recognized Chase but never saw the face of the man on the ground. "The young man I saw die, that was him right there."

"And my dad?"

Brienne didn't want to give him false hope, but she also couldn't know for sure. "What did your dad wear? Did he have a dark green military-type jacket on?"

"I don't know what he wore that night, but he does own one."

Rustling came from the kitchen doorway. "Are you going to eat these eggs or not?" Tanya asked, her arms folded, telling them she was guarded and angry.

Brienne swung around and replied, "Yes, I was just chatting with Mike."

"Good, because we don't waste around here," Tanya spat. She turned, but before going back into the kitchen, she said, "And his name isn't Mike, it's Michael."

"Sorry," Brienne said.

"It's okay. I don't mind Mike."

"I think your mom probably wants me to leave soon," Brienne said.

"I don't want you to go just yet. Please stay."

"I'm really sorry about Chase and your dad."

Michael put the photograph back and said, "Chase was hard on me, but I know deep down he loved me."

Tanya appeared again and said, "Michael, go take Nana her lunch."

"Yes, Mom," Michael said. He rushed off.

"I'd like to talk with you," Tanya said. She motioned to the side door.

The two exited the house.

Tanya leaned against the porch railing. Her eyes were red and swollen from endless fits of crying. Her once strong eyes now told of pain and sorrow. "When will you be leaving?" she asked.

"As soon as you want me to leave," Brienne answered.

Tanya looked up and said, "Don't make sense for you to leave at midday, but if you could be gone by early morning tomorrow, that would be great."

"Can I get the food and water promised?"

"You'll get what's due for bringing back my boy. But let me tell you something, the nerve of you to come into my home and just blurt out that my husband and oldest are dead is vile, grotesque and lacks any sense of decorum."

"I wasn't trying to offend anyone. I thought you should know," Brienne said defensively.

"You could have pulled me aside, but you didn't. You rolled in and made it a damn announcement. Now my mother-in-law is distraught and my baby boy is struggling."

"I mean no disrespect, but if what I said is debilitating, then you have no idea what's going on out in the world now."

Tanya's eyes widened with anger. "How dare you speak to me like that in my own home."

"Like I said, I don't mean any disrespect, but the world isn't a nice and pleasant place where you have the luxury of being offended by words. People are literally eating one another out there."

Tears welled up in Tanya's eyes. She pointed her finger

at Brienne and barked, "Tomorrow morning, first light, you're gone." She turned and raced back into the house. "And eat your damn eggs before I do!"

Brienne sighed. "Maybe this little house on the prairie isn't so pleasant after all."

One Mile South of Santa Rosa, New Mexico

Reid came to, but this time he wasn't just in a different room; he had the means of escape tucked into his pocket. His hands were bound like before to the frame of a bed, but were next to his body and within reach of his front pocket, where he had tucked the pair of surgical scissors. He twisted his hand, slipped two fingers into his pocket, and pulled out the scissors. He carefully manipulated them, ensuring he didn't drop them, until he was able to begin cutting the leather bindings. He wasn't sure how long he had to cut, adding to his anxiety. It wasn't his life he was concerned about, it was Hannah's. Hillary might be trying to help mankind, but she was doing so at the risk of Hannah's life. Being used as a science experiment wasn't what Reid had had in mind when he set out on this journey.

He cut the last part of the binding and pulled his arm out. He removed his other restraints, hopped out of the bed, and went to the door. He placed his ear against it and listened, but heard no one.

A cry sounded from the other room, jolting him. It was a woman, no doubt the young woman he'd seen strapped down like him. He began to wonder how many people had been Hillary's hapless victims over the years. How many had she taken prisoner only to kill them by experimenting on them? He didn't know, but if he, Hannah and the woman equaled three in the matter of a day and a half, that number could be large when stretched out over eight years.

He cracked open the door. He didn't see anyone, but by the amount of natural light coming in from the end of the hallway, it wasn't that late, meaning he hadn't been unconscious for all that long.

The woman cried out again, "Someone help me, please!"

"Where are you, Marvin?" Reid asked himself.

"Help me, please!" the woman begged.

Reid clutched the scissors, took a deep breath, and stepped into the hallway. He turned down the hall towards Hannah's room without incident. He threw open the door to find Hannah sitting upright, with Hillary injecting something into her IV. "Just stop what you're doing."

Hillary shot Reid a look and said, "Again?"

Reid held the scissors out like a knife and seethed, "Step away from my daughter."

She did as he ordered. Her glance shifted to something over Reid's shoulder.

Seeing her look, Reid suddenly felt a presence, but this time he was prepared. He stepped aside, pivoted and swung the scissors.

Marvin was there with a devilish smile on his face; however, he wasn't expecting Reid's swift move. Unprepared for Reid's action, he stood and let the scissors plunge into his neck. Startled, he moaned as he saw the blood pouring down his shirt. "Mama," he cried out, "the man hurt me."

Reid was stunned in a way at what he'd done, then quickly overcame his shock, pulled the scissors out, and again stabbed Marvin in the neck near the same spot.

Marvin reeled back, blood now spirting from the wounds. He lost his footing and slipped on the bloody floor.

Hillary wailed in grief and rushed to Marvin. "My baby, no!"

Still armed with the scissors, Reid grabbed Hillary and wrapped his arm around her neck and pulled her close. He placed the scissors against her throat and said, "Where are my belongings?"

"I'm not telling you anything," Hillary spat.

"I'll cut your fucking throat," he warned.

"I don't care what you do to me," she fired back. She looked down at Marvin lying in a pool of his own blood, his body flinching. "You killed my baby boy."

"Where are my things?"

"Kill me, go ahead," Hillary said.

"Daddy, don't," Hannah pleaded.

Reid looked at Hannah. "But she—"

"She's trying to save my life," Hannah said.

"You should have listened to your daughter from the get-go. Now look at what you've done," Hillary snapped.

"You kidnap people and experiment on them," Reid growled.

The woman down the hall screamed again.

"Listen to her, Hannah. There's another prisoner just down there she's testing her drugs on," Reid argued.

"But—" Hannah said before she was interrupted.

"You're wrong, Hannah, she's killed people." He turned back to Hillary and asked, "How many people have you murdered? Tell her."

"Hundreds, and I'd experiment on twice that, hell, ten times that if I could cure what has killed millions. You're looking at the small picture," Hillary preached.

"Daddy, don't, please," Hannah begged.

Reid gave Hannah a look and was about to protest when he decided he was wasting time. He dragged Hillary to the side, where he saw restraints dangling. "Put that on."

"No," she said defiantly.

"Do it!" Reid barked.

Hannah reached out and touched Hillary's arm. "Please do it."

Hillary stopped resisting. She put the restraint on her left wrist.

With her temporarily restrained, Reid took the other restraint, removed it from the bed frame, and walked back over to Hillary. He took her right arm and secured that a foot apart from her left arm.

"Thank you, Daddy," Hannah said.

He pocketed the scissors, removed the IV from Hannah's arm, and scooped her up in his arms. He gave Hillary a last look and asked, "Where's my belongings, my fob for the car, all of it?"

Knowing she was defeated, she sneered, "I'll tell you, but you need to shoot me. I don't want to live without my baby boy."

Frustrated with her resistance, he carefully stepped over Marvin's dead body and out the door. He went straight to Hillary's office and set Hannah down in a chair.

After a quick search of her desk, he found nothing. "Damn it."

"Daddy, I think our stuff might be in another room," Hannah said.

"You know where our things are?" Reid asked, surprised.

"When they brought me here, they also took our stuff into a room that way," she said, pointing in the direction of the front of the building.

He promptly picked her up and swooped down the hall.

"Here," she said, pointing to a door on the right.

Behind them he heard the woman cry out. "Help me, please."

"Daddy, we can't leave that woman," Hannah said.

"We don't have time," Reid said, going into the room she'd pointed out. When he opened the door, he found a room stacked tall on all sides with boxes, all were marked by year. In the center of the room were piles of clothes, gear, equipment, weapons, and an assortment of people's personal belongings. Sitting on a table near the front, Reid spotted their things, including the fob to the car. "Yes," he yelped in joy.

"Can we now go help that woman?" Hannah asked.

He paused and looked at her. "You care more about other people than yourself?"

"If everyone helped everyone else, none of what happened would have happened," she replied.

Reid stared upon Hannah's weakened state. Her face

was growing gaunt and her skin was ashen. When the bloody eyes were added in, she looked terrible. "How did you become so wise?"

"You taught me," she said softly. She could feel her body growing weaker.

"I'm going to set you down back in Hillary's office and drop you off. From there I'm going to go find the car, load it up and get you set inside; then I'll go let that woman go," Reid said. "Deal?"

"Deal," Hannah said.

Reid went and did exactly as he said. The car was easy to find. Hillary had it parked in front of the office building that masqueraded as her medical laboratory. He packed the car with his gear plus extra weapons, food and water that he'd taken from the storeroom. He got behind the wheel to confirm the car was able to drive and was charged. He turned it on and watched as the screen showed the car was fully charged with a range of just under four hundred miles. "Yes!" he hollered happily. "Finally something worked out smoothly." He was referring to Arthur's theory that the car could recharge itself if allowed to get sunlight. Confident that he could get on his way, he left the car and ran back inside.

He stopped at the office and found Hannah resting, her eyes closed. He had one last thing to do: let the woman loose. He went to room four and turned the knob. He pushed it open to find the young woman awake. She lifted her head and said, "Don't hurt me, please."

Reid looked at her and instantly felt regret that his instinct had told him to just leave her. It was as if Hannah was operating as his conscience. "I was a prisoner like you. I won't hurt you." He raced to her side, his knife in his hand, and cut her bindings.

She grabbed her wrists and began to rub them.

Reid cut her legs loose and said, "You'll find your stuff on the right, last door on the right."

"Thank you," she said. She threw her arms around his neck. "You saved me. I'm so grateful."

"You'll need to thank my daughter for that, not me," Reid said. He turned and raced from the room. He stopped just outside the office door when he heard the distinct click of a revolver. He snapped his head in the direction of the sound and saw Hillary standing at the end of the hallway, her revolver in her hand.

"You forgot to check to see if I was armed," Hillary said.

Reid was now armed, his pistol in a holster on his side. "Just let us go. You've done your test; it's over."

The young woman exited the room and saw Hillary standing feet from her. She gasped and leapt back into the room from which she came.

"I'm not going to hurt you; you go. Just know that I did this all for the greater good. Whatever evil you think I've done is justified when compared to the lives I could save. If your daughter is saved by what I gave you, look for her eyes to change back first. She's in day three now and I'm afraid to say past any hope for her body to be immune. In my office you'll find a safe. That's where everything is, my journals, data, everything I've done to help make what wrong I did right. The code is eight two eight seven. In there you'll also find a vial; give her a booster in two days, that's equal to half a syringe, you'll find them in there too."

"I don't think so," Reid said.

"Mr. Flynn, what do you have to lose now? Give her the booster," Hillary urged.

He nodded.

"If she doesn't die, it's because of what I've done for her; remember that," she said and put the pistol to her temple. "If she lives, those journals and all the data I've compiled will help others recreate that serum. It can save the world from that horrible disease." She pulled the trigger. In an instant she dropped dead to the floor.

The young woman slowly emerged from her room and looked down at Hillary's body sprawled on the floor, a pool of blood encircling her head. "She killed herself?"

"Yeah," Reid replied. "Don't forget, your stuff is down there." He pointed behind him to the storeroom.

He went to pick Hannah up, then recalled Hillary had talked about a booster shot. He paused several times as he thought about getting it, his mind spinning with the possibility that Hillary's drugs might work. He searched the office, found the safe, and opened it using the code she'd given him. Inside were journals stacked up alongside a pile of Polaroid photos. He looked at a few and saw they were pictures of people. At the bottom of the photographs, written in red ink, were numbers. He found a photograph of Hannah; at the bottom it was labeled #1913. He cringed at the thought she'd killed that many people in her quest to find a cure. He tossed aside the photographs and reached further in to grab a vial with the handwritten words *TEST*

BATCH T-36, and the syringes that were sitting next to it. This had to be the booster, as there was nothing else in the safe. He put it in his pocket, swung back to Hannah, scooped her up, and raced out of the room towards the exit.

The young woman was now outside looking around. "It's not here, it's not here."

Reid didn't pay much attention. He put Hannah in the passenger seat and ran around to the driver's door.

"It's not here. Where is it?" she howled.

Reid stopped and asked, "What are you looking for?"

"My ride, it's gone," she said, her tone sounding defeated. "How will I get there now?"

Reid watched her pace. He understood how it must feel for her. She was young, alone and without her vehicle. "Where were you headed?"

"Mexico, Baja more specifically," she replied.

He was torn as to what to do. She seemed innocent enough, but he had a car, she didn't. Could she be a threat, or was she just someone in need and he could help? So many questions, so many decisions and not a lot of time. So far he'd found himself batting five hundred, with Kaitlyn helping him and Hillary using him and Hannah. Figuring it would be nice to have another driver to help push the distance he could go, and with time running short, he gave in and said, "I'm going to Southern California. You can ride with me there, then find another way south."

"Are you sure?" she asked, her eyes wide with joy that she'd found a way to keep going. "You're not a bad person, are you?"

"I'm not going to stand around convincing you I'm a

good guy. I'm offering you a ride; you either want to go or not. But hurry up, 'cause I'm leaving in less than a minute."

"I want to go."

"But I need to tell you, my daughter is sick with the dog flu, so ride at your own risk," he warned.

"I've been infected before; I'll be fine. I'm immune now, they say."

He opened the rear passenger door and said, "Hop in."

She looked in the backseat. "There's barely any room."

"I know it's tight, so make up your mind because this bus is leaving."

She tossed in her backpack and slid into the tight space between the door and the electric inverter. "This thing is on, should it be?"

Reid was behind the wheel and engaging the drive. "Yeah, it's what helps power this thing all the time."

"This is one of those Tesla cars I heard about before the war," she said.

He pulled out of the driveway, saw a directional sign that read INTERSTATE 40 WEST, and turned towards it. "Yeah, it's a Tesla, and it's now powered by solar power as we go along."

"That's cool," she said.

Reid heard Hannah breathing and gave her a look.

She was slumped down in the seat, her chest rising up and down with her breathing, which itself sounded labored.

"How far along is she?"

"Three days if my count is right. Getting tangled with them back there has thrown me off a bit," Reid said. He turned the car hard to the right and swerved around a large chunk of debris in the road. Up ahead he spotted the on-ramp for the interstate.

"You don't seem concerned. Are you immune too?"

"Yeah, I got sick; it never progressed past the third day. She's getting worse," Reid replied. "Ah, what's in Mexico?"

"A safe zone, I hear," she answered. "What's in California?"

"I guess you could say it's the same thing you're going to find, but where I'm going they might have a cure for my girl," Reid answered. "There's an island off the coast; there might be a place there."

"I've heard those rumors too, but I also heard that the place is now gone."

He shot her a look in the rearview mirror. "You heard it was gone?"

Seeing that he was stressed about her comment, she retracted it somewhat. "You know how rumors have been over the years. It's hard to know what's real or not. I heard a rumor that the dog flu was really a bioweapon created by extraterrestrials to thin us down so there's fewer of us when they attack with their main force."

He turned onto the on-ramp and sped up. He raced onto the freeway and immediately saw a sign that read ALBU-QUERQUE 118 MILES. He quickly calculated how long it would take him and came up with two hours easily if he had no issues.

"Why are you helping me?" she asked.

"I normally wouldn't. You could say I've had a mixed

track record. But I looked at you, and you, well, you seem nice enough. Please tell me I'm correct," he joked.

"I'm harmless," she said with a sweet smile. "I just need to get to Mexico via Yuma."

"Yuma, eh? Have someone in Yuma?"

"Yeah, you could say that," she replied. "What's your name?"

"I'm Reid and this is Hannah."

"My name is Emily. Nice to meet you."

Five Miles West of Logan, New Mexico

From left to right, the dining table was full of Brienne's gear. She rarely had opportunities to lay everything she owned out and do an inventory, so given the chance, she was going to do it. Knowing she had many miles ahead of her, she wanted to ensure that when she departed the farm, she'd have most of what she needed.

Michael walked in to find Brienne wiping down her rifle. "Is this all your stuff?"

She smiled. "Hard to believe, but yeah."

The flames of several candles set sporadically around flickered and danced, casting multiple bouncing shadows on the walls.

"I don't want you to leave." Michael sighed. He pulled a chair out and sat down.

"Even if your mom wanted me to stay, I can't. I need to go find my family," she said as she opened the receiver of the AR, pulled back on the charging handle, and removed the bolt carrier group.

"Have you always known how guns work?" Michael asked. He found her knowledge of firearms fascinating.

"No, I learned along the way. My first winter after landing back in the States, I settled down in the mountains of North Carolina. It was there I met an old Marine living up there. He was a salt-of-the-earth kind of guy. I knew I wasn't going to be able to make it across the country just on my good looks, so I had him teach me the skills and knowledge I was missing."

"That sounds cool," Michael said, his eyes wide at the marvel of it all.

"I never gave much attention to knowing things like this before. I was like most people, who thought our way of life would never come to an end. Well, it did and I was left flat-footed. I managed to survive living in Europe and during the sail across the Atlantic because of my mindset. The mind is a very powerful thing."

"Nana has talked about that," he mused as he recalled little snippets or phrases Nana would say, and even some of her sage advice.

"Old Sam said that survival is built upon four pillars, think of it as the four legs of a chair. You have skill sets, that's stuff you know or have learned. Then you have resources, that's stuff you acquire, like food, water, gear like this on the table. Then fitness comes into play, and I'm not talking about fitness from before with bikini bodies or six-pack abs; I'm talking about having the physical ability to do something. And finally there's mindset, and do you know what mindset is?"

"It's how you view things?"

"Yeah, that's it. It's an established set of attitudes or beliefs. Take, for instance, if your attitude to do something is so engrained, I guarantee you will find a way no matter what the obstacles are," she said then paused for a moment to gather her thoughts. "My mindset is I'll never quit trying to get to my family. I can have nothing, but I'll keep pressing forward. If someone had a defeatist mindset, then they could have the gear, skills and be a stud, but they'd fail to achieve what they were after all because they chose to opt out. They quit because their mindset was fixed on failure right from the start. As Old Sam used to say, mindset is the key to survival."

Michael sat fixated on her, mesmerized by the conversation.

Giving her attention back to the bolt carrier group, she carefully, using her fingernails, pulled the firing pin retaining pin, set it on a napkin, tipped the bolt carrier group up, and shook it. The firing pin dropped out into her hand. Like the retaining pin, she set it on the napkin. She rotated the bolt and pulled out the cam pin then removed the bolt assembly and set all the pieces on the napkin.

"What is that?" Michael asked.

"My memory may not be that good, but that is the bolt housing—no, it's the bolt carrier. This little silver dart thing is the firing pin; the tip of this little bad boy is what strikes the round and creates the explosion, for lack of a better word, that ignites the gunpowder in the cartridge, which then propels the bullet."

"Cool," Michael cooed. "I wish you were staying so you could teach me all this stuff."

"Can I ask you a question, a personal one?" Brienne asked.

"I suppose."

"I've heard you mention a few times that you think you're weak. Why do you look at yourself that way?"

His enthusiasm evaporated. He recoiled and sat silent.

She sighed and said, "I'm not here to pick on you. I want to help."

"'Cause I'm different," he muttered.

"When you say different, what does that mean? How do you define that?"

"My brother, Chase, is...was tough. He liked to play ball and do rough stuff. I liked to play, but I was more focused on computers, puzzles, stuff that involved, I don't know, not rough stuff."

"So you look at this rifle here disassembled and that gets you excited?" she asked.

"Yes, very much."

"And when you showed me the plane earlier today, you probably helped your dad take it apart?"

"I did."

"Did your brother?"

"Yeah, he was there, but he always gets distracted. He's just more physical than I am, sorry, was more physical. I'll never get used to talking about them in the past tense," Michael said.

"I still don't understand the weak thing."

"Do we have to talk about this?"

"Michael, we don't have to talk about anything, but if I can help you get rid of that negative view of yourself, your mindset—and remember how important that is—will be enhanced."

"I've always liked to tinker, play games, and I even used to help, I suppose I still do, help my mom cook because I loved to follow recipes. I always found it fun to look at something, look at a bunch of ingredients, parts like that rifle, put them together and create something."

"That's sounds really awesome, but still I don't get why you think you're weak."

He crossed his arms and grunted.

"Someone has told you that that stuff was weak, didn't they?" Brienne asked.

He shook his head.

"Someone did, right?"

Tears welled up in his eyes.

"Who?"

"Everyone, they all used to say things; most of the time it was just joking, but they kept going on and on. My dad was a really good football player, and he wanted me to play, but I was never really that good. I never could throw the ball just right, but Chase always could. My dad would praise him—"

She interrupted him and said, "And he'd put you down?"

Michael wiped the tears from his eyes and answered, "No, it wasn't like that. He was always nice, he just would say that I'm special, to me that said I was different but in a bad way. He never really took interest in the stuff I did."

"And your mom?"

"Sometimes, but she was always so busy. Then Nana

came to live with us, and she got even busier taking care of her. So I just spent more time being me and doing my stuff. There was this one time when they had to put down one of our horses. I begged my dad not to, but the horse had broken its leg. I get now why, but my heart broke for Maggie, she was so beautiful. Chase made fun of me and called me a little girl for crying, but I swear when I looked into Maggie's eyes, I could feel her pain."

A cascading wave of emotion began to build in Brienne as she sat and listened to Michael tell his story. She wanted to give him a hug but knew that now wasn't the time for such a thing.

"My dad said Maggie needed to be put down and told me to be strong, but I couldn't be strong. I cried and cried. So I took that as being weak. And after I added up all the things my family always said to me—even recently my mom said I needed to be strong, as if I'm some wimp. I'm not a wimp. I just look at things differently."

"Would you like me to teach you how to reassemble this rifle?" she asked with a smile.

He sat without saying a word.

She picked up the Glock 19 and waved it. "And I can show you how this works too."

He wiped his eyes dry and said, "Yeah, I'd like that."

She put the Glock down, pointed at the rifle disassembled on the table, and said, "First let's talk about what we have here, and then we'll go into the nomenclature. This is an AR-15..."

Three Miles East of Gallup, New Mexico

REID WAS happy to reach the outskirts of Gallup. The trip since leaving Santa Rosa had been uneventful, with the pass through Albuquerque easier than he imagined it would be.

He and Emily had chatted, but didn't cover much in the way of a substantial conversation. They talked mainly about life before, the things they missed, like music, food, drink and a common longing for the world to return to some sort of resemblance to what it was.

He enjoyed the casual banter with Emily; he found her smart, witty and charming. And he felt happy that he'd asked her to come. He even found her to have an uncanny resemblance to Evelyn now that he'd had a better chance to look at her. Evelyn had had brown hair while Emily had dirty blond, but they both had slight dimples and a crooked smile at the end of their mouth that gave them cuteness and character.

Hannah, though, was not doing well. She had been slipping in and out of a deep sleep. Her fatigue had become crushing, and the rash on her belly had now spread to cover her entire chest and back and was creeping down her arms. Her temperature was elevated, and at one stop just east of Albuquerque, he gave her some ibuprofen to ease any pain she might be experiencing and to reduce her fever.

"How far can this car go?" Emily asked.

"The guy who retrofitted said that it had a range of five hundred miles, but to be honest, I don't know. It does slowly recharge as you drive but not enough for what it uses. We're going to have to make a stop for some time to get it fully charged again," Reid replied, then remembered the map of charging stations.

She looked around the car and said, "This car is really cool."

Hannah's body went rigid and her jaw clenched so tight her teeth began to grind.

Reid watched in horror as she was having the first of what would be many seizures.

"What's wrong with her?" Emily asked.

Reid pulled the car over fast. The tires hit the loose gravel, causing the car to skid hard to the right. Reid countered by turning the opposite way, but the car's rear end swung out the other way. He again corrected and came to a full stop. He immediately gave Hannah attention.

Her body was still rigid, and the grinding of her teeth sounded awful, like nails on a chalkboard. "Get me something to put between her teeth."

Emily looked around in the back and found a line of rope. "How's this?"

He snatched it from her and carefully pried open Hannah's jaw and placed the one-inch nylon rope. He opened her eyelids to see her pupils were rolled up into her head. Saliva streamed from the side of her mouth now that it was open slightly due to the rope.

"What can you do for her?" Emily asked.

"Just wait now. This should subside shortly," Reid said, his voice cracking with emotion. Seeing Hannah's latest symptom filled him with terror that she was progressing fast, maybe too fast for him to reach California.

Emily sat back and watched Reid caress Hannah's arm

and sweetly talk to her. She didn't know what to expect when she'd hit the road after life in the compound, but finding a man like him, who appeared kind, wasn't on the list of what she expected.

Hannah's body went limp and relaxed back into her seat. The rope dropped from her open mouth.

Reid opened her eyelids and could see her pupils. "Thank God, it's past." He turned to Emily and said, "There's a small bag back there; hand it to me."

She did as he asked.

He opened it, found the bottle of Artane, removed two small white pills, and held them in his palm.

"How are you going to get her to swallow those?" Emily asked.

"That's a good question."

"What are they for?"

"They're supposed to help with the tremors," he replied.

"Try lifting her chin, opening her mouth and dropping them on the back of her tongue, then dump water in," Emily said.

"I'll try to wake her," Reid said. He shook Hannah, but she didn't move. "Hannah, wake up, honey, c'mon, wake up." He shook her some more, but she still wouldn't wake.

"Hannah, wake up!" Emily shouted.

Reid recoiled from the loud shout and gave her an annoyed look.

Hannah stirred.

"Hannah?" Reid asked. "Honey, I need you to wake up just a second and take something."

"Daddy," she said, her voice barely audible.

"Honey, open your mouth," Reid said.

Hannah did as he asked, her eyes half closed.

Reid placed the tablets on her tongue and poured some water in her mouth.

Not expecting the water, Hannah coughed and choked. She spit up the tablets.

"Damn it," Reid snapped.

Hannah's eyes widened. She looked at Reid and said, "I'm sorry. I'm…" Tears started to flow.

"You made her cry," Emily said, as she felt sorry for Hannah.

"Stay out of this," he snapped at Emily. "Hannah, honey, I need you to take these pills."

"Daddy, I don't feel good. I don't…" Hannah stopped talking, her eyes rolled back into her head, and her body again went rigid and began to convulse.

"No, no, no," Reid cried out. He took the rope and, like before, slid it between her teeth.

Hannah convulsed for a minute before it subsided again. When she was done, she opened her eyes, looked at Reid and sobbed, "Daddy I don't feel good. It hurts, it hurts real bad."

"I know, sweetheart, I know," Reid said, tears now streaming down his face. "Honey, I need you to take these pills and…" He looked through the bag and removed the bottle of Roxanol. He opened it and dumped a pill into his hand. "And take this too. This one will help with the pain."

"I don't want to die," Hannah cried.

"We're about halfway to the ocean, honey. We'll be there soon," Reid said. "Open your mouth for me."

She did as he asked.

He put one tablet of Artane on her tongue instead of both. "I'm going to pour a little bit of water; please swallow it."

When he poured a cap full of water into her mouth, she focused on what she was doing and swallowed the pill.

"Good girl," Reid said. He proceeded by giving her the rest.

She took the other tablet and pill with no issue, then asked as she looked outside, "Where are we?"

"New Mexico still, but we're almost in Arizona."

"Wake me when we reach Arizona," she said then closed her eyes.

Exhausted from the drama, he melted into the seat and sighed. Tears trickled down his cheeks.

Emily too felt the wave of emotion. She reached over the seat and touched his shoulder. "You're a good dad."

Reid wiped his tears from his face and said, "I don't know about that."

"How many dads would do what you're doing? Most would have probably been resigned to the fact their kid would die."

"Maybe so."

"Sorry for being rude a bit ago," she said.

"It's fine, no worries," he said. He handed her back the bag, put his attention back on the road, and proceeded ahead. What he'd just witnessed was the worst she'd been.

She wasn't getting better, and whatever Hillary had tried definitely didn't seem to be working. He needed to get to San Clemente Island, but at her rate of decline, he was now beginning to think she wouldn't make it.

CHAPTER 6

Five Miles West of Logan, New Mexico

BRIENNE WOKE early with the hope that she could slip out without having to say goodbye to Michael. She wasn't good at goodbyes. Even when she had left Jake and Dustin all those years ago, she took an Uber versus having Jake drive her to the airport. It had been her way of doing things since she could remember, and for the life of her, she couldn't recall why.

She slung her pack over her shoulders and slipped out of Chase's bedroom, took two steps, and found Michael sitting in a chair in the living room. Seeing him startled her. "Why are you up?"

"I wanted to say bye," Michael answered as he fiddled with a loose thread on his sweater. "Plus I didn't want to miss seeing you again."

She stiffened her back, cleared her throat, and said, "Thank you for the stuff."

He got to his feet and gave her a pensive look.

"You take care of yourself, kid," she blurted out then shuffled past him.

"Is that it? Will I ever see you again?"

She stopped at the entry to the kitchen and replied, "I doubt it."

"You said this place was nice, that we had it lucky here. If you find your family, why not bring them here? We have plenty of room."

Her heart melted. She turned towards him and said, "I'll consider that."

"I'm really happy to have met you."

"Nice to have met you too," she said and continued on her way through the darkened kitchen to the doorway. She grabbed the knob, turned and, just before she opened the door, said, "Tell your mom I'm grateful too."

Michael had followed her and was a few feet behind her. "I will."

"And I hope your nana gets better," Brienne said, opened the door, and walked out as the light of the new day was just beginning to show itself in the east.

Michael went to the door and looked for her, but she'd vanished.

A tear had come to Brienne's eye, which she quickly wiped away. She still had a long way to go, and any feelings like this could make her weak. With her rifle slung across her body and her pack snug to her back, she marched down the gravel drive towards the gate.

Lights flashed down the road past the gate, followed by the rumble of an engine.

Brienne paused and listened.

The lights grew closer and the engine sound louder. Voices now came into earshot.

Fear gripped her. She unslung her rifle and held it firm as she stayed frozen, her senses heightened.

The lights came into full view. They were the headlights of a vehicle. The voices boomed and carried around the area.

Brienne had the sickening feeling that these people had a connection to the ones she'd shot a couple of days ago. And if her suspicions were correct, they were here to seek revenge and raid what they had. She spun around and sprinted as fast as her legs would take her to the house. She leapt onto the porch, took the door handle in her hand, and went to turn it, to find it was locked. She banged with her fists against the door. "Michael, open up!"

Seconds passed and the door opened. "What's wrong?"

Brienne pushed past him, slammed the door behind them, and exclaimed, "Hurry, get your mom and Nana up!"

Michael saw the fear in her eyes. "What's going on?"

"There are people coming. We have to hide; we have to go!" she roared.

All Michael could imagine was these people torturing his mother and his nana, much less him. Never in the years since the war had they had anyone show up. Now someone was here, and they most likely presented a grave threat.

"Go!" Brienne shouted.

Michael turned on a dime and raced away. "Mom, Nana, wake up, wake up!"

Tanya emerged from her bedroom holding a lantern. "What is up with all the noise?"

Seeing her, Michael ran up and said, "There are people coming. Brienne saw them!"

"People coming?"

"Gather what you can, and get Nana. We have to go hide," Brienne shouted from the end of the hall.

"Who are they?" Tanya asked.

"It's best we don't stand around and wait to find out," Brienne said.

Nana appeared at her door. "What is all this racket?"

"Nana, we need to go. Someone is coming," Michael said.

"Go? I ain't goin' nowhere," Nana said defiantly. "This farm has been my home since I was a little girl. I'll be damned if I'm running from it."

Brienne, Tanya and Michael approached Nana.

"This is not a time to act gallant or cavalier," Brienne said.

"Young woman, I'm old and I won't be run off by whoever is coming," Nana shot back.

"Mom, this is foolish. We should go hide in the creek bed to the south of the property," Tanya said, her hands trembling.

"Nope," Nana said.

Annoyed, Brienne walked to a window in the living room and pulled aside the curtains to see the lights of the truck parked in front of the gate. She saw movement; no doubt they were trying to open the gate. "They're at the gate. We need to go now before the sun rises. We still have a bit of darkness to hide in."

Nana stood her ground. "You go; I'm staying. If those bastards want to drive me out of my house, they'll have to take my dead body out of here, but not before I put some lead in their asses."

"You're talking nonsense, Mom; we need to go," Tanya snapped. She too was growing annoyed with Nana's attitude.

"Tanya, you take Michael and go. I'm an old woman, I'm tired, and I ain't leavin'."

Brienne came back and said, "She's made up her mind. Michael, Tanya, let's go."

"No, I won't leave Nana," Michael said, his voice cracking with emotion.

Nana reached out with a shaky hand and touched his cheek. "Go, protect your mother."

"But, Nana," Michael said.

"I love you, Michael. You've always been my favorite," Nana said.

Brienne raced back to the window. She peered out to see several men moving the nail strip from the drive. "They're inside the property. They're coming this way."

"Go," Nana said.

"Michael, she's made up her mind. Time for us to go hide," Tanya said. She pulled on Michael's arm.

Brienne came back and asked, "Is there a way out the back?"

"We can climb out my window," Tanya replied.

Brienne turned to Nana, pulled out her Glock, and offered it.

Nana shook her head and said, "I've got something, my husband's old service revolver."

"You have a pistol?" Tanya asked, shocked upon hearing the revelation.

"I've always had it, kept it in a safe place just in case and, well, this is one of those cases. Now you all hurry and go hide. When those bastards come in the door, they'll get a surprise," Nana said with a smile.

Michael embraced Nana, tears in his eyes. "I love you."

"I love you too, and remember what I told you. Now go, please hurry," Nana said, pulling him off her.

Voices from outside were now carrying inside.

"They're here," Brienne said. "Come on."

The three climbed out of Tanya's bedroom window, hit the ground, and sprinted for the dry creek bed two hundred yards away. The light from the vehicle lit up the house, and the sun's light was growing with each passing minute.

After settling into a good hiding spot with a vantage point of the back and side of the house, they watched as six people emerged from the old 1968 Ford F-100 pickup truck. They dispersed, with three looking around the property and three going inside.

Brienne had her rifle in her shoulder.

"Nana is going to die, isn't she?" Michael asked. "We have to fight back, we must."

Brienne pulled the Glock 17 out and handed it to Michael. "Remember how I told you to shoot this?"

He looked at her, shocked to be given the pistol. "Yeah."

"Good."

"You can't give my son a gun," Tanya spat.

"I'm not here to get into a pissing contest, but he might need it," Brienne said.

"He's a boy," Tanya said before Brienne interrupted her.

"He's a young man who needs to know how to fight for himself and defend what is his. You've spent all this time living behind that gate thinking the world was the same. Well, Tanya, that there breaking into your house is the new world, and they kill people for no reason at all."

Tanya sneered but decided not to respond.

"We need to fight back," Michael said.

"Right now, we'll stay put," Brienne said.

Several gunshots sounded from inside the house.

Michael jumped. "Nana, no."

Brienne got back behind her rifle and steadied herself. Through her scope she saw the three who remained outside rush back towards the house. Seconds later two men came out dragging Nana, who was kicking and screaming.

"Nana, no," Michael again whimpered.

"Remain calm," Brienne urged.

The man dragging Nana was known to Tanya.

"That's Jon Wilkins," she gasped.

Wilkins threw Nana to the ground, snatched her by the neck, and smacked her across the face. "Where is everyone else?"

Nana smiled, blood dripping from a cut lip. "I'm here all alone."

"That's not what Will told us before I slit his throat," Wilkins said. He was tall, lean, and a thick black beard covered his face. His piercing pale blue eyes gave him an ominous appearance. "He said you all were doing okay out here and promised to give us some provisions if I didn't kill him."

"There ain't no one else out here but me. Will went to town to get me some medicine," Nana smirked.

"I warned him to stay out, but he came back. I told him what would happen if he stepped foot back in my town to scavenge," Wilkins said.

"Your town, since when did you come to own Logan?" Nana chuckled. "You're just a two-bit thug. I remember you. Didn't you used to pump shit out of those portable toilets? Now look at you, you think you're some sort of kingpin. Son, you were and will always be a shit sucker."

Tanya, Brienne and Michael could all hear what was being said. After Nana's snarky remarks, they all cringed, knowing nothing good would be the result of what she just said.

Wilkins reeled back his clenched fist.

"Stop!" Michael shouted.

Wide-eyed, Brienne grabbed at Michael's pant leg. "What are you doing?"

"Michael, no," Tanya cried out.

Michael brushed off Brienne's grasp and walked out of the dry creek bed, the pistol tucked in the small of his back.

"Get back here," Tanya snapped.

"No, Mom, we need to stand up and fight people like this. Nana is my family, and I won't see her hurt by these people," Michael declared.

Hearing Michael's shout, Nana sighed.

Wilkins spun around and looked into the dimly lit distance. "Who's that?"

Michael approached until he was in view. "I'm Michael, her grandson."

"Ah, I suppose you were that brat we went chasing after the other day. Tell me, where is your mother? I know that pretty little thing is here," Wilkins asked.

Michael's arms were raised. "What do you want? Is it the farm, our stash? What is it?"

"I didn't come here to take your stuff, though I will have it once I'm through here. No, I came to get a pound of flesh as payment for killing my brother and cousin."

"I didn't kill them," Michael shouted back.

"Someone with you did. Now how about you turn them over and we can call us even—that is, after I take what I want," Wilkins barked.

Michael took a few steps farther. "I need you to leave."

Wilkins raised a brow, cocked his head, and laughed heartily. He turned to his right-hand man, Curt, next to him and said, "He wants us to leave. What do you think we should do?"

"I say we kill that little pipsqueak, shoot this old hag, and burn the fucking place down," the man answered with a sinister tone. Curt was a short man, he stood about five feet six inches, but he made up for his limited height by being stocky and muscular. He was known for his strength and had at one time been the New Mexico arm wrestling champion.

"I like that. Hey, pipsqueak, I don't think we're gonna leave. Now how about you just get whoever killed my brother and cousin to step forward, and maybe I'll consider not killing you," Wilkins said.

The entire time Michael and Wilkins were going back and forth, Brienne scoped who she would shoot first, and settled on Wilkins.

Tanya knelt frozen. The shock of seeing Michael confronting Wilkins and his people was too much for her already fragile mindset to take.

"Michael, you go, run. These scumbags can't do anything to me; I'm already dead. Now go, run," Nana yelled.

"Would you shut that old cow up," Wilkins said to Curt.

Happily, Curt cocked his arm back and readied to strike her but paused when Nana gave him a big smile. "What are you smiling at, bitch?"

"Curtis Marlow, aren't you the fella all the girls snickered about? It was you with the micro penis, wasn't it?" Nana quipped.

"Fuck you," Curt said and pulled his pistol from his waistband. He placed it against Nana's forehead and barked, "Take that back, you hear me."

"Why so mad, Curtis?" Nana laughed. "It must be true based on how angry you are about it."

Wilkins turned back to Curt and said, "Shut her the fuck up."

"Fine," Curt said and pulled the trigger.

Nana's head snapped back when the round passed through it. She crumpled to the ground dead.

Rage welled up inside Michael. He reached for the pistol tucked in the small of his back.

Tanya couldn't sit idle any longer. Nana was dead, and Michael was not far away from them. She jumped to her feet and ran toward Michael. "Michael, no, don't do anything

"Shit," Brienne growled as she watched Tanya run towards Michael.

Wilkins peered out. "Who is that?"

Brienne was done. She knew there was no way they were getting out of there without having a gunfight. She put her reticle back on Wilkins and squeezed the trigger.

Curt, who was still angry from the stinging words from Nana, pushed his way past Wilkins, leveled his pistol in Tanya's direction, and pulled the trigger.

The 9 mm round exploded from the barrel and ended its journey buried in Tanya's chest. She dropped to the ground, alive but barely.

"No!" Michael screamed. He looked back at his mother and wailed in anger and pain.

That was Brienne's official cue. She applied that last bit of pressure to the trigger and fired the first round from her rifle. The 5.56 mm round exited the barrel and in less than a second passed through Wilkins' chest, out his back, and impacted the side of the house.

Wilkins clutched at the wound, looking down as his shirt began to turn red with blood. "I'm shot," he muttered.

Curt looked for where the gunfire had come from, but before he could do anything, Brienne unleashed another round, this one hit Wilkins in the neck, then a third struck him in the solar plexus region. He stepped backwards two steps, fell down and choked on his own blood.

The remaining group lifted their rifles and began to fire towards the creek bed.

Enraged, Michael began his advance on the others, his pistol out in front of him.

Brienne spotted a woman who had pivoted with her rifle and was taking aim on Michael. Brienne squeezed off a round and struck her in the stomach, then a second that hit her in the upper chest. The woman fell to the ground dead.

Bullets ripped past Michael, but it was like he was immune to getting hit. He aimed at one man and pulled the trigger several times, each round hitting the man, and killed him. He turned and took aim on another and did it again.

Brienne watched Michael's rampage with respect and awe, then went back to surveying the area to ensure that Wilkins and his people were dead.

A man came around the corner of the house. He hollered as he came at Michael.

Michael turned quickly and unloaded the remaining bullets into him.

The man toppled to the ground feet away.

Brienne looked but found no one else; however, she swore there had been another person.

Smoke began to billow from the house.

"The house is on fire!" Michael cried out. He ran to the side door just as the last of Wilkins' people burst from it, a pistol in his grip.

Brienne sighted quickly and pulled the trigger. The well-placed shot struck the man in his chest and dropped him where he was.

Michael looked over his shoulder in Brienne's direction

and nodded his appreciation for the save. He stepped over the dead man and went inside only to find the entire living room and kitchen were engulfed in flames. Seeing there was nothing he could do, he retreated out the door and stood a safe distance away.

With the area safe, Brienne stood and walked from her hide position. She advanced slowly, her eyes darting from one body to the next. She wasn't going to take any chances that one couldn't be feigning death.

With the battle over, Michael turned and went to Nana's side. He leaned down and gave her a kiss on the cheek. "I'm sorry I couldn't save you, Nana."

Brienne checked on Tanya, but like Nana, she was dead. A bullet had passed through her heart.

Michael raced back to Tanya, but this time, he lifted her and placed her motionless and dead body in his lap. Tears poured from his eyes, and the heat from the flames now engulfing the entire house was intense.

Brienne stared at the sad scene. She had no words and found that if she did say something to Michael, it was meaningless. The poor boy had lost his entire family in the span of days. He was alone in the world, a world she despised above all else. She stopped trying to understand how it worked, as doing so was incomprehensible.

It took only minutes for the house to be devoured by the flames.

Michael craned his head back and watched as the roof collapsed. His entire life had been spent there, all those years, all the memories gone in a flash. He was not only alone, he was homeless.

Brienne walked up to him and knelt. She placed a comforting hand on his shoulder and said, "I can't imagine what you're feeling, but know I'm not leaving you."

"You won't go? You'll stay here?"

She looked around and replied, "There's nothing here to stay for now."

"So you want me to come with you?"

She looked as the house began to crumble and said, "Well, you're not staying here."

Three Miles North of New River, Arizona

Emily woke suddenly. She lifted her head and noticed they were pulled off the road. In the front seat Hannah was fast asleep. It was daytime but hard to tell if it was morning or afternoon due to the cloud cover. The driver's seat was empty, and Reid was nowhere near the car.

She opened her door, stepped out and stretched. The distinct smell of the desert hit her. She inhaled deeply and reached even higher as she extended her arms to the sky. Sitting in the backseat was not a comfortable situation, yet she was thankful not just for the ride but for being a small woman.

"You're awake," Reid shouted. He was atop a rise about seventy-five feet away and looking south, a pair of binoculars in his hand.

She made her way up the rocky slope. She was curious as to what he was doing, but when she crested the hill, she saw it with her own eyes. "What is that?" She could tell it was a city, but something seemed off about it.

"That was Phoenix," he answered. He handed her the binoculars.

After she adjusted the focus, she saw the destruction more clearly. The skyscrapers that once dotted the skyline were charred and broken. Glimmers and glints of glass appeared strewn all across the valley floor for miles. "It's glimmering."

"The bomb literally turned much of the valley to glass," Reid said.

"I don't understand."

"Intense heat and sand make glass," Reid explained.

"Oh, that's right."

"Needless to say, we won't be traveling through Phoenix," he said. "We'll find a different route. I'll check the map and see what's best."

Voices echoed off in the distance.

The two snapped their heads around and looked for the source.

"Am I just hearing things, or is that people talking?" Reid asked.

"I hear it too," she replied.

They crouched down and moved to cover behind a boulder.

"Over there," she said and pointed to the east about a few hundred yards past the freeway.

He took the binoculars back from her and looked to see a small band of people walking. They had packs on their backs, with rifles slung. He counted four: two adults and two children approximately in the early teens. He assumed they were a family.

"Best we get back to the car," she said.

"I think they're harmless, just passing through, but we can't take any chances," he replied. "Let's get back to the car."

They made their way back to find Hannah awake. She was sitting up and bloody tears were streaming down her face.

He opened her door and knelt beside her. "What's the matter?"

"I woke and you weren't here," she sobbed. "I got scared."

"I'm sorry, I was trying to get an idea of what's ahead of us," Reid explained.

"Did you?" she asked.

"We did," he answered.

"I need to go," Hannah said.

"Me too." Emily smiled. "I can take her just over there."

Hannah nodded.

The two walked a few feet off the road and, using a shrub for privacy, went to the bathroom.

Emily helped Hannah walk back. She was very weak, and just the short distance had taken its toll on her strength. "I'm tired."

"I am too," Reid said. He turned to Emily and asked, "Do you mind driving for a bit?"

"Yeah, of course, you'll just need to show me how this works."

"It's like driving any other car," he said, then proceeded to tell her about the specifics. It was then that he noticed the gauge had the power at less than half, and with the cloud cover, they weren't generating any new power. "We need to find one of those charging stations and hope they still work."

"Where's that map?" she asked. "You said you had a map of where those stations were."

He dug through the console and found the map Arthur had given him. "Here." He unfolded the single sheet and pinpointed where they were. "There's one in Wickenburg and one in Quartzsite. Let's keep our fingers crossed."

"Let's."

The two got into the car, with her in the driver's seat and Reid in the back. Emily adjusted the seat up, giving him more room.

"Hey, before we go, I want to say it's been nice having you along for the ride," Reid said.

"I've enjoyed it too, considering. Hannah is lucky to have you."

He reached up and rubbed Hannah's arm. "I'm the lucky one."

"I haven't asked, but where's her mom?" Emily asked.

"She's dead. The dog flu took her," Reid answered.

She turned around to face him and said nicely, "I'm sorry, I know what it means to lose someone close."

"Were you married too?"

"No, not that, I lost my brother recently," Emily said.

"My condolences."

Emily turned back to face the road. "Shall we?"

"Hey, I've plotted the route to take us through Yuma, so—"

She spun back around and asked, "You'll take me to Yuma?"

"Yeah."

"Thank you, I've been wondering how I'd get there."

He gave her a smile and said, "Shall we?"

"Yes," she said, returning his smile.

Reid got as comfortable as he could, placed his pack so he could use it as a pillow, closed his eyes and drifted off.

Quartzsite, Arizona

When Reid, Emily and Hannah reached Wickenburg, they found the Tesla charging station, but it wasn't operational. With the charge on the car down to a range of one hundred and twenty-two miles and with no sun to help provide a supplemental charge, Reid began to lose hope. They traveled the distance to Quartzsite in less than an hour and hoped to find something different.

"The map says it's off West Main Street. Look for a Carl's Jr.," Reid said, his finger on the map.

Emily was still driving, a choice made by Reid, as he needed more time to rest. Even though he couldn't sleep, he wanted the time to relax in the backseat.

Hannah was asleep. She'd had one small seizure, which lasted less than a minute, and it appeared the Artane had helped in that regard. While she was awake after, Reid gave her the drugs recommended by Thomas. While he was repacking the bag with the drugs, he spotted the vial from Hillary and recalled that she'd told him to administer the booster shot in two days.

With the days bleeding into each other, it took him a few seconds to realize that he'd have to give her the shot tomorrow. While he was skeptical, he figured why not?

Emily slowed the car.

Reid looked up and saw the freeway exit sign for Main Street, then saw the restaurant sign to his right. "It's right there, see it?"

"Yep," Emily said. She navigated the car slowly around some small debris and garbage and brought it to the stop sign. She turned right and pulled the car into the Carl's Jr. parking lot.

"Back there, at the end of the parking lot," Reid said, pointing.

"I see it," Emily said and proceeded ahead.

Reid's heart filled with hope when on top of the charging station he saw a large solar array. "I think we might be lucky this time."

Emily stopped the car a foot from the charging station.

Reid didn't hesitate; he jumped out and walked up to the tall white tower. There were three in a row, but nothing that told him if they worked. He'd never had to charge the car manually but figured it couldn't be that difficult. He went to the rear end of the car and pulled on the charging cable. It popped out easily. He took the cable from the tower then realized it wasn't long enough. "You need to back the car in," he said to Emily.

She did as he asked.

With the car now backed in, he inserted the charging cable. "Anything?"

"I don't know what I'm supposed to be looking for," Emily said.

Reid went to the driver's side and said, "Look at the screen; see if the mile range increases."

"Okay."

He walked back to inspect the cable.

"Nothing," she said.

"Give it a little bit of time. This thing doesn't charge like a car getting fueled with gas," Reid said.

Bored, Emily got out of the car and stretched. "So this is the metropolis of Quartzsite, huh?"

Reid wasn't interested in casual conversation. He went back to see if anything was changing on the screen, to find the range was up a few miles. "It's working, it's working." He grabbed his map and quickly calculated the distance to Oceanside with the detour through Yuma. "It's enough, it's enough."

"What's enough?" Emily said as she paced back and forth in the parking lot.

"If we can get a full charge, I'll be able to make it to Oceanside," Reid replied.

"Does that include taking me to Yuma?"

"Yeah," Reid answered happily. He gave Hannah a sweet gaze and said, "I'm gonna get you better, honey, I promise."

"So you really think there's some place that has a cure?" she asked.

"Is it any crazier a concept than you thinking you'll find a utopian society in Baja?"

"Yes, on account you're from a utopian town in Oklahoma," Emily quipped.

"Touché." He chuckled. His spirits were lifted now that he'd found a charging station that worked. "Why don't you just stick with us? After we find what I'm looking for, we'll probably head back to Deliverance."

"I ran into someone recently who said your town was real. I thought they were wrong," Emily said, referring to her initial conversation with Brienne.

"It's real, but a place in Mexico—I suppose if a town in Oklahoma can survive and thrive, why not a small fishing village in Mexico?"

"All things are possible even if they don't seem so," Emily said.

"I'm hungry," Reid said and poked his head in the backseat.

"I've got some snacks in my pack," she offered.

He searched through her pack and pulled out the bag of human jerky. "I love jerky," he said walking up to her.

She saw what he had and rushed over. She smacked it out of his hand and barked, "Don't eat that."

"But it's jerky," he replied, shocked by her action.

"You don't want that type of jerky."

He looked at the piece on the ground then to the bag still in his hand. "What's wrong with it?"

She snatched the bag out of his hand and tossed it away. "Just trust me, you don't want to eat that."

He shrugged his shoulders and went back to dig through the backseat. He produced a bag of chips and asked, "Is this acceptable to eat?"

"Yeah, sure."

He rolled his eyes and opened the bag. After he took his first bite, he said, "Stale."

"It might be stale, but it's better than that jerky," she said.

"What's wrong with it? Is it made from dogs or something?"

"Let's just say it's not the kind of jerky you want to eat," she said.

"You're odd."

"That's an understatement."

"Why don't you want to join us to California, then come back to Deliverance with us? You'd fit in," Reid offered, genuinely desiring her companionship for the rest of the journey.

"I'm afraid I have to go to Yuma then on to Loreto," she said, although she did give the idea honest consideration. "But I don't think I'd be as welcome as you think I would be. My life has been complicated."

"Whose life isn't complicated?"

"Believe me when I say mine has been very unusual."

He gave her a curious look and wondered what she'd seen or done that made her think the way she did. She couldn't be that old; he guessed mid-twenties. He found her attractive, something he hadn't found in anyone in a very long time.

"Why are you looking at me that way?" she asked. She could feel his energy had shifted to something she wasn't used to. She enjoyed his stare; it made her feel good. She then thought about him in a way she'd not thought of. "Are you married?"

"No, my wife died shortly after Hannah was born," Reid replied, his tone changing from joy to remorse.

"How?"

"The virus, like many others. I mean, look around; I thought we'd encounter more people than we have."

"It all does seem empty, doesn't it?" she said, looking around.

He walked back to the car and glanced in to see the range was at two hundred and fifteen. "We're getting close." He turned around and found her standing just behind him. He recoiled at first then realized she wasn't there to harm him; she wanted something else.

She touched his chest and ran her hand up to his neck. "I've never been with a man before."

He suddenly became nervous. It had been so long since he'd had sex that he might as well be a virgin; he laughed to himself.

She ran her hand from his neck, down his chest, and rested it on his crotch.

Reid stepped back, but the car stopped him from retreating out of her reach.

She closed the distance, lifted her head, and planted a kiss on his lips.

He didn't know how to act. He was aroused but also felt odd because he thought she was probably fifteen to twenty years his junior; also Hannah was in the car.

She kissed him again, her hand wandering over his body.

"Ah, no," he said softly as he gently pushed her away. "I'm sorry, but I can't."

Hurt and confused, she asked, "You don't like me? I thought you liked me."

"I do, I, um, I find you very attractive, but I…"

"Is there something wrong with me?" she asked.

"No, it's not you. I, um, I…"

"You want me to come back with you to Deliverance? Why would you want me to come with you if you don't want me or like me that way?"

She made a good point and one he found hard to refute. "I like you, I do. I find you very pretty. I, um…How do I say this? I haven't been with a woman since my wife died. I guess I don't know how to anymore. And Hannah's right there. I just feel awkward, but believe me it's not you. You're very…you look very nice. I'm flattered."

"I don't care if you're flattered. I want to be loved. I want to feel someone, be a woman," she snapped.

"Please don't take me not wanting to have sex with you as it being about you. It's all about me."

"Why did you take me with you? Why did you invite me to go to Deliverance if you didn't want me?" Emily asked.

"I'm confused. I took you with me to help. I asked you to come back to Deliverance to give you a home. I never had an ulterior motive," Reid confessed.

She spun around and stormed off, her fists clenched.

As she headed away, he couldn't help but think he was the cause of her confusion.

Hannah cried out in pain from the car.

Hearing Hannah moan, Reid was torn away from his thoughts about the incident with Emily. He raced to find her body rigid and in the middle of a seizure. He looked around for the rope he'd been using to help but couldn't find it. "Hold on, honey."

Hannah shrieked. Her nails dug into her palms and cut them open.

"Where is it?" Reid growled in frustration. He looked on the floorboard underneath Hannah and found it. He picked it up and went to slide it between her teeth, when she relaxed.

Hannah opened her eyes, looked at Reid and cried, "It hurts, Daddy."

"I know it does, baby, I'm sorry," he said.

Emily appeared behind him. "Is she okay?"

"She had another seizure," Reid said.

Emily looked past him and at the screen. "We're at three hundred and eighty-five miles. Is that a full charge?"

"Ah, yeah, that's it," Reid answered. He turned back to Hannah. "I'm going to give you some more pain meds." He reached back and grabbed the bag, found the drugs, and gave them to her.

Shortly after taking the drugs, Hannah closed her eyes and fell asleep.

Reid stepped out of the car. "Can we talk?"

"Why?" Emily asked.

"About what happened?"

"There's nothing to talk about. Let's get back on the road," she sneered.

"Very well," he said. He unplugged the car from the charger and got behind the wheel. He peeked at her in the rearview mirror to find she was staring back at him.

"I don't want to talk about it. Just drive," she snapped.

He nodded, put the car in gear, and drove towards the freeway.

Five Miles West of Logan, New Mexico

While Brienne packed what she could find in the barn and other outbuildings for the trip ahead, Michael stood frozen above the freshly dug graves for his mother and Nana. He stared at the dirt and wondered if it all was just a nightmare that he would soon wake from. How could his entire life be upended so quickly? he thought.

Brienne loaded the bed of the truck with everything of value she found, including jugs of water, which she filled from the well; long-term storage food she found in the barn; tools; extra fuel, which she prayed wasn't worthless; a hose to siphon more along the way; a medical kit she also found in the barn; all the weapons she could find, including those of Wilkins' people; and assorted miscellaneous items she thought could be useful. She put the last item in and shot Michael a look. Her heart melted for him. Even though she'd not seen her family in a long time, she still hadn't had to deal with death as far as facing it. Without really knowing what happened to her family, it was as if they were still around.

Michael placed some personal effects on the graves, turned, and walked up to the truck. "I'm ready to leave."

"I'm packed, so if you're ready, I'm ready."

He looked at the graves again then to the charred and

smoldering remnants of the house. The only thing left standing was the brick fireplace.

Michael opened the door to the truck and got in. He slammed the door and sat silent, staring out the cracked and bug-splattered windshield.

Brienne got in the cab but didn't start the truck. She shifted in her seat to face Michael. "How are you doing?"

"I don't want to talk," Michael growled, anger showing in his sharp response.

"I know what you're feeling must be—"

He glared at her and snapped, "I don't want to talk."

She raised her hands as if surrendering. "Sorry. I thought you might want to talk."

"Well, I don't. Can we just go?"

"Listen, Michael, I know you're hurting, just know that I'm here to listen if you want," Brienne offered.

"Can we just go?"

She turned the key and fired up the truck. "We're fortunate to have a truck though. That will make traveling much easier."

"Well, I'm glad you feel we're lucky. I just lost my entire family. I watched my mother and Nana die right in front of me. But hey, you got a truck, so you can drive to see your family!" he cried out.

She was tempted to reply but kept quiet. She knew anything she said now would only fall on deaf ears. Michael was suffering deeply and needed time to process.

"So if you're done feeling lucky, can we leave? If I stay here any longer, I'll just go and jump into the hot coals of what was my house."

Brienne put the truck into gear and drove down the driveway. As they passed through the gate, Michael started to cry quietly. He turned away so she wouldn't see. A motherly desire to comfort him welled up inside, but she kept her distance. She saw there was an aftermarket CD player in the truck. She turned it on, and instantly rap music began to blare.

Angrily, Michael hit the player and turned it off. "I want peace and quiet."

"Sorry," Brienne said. She rolled down her window a crack to let in some fresh air.

"Can you put that up? It's cold in here," Michael spat.

She'd had enough. She slammed on the brakes, bringing the old squeaky truck to an abrupt stop. She shifted in her seat to face him and said, "It's perfectly fine for you to be upset, angry, pissed, you name it, but you don't get to treat me poorly. I didn't harm you. I wasn't the one who killed anyone in your family. I've helped you since day one. I'll not play music or roll down my window or even talk to you after this, but please don't think you have the right to take your anger, your sorrow, out on me."

He sat sulking and staring out the passenger-door window.

"Do you hear me?" she asked.

He sat silent.

"Michael, do you understand?"

"Yes."

"Good, and believe me when I tell you that I'm on your side, I'm here for you. We're in this shit show called life together now."

He remained quiet. Tears gently slid down his cheek and clung to his jaw and chin.

Brienne positioned herself behind the steering wheel again, adjusted her ponytail, and drove off.

CHAPTER 7

Two Miles North of Yuma, Arizona

"YUMA CITY LIMITS! We made it, it's hard to believe, but we're here," Reid said. He gave Emily a glance in the rearview mirror to catch her response, but she glared at him. It appeared to him she was still upset about being rejected. He hated that he might end their time together on such a sour note. "Ah, tell me, where exactly am I dropping you?"

She remembered the address, as she had it seared into her memory. "14587 Fort Yuma Road."

"You don't know how to get there?"

"No, I only have an address," she answered. Her tone matched the harsh glances she had been giving him.

"Best I pull over," he said and slowed the car down to a stop on the highway. "This bridge should be safe," he said, referring to where they'd stopped. It was still dark outside, but soon the sun would be rising. He took out a map he had of the southwest and checked to see if it had a detailed map of Yuma, but it didn't. "Nothing."

"Do you think we're safe here?" she asked.

"I don't see anything, but this is an overpass. I didn't pass anyone coming onto it, and there's no one ahead of us, nor are there cars or stuff to hide behind. Yeah, this is probably okay."

She opened her door and stepped out.

"You taking a break and a stretch?"

"Yeah," she said and slammed the door.

Reid continued to look for any map that might show a detailed view of Yuma but came up short. He then thought of stopping by the first gas station and finding one. He then recalled it was a new day and that it was time to give Hannah the booster from Hillary. He grabbed the bag, opened it, and removed the vial and syringe. He filled the syringe half way per her instructions. Using an alcohol swab, he cleaned her upper left arm and stabbed the needle into her arm.

Hannah squirmed and opened her eyes. "Daddy."

Reid quickly injected the dose and removed the needle. Using another alcohol swab, he wiped the area he'd injected.

"Daddy, where are we?" Hannah asked.

"Yuma, that means we're close to California. We could be seeing the ocean by midafternoon at the earliest."

Hannah smiled, her eyes half open, and said, "I can't wait." She rolled onto her right side and dozed off.

Emily walked up and tapped on his window. "I need you to see something."

"What is it?" he asked.

"Let me show you."

He checked on Hannah, who was sleeping, and got out of the car. He closed the door and was face-to-face with the muzzle of her pistol. He laughed. "Is this your way of flirting? Because it might work."

"Give me the fob," she ordered.

"Wait, you're taking the car?"

"Yeah, I'm taking the car and your stuff, minus the drugs for Hannah," Emily said.

"Don't do this, please. I need to get to the coast. I'm probably only a half day's drive now. Please don't do this."

"I'm doing it. Now give me the fob," she said and moved the muzzle closer to his face.

"This isn't you. You're not this kind of person," he said, his hands raised.

"You're a fool. I am like this. I'm a broken person. You just saw a pretty face and thought I was something you wanted me to be."

"Emily, I need this car to get me to the coast. Please don't abandon me and Hannah."

"You can take the drugs, some water and food, but I get the car."

"You're killing her by leaving us here. You're killing her," Reid said.

"I won't ask again," she said, this time placing the muzzle against his forehead.

"So you'll shoot me, then what, kill Hannah?"

"Maybe I will."

"No, this isn't who you are, I know it; you're angry, you feel rejected."

She laughed heartily. "You think I'm mad because some old man won't fuck me?"

"Can we please talk about this? I'll take you to find a car, okay; but please don't leave us here."

"This is my last request. Give me the fob, now."

"Emily, please," Reid urged.

Frustrated, she shifted the muzzle off his forehead, pointed it just slightly away from his face, and pulled the trigger.

The roar of the gun firing was deafening.

"Fine," he said as he dug through the front pocket of his pants. He pulled out the fob and held it out in his open hand. She went to snatch it, but he turned his hand and dropped it on the ground.

"I'm not fucking around, Reid. Now pick it up."

"You're right, that was stupid, but you have to understand that car is my little girl's life," he said.

"Pick it up," she barked, her frustration growing.

"Okay, okay, I'll pick it up," he said and bent down. He scooped it up and looked at it for a brief moment. He probably wouldn't get any closer to her than he was now. If he gave her the car, Hannah would certainly die and he might too. Letting Emily leave them was a death sentence for Hannah, which meant he had to fight back. Giving in gave him zero options. His only sure bet was to try to disarm her. The second he needed to pick up the fob was enough time to make this critical decision. As he began to stand, he lunged forward, wrapped his arms around her waist, and launched them both through the air.

They came down on the hard pavement; she landed on her back.

The force of the tackle caused her to accidentally discharge the pistol, the round shooting high into the sky.

He straddled her. With his left hand he held her hand with the pistol down on the ground; then he cocked his right fist back and punched her as hard as he could in the face.

The single punch dazed her, but she was still conscious.

Seeing that she was still capable, he leveled another punch. This time it knocked her out. He pulled the pistol from her grip, tossed it aside, and checked her for any other weapons. He found two knives and tossed them as well. With her out cold, he now got to his feet, opened the back door, grabbed her backpack, and tossed it out. He looked at her sprawled out on the ground and felt the opposite of what most people would: sympathy. He did truly believe she wasn't a bad person, but a good one making horrible decisions. What he didn't know, though, was this was the second time in a week that she'd been left on the side of the road. He jumped back in the driver's seat, engaged the car, and sped off.

Hannah opened her eyes and asked, "What was that noise?"

"It was nothing. Now go back to sleep," he said. He saw the road sign for the interstate, made the turn, and roared onto the freeway. Within a mile he was crossing the

Colorado River and passed a large blue sign that read *WELCOME TO CALIFORNIA.*

Six Miles East of Holbrook, Arizona

Brienne's back was sore from the twelve-hour drive, which only saw one stop to refuel. She needed a break and thought the open desert was as good a place as any.

The cloud cover that had hidden the blue sky for days was gone. She marveled at the deep blue and the crescent moon that still lingered just above the horizon to the west, with the sun just making its appearance to the east.

"I need some sleep," she said.

Michael looked around, taking in the scenery. "Sure."

"I wish you could drive," she said, not thinking about his answer.

"I can try."

"Best not, could you stay up, though? Be my eyes while I shut mine," she said and leaned down to rest her head against the top of the seat. She yawned and shifted around until she found a comfortable position.

"I'm sorry," Michael blurted out.

She opened one eye and gave him a look. "About what?"

"You know, back at the house."

"Don't think anything about it."

"I was afraid. I still am, I suppose," he confessed.

"Seriously, it's okay. I understand."

He rested his head on his hand and peered out at the rolling hills dotted with shrubs and brush. "What scares you? I mean, what are you afraid of? I ask only because you don't seem afraid of much."

She wanted to protest his questions then thought that he was now ready to talk, so she'd better oblige. "A lot scares me."

"I don't believe it."

She yawned again. "I'm more afraid than you think I am. I just channel my fear, let it work for me. You have to remember that fear doesn't exist; it's only in your head."

"You're always afraid?"

"Not always, but a lot. I'd be lying if I said I wasn't afraid of this trip we're going on. Heck, I'm afraid whenever I'm on the road. I've noticed that I've seen fewer and fewer people over the years, but the road can be a very dangerous place. I channel my fear, use it to be more diligent about what I do, I focus more; but if I lived in a constant state of paralysis from my fear, I would never have left Germany."

"That makes sense."

"It's okay to be afraid. It's how you handle that fear that says everything about you and your character as a person," Brienne said.

He nodded, showing he acknowledged what she was saying.

"My greatest fear, finding that my family is dead and that I could've been there to prevent it," she confessed.

He shot her a look of surprise. "That's your greatest fear?"

"It sure is. I can handle running into bad people on the road, but to find my family dead when I get there is definitely the most frightening thing I can imagine experiencing."

"Do you regret leaving?"

She was now growing weary of the conversation but decided to keep going for his sake. She knew he was the one getting therapeutic help from it more than her. "I do regret leaving."

"You left for a job, right?"

"Yeah, but when I look back, I see how foolish it was. I was shortsighted, thinking that while the world was suffering from the virus and the war, it would eventually go back to being normal. It clearly didn't, and I became a prisoner of my own arrogance and ignorance. Now I've been separated from my family for almost nine years. I haven't heard from them or seen them," she said and sighed heavily. "If I could do it all over again, I would have stayed. People used to say you can't have regrets in life, but that's a nice meme when the world is predictable and safe, but when your actions lead you to not seeing your family for such a long time, then I think it's safe to say it's a regretful act."

"I regret not acting sooner yesterday. I should have stood up and gone after those men before they had a chance to shoot Nana."

She sat up slightly and said, "You can't do that to yourself."

"Why not? My inaction led to her being shot. I could've probably stopped it if I had gotten up sooner."

"You'll eat yourself alive with guilt if you think that way," Brienne said.

"But you just said that some actions are regrettable. My inaction yesterday might have cost their lives," Michael said.

"Or you could have stood up, been shot, then they could have been shot right after you," she said, posing him another possibility.

"I've been running every scenario, and I could've stopped them, I know it," Michael declared.

"If what happened yesterday makes you a better person today and tomorrow, then I'd be good with that."

He looked at her and asked, "Did you really save me because I reminded you of your son?"

"I said you're about his age today, so yeah, I saw him in you and thought that if Dustin was being chased, I hope someone would save him too," Brienne answered honestly.

"I look forward to meeting him and your husband."

She yawned deeply. "Listen, I need to get some sleep. Keep your eyes peeled and wake me for anything that's out of the ordinary or if someone is coming our way."

"Okay."

She slid back down in the seat, rested her head against the back of the seat, and quickly dozed off.

Yuma, Arizona

Emily's feet ached and she prayed that the sign ahead was for the road she was looking for. She covered the distance, and when the words came into focus, she smiled. "Well, hello there, Fort Yuma Road." She was close now, close to seeking her revenge and closer to her final destination, Loreto. She'd been through a lot to get here, and hopefully what she was about to do would give her satisfaction, but she wouldn't know until she did the deed.

Happy to have this leg of her trip almost over, she proceeded down the long and straight single-lane road straddled by desert. In the distance she spotted a lone ranch-style house. Was that the house? she thought.

She approached the mailbox, and there in bold black numbers was the address she was seeking. She glanced to the house, which sat about two hundred feet off the road, but saw nothing that told her anyone was there. There was a chance that Brienne had beat her there, but she doubted it. For some uncanny reason she felt she'd gotten there first.

"Well, only one way to find out if anyone is at home," Emily said and headed down the gravel drive. Her situational awareness was high as she scoped each window, watching for a blind to move or a head to pop into view, but nothing.

Now mere feet from the front door, confidence started to wash over her. She could feel that she'd beaten Brienne there, giving her the upper hand she wanted. She walked down the concrete sidewalk and up to the front door. A small window next to the door gave her an opportunity to peek inside, which she did but saw no movement. In fact, the place looked like it hadn't been lived in for years. She tried the front door and surprisingly found it unlocked. She pushed the door open and called out, "Hello?"

No reply.

Cautious, she removed the Glock 17 from her waistband and held it firmly. She had been shocked to find it on the road. She could only imagine that Reid was still looking out for her. She had plenty of time to think about what she'd tried to do, and she wished she hadn't.

She took a step closer and called out, "Hello? I'm here as a friend, so don't hurt me."

Silence.

She stepped over the threshold and into the tiled-floor foyer. A small table to her right held a small basket, and in it were car keys, mail, pocket change and an assortment of other items one would dump from their pockets. She glanced down at the mail and saw the name she was hoping to see: Brienne. "Looks like I found the right place."

Taking a quick look from the foyer into the open-space-concept house, to the right was a dining space; beyond that was the living room and kitchen. To her right was an office, and a short hall led to three other doors; she guessed they were bedrooms. She saw nothing that told her anyone had lived there for some time. The house, in fact, looked like it had been sealed up since before the war. She stepped left past the dining space and into the living room. A long sectional couch spanned from the corner and turned at a forty-five-degree angle, ending where she now stood. On it were blankets and bed pillows; on the coffee table dirty dishes sat along with food wrappers. She turned her head to the right and looked into the kitchen. A counter-height bar was the only thing that separated the spaces. On it were more dishes and more wrappers. By the look of the dried mold, the dishes had sat for a while. She spotted movement on the floor near the refrigerator. She pivoted and saw a cockroach race across the tile floor. Curious if there were any canned or dried goods, she began opening cabinets until she found a pantry closet, and in it were stacked cans of food, anything from beans to fruit and vegetables. "Jackpot."

Finding the food was the biggest clue that Brienne's husband and son weren't there unless…

She cut through a small hall and into the longer one. She opened the first door and found it was the master bedroom, but she also discovered what she'd come all this way for: a partially mummified body lying in the bed.

She holstered her pistol, knowing she wouldn't need it, and stepped farther into the room. A musty odor hung in the space and was too much, so she covered her nose with the neck of her shirt. To her left was a window; she drew the blinds and opened it fully to allow the fresh air to come in.

On a nightstand she saw a pad of paper with a pen on it. She walked over and picked it up. Her eyes glanced over the words. It was a farewell letter to Brienne from Jake.

"Dearest Brienne, I'm not sure if you'll ever come home, but I do know that we'll never see you again. A week ago Dustin showed the first symptoms of the dog flu. I don't know how he got it, but he did. We had been so careful all this time; then the bombs were dropped and we lost contact with you. I can only assume that in his anger at missing you, he slipped out one night to visit friends down the road, something I forbade him from doing. All I know is he woke with the bloody eyes a week ago exactly. I took him to the hospital, but they turned me away. Can you believe it? They told me there was nothing for me to do and that he'd either survive or not. I took him home and we've been here since. It's day seven now and he's fallen into a coma; I fear he only has hours to live. I'm so sad that you're not here with him during this time and pray that you're safe. As if it couldn't get worse, I showed the first symptoms earlier today. My plan? I will see if I'm one of the lucky ten percent, and if I'm not, and if you're reading this letter, that will say it all. I'm also writing this letter before I can't. I want to make sure I get my words on paper before the virus prevents me from doing so. Anyway, I don't know how I'm going to bury Dustin. It just doesn't seem right or natural to bury your child. The whole world has gone crazy, it's upside down. How did it come to this? Why did you have to leave us? Know this, I have loved you since the day we met, well, maybe the *third date, wink, wink. I still love you and always will. Again I pray you're safe, and if you ever do come home, I'm sorry I didn't clean up like you like it. Love always and forever, Jake."*

A tear came to Emily's eye. She'd never had anyone feel the way about her that Jake felt about Brienne. She then wondered if anyone would ever have those feelings for her. She thought it possible and considered Loreto the one place it could happen. She put the letter back on the nightstand and looked at the body. "I didn't know you, Jake, but you write nice letters," she said and wiped the tear on her cheek. Her expression quickly morphed from sadness to anger as she remembered having to kill Emile, all because Brienne had kicked her out of the car. If that hadn't happened, she wouldn't have been caught by her brother's men and so forth. She quickly reminded herself why she had come to Yuma. She was here to take revenge on Brienne, and she still planned on doing so. She picked up the letter again, folded it, and headed out of the room.

———

SHE PORED THROUGH THE PANTRY, looking for something to eat. "Hmm, fruit cocktail," she said. "I hope it's still good." She examined the can, looking for any telltale signs that it had gone bad, but didn't see any. She pulled the tab and pulled the steel top off. The juice looked fine. She sniffed it and didn't smell any off odor. She put the can to her lips and took a small sip. "Hmm, tastes alright."

Satisfied, she found a spoon, went to the living room, and plopped down. The second her butt hit the cushions, a cloud of dust flew into the air. "Damn it," she barked as she covered the exposed fruit cocktail with her hand.

She settled in, dug the spoon into the can, and pulled out a heaping portion. She devoured it with a few chews. She continued until she emptied the can.

With her hunger satiated, she removed her pistol, set it on her lap, and kicked her feet up on the coffee table. "I can't wait to see the look on your face, Brienne, when you come through that door and see me."

CHAPTER 8

Vista, California

REID PASSED the road sign that read *OCEANSIDE 7*, meaning that after a thousand long miles, he was now only seven miles away from the marina, then another thirty-seven miles across the channel to San Clemente Island.

Hannah shifted in her seat.

He took his eyes off the road and shot her a quick glance. "Almost there, honey, just hold on."

She sat up; her face was drenched in sweat. She craned her head in his direction and mumbled, "I don't want to die, Daddy. Please, I don't want to die."

"Honey, I'm doing my best. Now please just lie back. We've only got a few miles to go," he said.

She sank back into the leather seat and turned her head away from him.

He reached out and touched her leg. He could feel the

heat emanating from her body. "You're so hot. I need to give you something to reduce the fever."

"I don't want to die," she mumbled under her breath.

The car shuddered violently.

He tore his eyes off her and put them back on the road just as they were about to collide with debris in the road. He jerked the steering wheel hard to the right just in time to avoid the debris, but it only put him in the direction of striking something else. He swerved back to the left, and again something lay in the road. He slammed on the brakes. The car skidded to a stop just feet from ramming into a truck that had been parked diagonally across the road. He looked to Hannah and asked, "Are you okay?"

She lifted her head. The effort was a lot for her to accomplish. She looked out the window and saw something moving towards them. "Daddy."

He looked in the direction of where she pointed and saw two men running towards them with rifles in their hands. "No, no, no," he said as he put the car into reverse. He smashed his foot against the accelerator.

The car lunged backwards.

He couldn't see out the back window, so he had to use the side mirrors. He swerved it right, then left to avoid the obstacles, which he now assumed had been left deliberately. "I'm not going to get stopped this close."

"Daddy, I'm scared," Hannah whimpered.

"It'll be fine. Just keep your head down," he ordered. He spun the car around one hundred and eighty degrees and pressed down on the accelerator.

The car shot forward at a high rate of speed.

A man with a rifle stepped out from an abandoned car in front of them, aimed his rifle at them, and fired.

Two rounds penetrated the windshield and impacted into the backseats.

Reid had nowhere to go but forward, so he aimed the car for the man.

The man fired several more shots. Like the first two, they passed through the cracked windshield and hit the backseat, with one going through the back window.

Reid didn't flinch or swerve. The man was in his sights and it was either him or them. He slammed the car into the man.

The man flipped onto the hood and slid into the already shattered windshield.

Reid pressed forward, but he couldn't see where he was going. He slammed on the brakes.

The man, now dead, slid off and hit the ground.

Pings could be heard. It was the car getting hit by other bullets.

Angry, Reid swung the car behind an abandoned car for cover, got out with his rifle, and took up position. He was more determined than ever. He knew he had to fight his way out of this or else die. He spotted three men coming his way. He took aim on the first he saw, flipped off the selector switch, and squeezed the trigger.

The first round exploded out of the barrel, traveled the short distance, and smashed into the man's face. He recoiled backwards and dropped to the ground dead.

Reid transitioned to the next man he saw, aimed, and

fired. Like the first shot, his aim was true and struck the man in the forehead.

Debris next to him flew into the air, the results of the third man engaging him.

Reid pivoted, found the third man taking cover behind one of the obstacles laid out, and fired several rounds. The first missed; the second hit the man in the shoulder, with the third hitting him fatally in the chest.

The man toppled back and fell down. He looked down at his chest wound for a second before falling over dead.

Reid paused. He scanned the area for further threats, but no one else was out there. With the area presumably clear, he went back to the car to check on Hannah.

She was lying in the seat, her eyes half open.

"Are you okay?" he asked.

She nodded weakly.

With no time to waste, he tossed his rifle in the car and got in. He tried to put the car into gear, but it wouldn't go. He thought it odd since he hadn't turned the car off when he got out. He tried to start it, but nothing happened. "Oh, c'mon, no." He tried again and again, but it was as if the car didn't have any power left, as if it was dead. "Please, God no." He tried several more times, got out the fob, inspected it, made sure the car was in park, but still nothing. The car was literally dead. He got out and walked around it to find that the back end had about a dozen bullet holes. All he could think was a bullet had hit the right spot. What were the odds? he thought. To be so close only to lose the car that he needed to carry him over the line. He looked up into the haze-covered sky to get an idea of the time of day, and by the glow, he assumed it was late afternoon. With time ticking away, he had only one choice now, carry Hannah the rest of the way.

Reid raced to her door, opened it and said, "Honey, I'm going to carry you the rest of the way."

She nodded and said, "I can walk if you want."

"Not a good idea," he said. He opened the rear door, found his pack and put it on, then slung his rifle. He went back to her, scooped her up in his arms, gave her a kiss and said, "Time to walk."

She wrapped her slender small arms around his neck and nestled her face into his neck. "Love you, Daddy."

"I love you too, honey."

Yuma, Arizona

After spending a day and a half at Brienne's house, Emily began to wonder how long she'd have to wait. Bored, she began to look through Brienne and Jake's personal belongings. In the master bedroom she found a box in the nightstand drawer that had letters and cards each had written to the other. She spent the next few hours reading the sweet nothings.

With each card she was left with two feelings: one that Brienne and Jake loved each other deeply, and two, that she'd never experienced this sort of feeling for someone nor had anyone felt this way towards her. She then realized that the main reason she was having an emotional reaction reading the letters and cards was because she longed for the type of relationship Jake and Brienne had. In the compound

Emile had isolated and sequestered her; no man was allowed to touch her much less even look at her sexually. Emily never understood why he was so protective. She was a woman, after all, and had desires, but she was never allowed to express those.

Underneath a box of tissues on the nightstand, she found another card. This one wasn't complete. It was a birthday card to Brienne, and according to the date at the top, it had been written during the time of the last letter she'd found. As she read it, she found the same expressions of love that he'd written earlier. "Why did you leave him?" she asked out loud. "If I had a man love me like this, I wouldn't have gone anywhere."

She tossed the card back on the nightstand and stood up. She spotted crumpled papers behind the nightstand. Curious, she reached behind and pulled them out. They were covered in dust. She opened them up, smoothed them out and began to read; by the end of the first sentence she discovered it was a different draft of his farewell letter to her. She opened the others and they were the same. She carefully read. His words weren't as sweet as his final letter. In these he expressed his anger towards her. He pinpointed how he felt abandoned and alone. That her leaving was tantamount to having an affair, but instead of a person, her affair was with her career. He wrote that her devotion to her job was more important than their marriage or their son, Dustin.

Shocked by how harsh he was, she lowered the letter and thought about the words he used. She then realized that she didn't have to kill her; no, all she needed to do was show her these letters. Why kill her when she could let her live with her own guilt?

She exited the bedroom and went to the sectional couch and sat down. She again read the letters. They were powerful testaments to a world long gone, to people's selfish needs, to careers that were now meaningless. Many things in life are about time and place, but love is ever present. It outlives changes; even the apocalypse doesn't alter it. A job can come and go, yet the love for someone doesn't go; in fact, when put under stress, that love can grow and become stronger.

It was apparent to Emily now that Brienne had put her own needs for something that was meaningless now above the love of her family, and they'd paid the price. "You helped kill your family, you selfish bitch."

That devilish smile returned to Emily's face. She could not wait to see Brienne and give her the reality that she had been the inspiration for her family's death. If she hadn't left, Dustin wouldn't have fled to a friend's house and wouldn't have gotten sick, which then got Jake sick. No, if she had stayed, they wouldn't have gone out that way. Of course, they still might have perished, but that timeline would never be known, Brienne had made sure of that the day she left.

Kingman, Arizona

"I just inhale until I taste the gas?" Michael asked nervously, looking at Brienne.

"Yeah, I'd do it, but it's now your turn, sorry," she said, smiling.

Michael placed his mouth around the hose and inhaled. He kept doing so until he tasted the gasoline in his mouth. He choked slightly, almost dropping the hose before Brienne grabbed it from him and stuck the open end into a five-gallon fuel can.

The gas poured from the Buick minivan. The reddish color denoted that the fuel had degraded. She just hoped the old Dodge would take it without causing any issues.

She had noticed the performance of the truck was more sluggish than normal, but being that it was the only vehicle they had, she supposed that a poorly performing truck was better than no truck at all.

They filled two cans before tapping the minivan dry.

He closed one can and put it in the bed of the truck while she poured the contents of the other into the tank of the truck. "We're not far now. Maybe six to eight hours. Back in the day it would only be a four-hour drive, but the road conditions suck, and of course, some of the roads are impassable now."

"Did you like living in Yuma?" Michael asked.

"You want the honest answer?"

"Yeah."

"Hell no, I hated it. It's a shitty little town. We only lived there because Jake got a government contract job after his stint in the Air Force. I was in between jobs at the time, so it was the best thing for the family. Then I got a job locally selling pharmaceuticals and then that grew from there."

"Hello," a wisp of a voice cried out from behind a taco shop.

"Did you hear that?" Brienne asked.

"I sure did," Michael said. He ripped his pistol from his jacket pocket without hesitation and held it out in front of him.

She put the fuel can down and removed her pistol as well.

"Hello," the voice cried out again.

"Sounds like a child," Brienne said.

"It's coming from behind that taco place." Michael pointed. "We should get going."

"No, let's see if they need help," Brienne said and advanced towards the voice.

"Brienne, no, what if it's a trap?"

She looked back and said, "Get in the truck and start it. If it is a trap, drive off."

"But I'm not good at driving," Michael shot back.

"Then I hope you're a quick learner," she said. She made her way to the front right edge of the building and paused.

"Food, do you have food?" the voice asked.

"I do, but why don't you come out so I can see you," Brienne said.

The sound of shuffling feet came from behind the taco shop. A small girl appeared moments later. She was about six years old. "Do you have any food?"

"Hi there, I do have food, but first I need to know if you're alone," Brienne said.

Michael was in the cab of the truck, one hand on the

steering wheel, the other on his pistol. He hated waiting, so he got out and slowly began to walk towards Brienne.

"It's just me and my little brother," the girl said.

"What's your name, sweetheart?" Brienne asked.

"Mama called me Shelly."

"And your brother?"

"He's called Frankie," Shelly said.

Brienne stepped out from around the corner, kept her pistol ready, and advanced towards the girl. "I'm coming to you, okay?"

Shelly nodded.

Brienne reached her and peered around the corner to find a boy, not older than two, sitting next to the rotting carcass of a dog. "Where are your parents?"

"Mama was taken a week ago. Some men came by and took her. She told us to hide with the dog, so we did."

"And your papa?"

"I don't have a papa."

"You don't have any parents, no one to watch over you?" Brienne asked.

"No," Shelly answered.

"How about you and your brother come with us? We're going to my home; you'll be safe," Brienne said.

"No, we want to stay and wait for Mama to come back."

"I don't think your mama is coming back, sweetheart, best you come with us," Brienne said and reached for Shelly.

Shelly got spooked and ran back to where her brother was sitting.

"I'm not here to hurt you. I'm here to help," Brienne said.

"We're hungry. Do you have food?" Shelly asked.

"I do, but I need you to come back to the truck. I have some in there."

Shelly shook her head. "Bring the food here."

"Is that your dog?" Brienne asked.

"Yes."

"What happened to him?"

"I killed her so we could eat," Shelly said.

"Oh," Brienne said, shocked by her honest and brutal answer.

By the condition of the dogs remains, it had been killed a week or so before. "How long ago did your mom get taken?"

"A while ago."

Brienne took a couple of steps closer.

Nervous, Shelly got her brother to his feet and said, "Stay back."

"I just want to check to see if you're alright."

"Stay back."

"Fine," Brienne said.

"We need food, and then we'll wait for Mama to come back," Shelly said.

Michael came around the corner holding a case of MREs that Brienne had found in his barn. "Here, this is enough food for about two weeks if you ration." He tossed it towards them; the heavy box landed a couple of feet from Shelly.

Seeing Michael startled Shelly. She spat, "Stay back."

"They don't want to go with us. I gave them food. How about we get on the road?" Michael said.

Brienne snapped, "They need our help."

"They don't want our help except food. You can't save people who don't want to be saved."

"They need our help," Brienne scolded him.

"And we've given it. Now it's time to go."

"They'll die out here. They need our help."

While Brienne and Michael were arguing, Shelly managed to sneak away, dragging the box while Frank followed her.

"They need to come with us or they'll die. Look at them," Brienne said and pointed but saw they weren't there anymore. "Wait, where did they go? Hello? Shelly, Frank, don't go. I'm here to help you." She raced around back, past the rotting corpse of the dog, and reached the opposite side, yet she couldn't find them. "Shelly!" she called out.

"Brienne, they're gone. Be proud, be happy, we gave them what they wanted."

"You're callous."

"Huh, the girl wanted food, we gave it to her. She wants to wait for her mother, end of story," Michael said.

Brienne marched back and got inches from his face. "They're just little children. They're innocent, vulnerable."

"I'd say that little girl was capable. She killed her dog and ate it, then got us to give them a case of food."

Disturbed by the encounter, Brienne couldn't help but think about Dustin and him trying to survive if something happened to Jake early on. It only made her regret leaving. What if Dustin's life was like Shelly and Frank's?

Michael put his hand on Brienne's shoulder and said, "You're a good person, Brienne, but we can't help those who don't want to be helped. Let's get back on the road and go find your family." He turned and walked back to the truck.

Brienne turned back towards the back lot of the taco shop with hopes that Shelly or Frank would reappear, but they didn't. They'd probably gone back to whatever shelter they had so they could eat the food. She knew she'd never see them again; it was an odd thought. Maybe their encounter was enough to keep them alive. Maybe all those children needed was that brief meeting with her. Just that one moment, that one case of food could be what separated them from life and death. Maybe she had done enough to keep them alive. Thing is, she'll never know. Frustrated, she went back to the truck.

CHAPTER 9

Oceanside, California

THE WEIGHT of carrying Hannah was beginning to take a toll on Reid. His muscles ached and his feet had blisters. He'd walked all night and morning, only encountering a few people, who didn't seem concerned about him. At times he thought he wasn't going to make it, but when the sun rose he was in view of the marina. The last time he'd seen it was during his time in the Navy. He'd spent many weekends there, sailing with friends, one of whom owned a boat. He wondered if it was there, although it wasn't one he would try to take. While Reid had been in the Navy, contrary to some popular belief, he wasn't taught how to sail. He was fine operating powerboats, but if he had to operate a sailboat, with all its rigging, he'd end up capsizing.

He breathed a sigh of relief as he glanced across the inlet to the rows upon rows of boats, from forty-foot powerboats to thirty-five-foot sailboats and various smaller craft in between, all moored in slips like they had been the day the bombs dropped.

He spotted a blue two-wheeled cart, used by boat owners to haul things down the docks to their boats. He set Hannah in it and pushed it towards the first dock gate he came to then froze when he saw the handle had a keyhole. Was the door locked? Was he going to have to swim to get to a boat? Before he was going to get wet, he reached out and tried it. He turned the knob right and it opened. His heart skipped a beat. Once more fate, or luck or whatever, had been on his side.

Reid swung the gate wide, pushed Hannah through and down a long gangway to the dock. He went to the first powerboat he saw and hopped on. He couldn't find the keys, so he went to the next, nothing; the next, still nothing. Frustrated, he thought about where he could find keys; then he realized even if he found them, the boats' engines might not even turn over. He'd come so far, to not be able to cross the channel for lack of a boat was beyond horrible to fathom, but from a tactical standpoint for the government, it made sense to have secret laboratories there because it had limited access.

Hannah jolted and twitched. Her eyes fluttered underneath her eyelids.

Hearing her stir, he looked over at her. "It'll be fine, sweetheart. We're close, very close." Frustrated, he stood looking at each boat. He had a selection, but he didn't have the luxury of time. He heard a knocking sound, turned, and saw a ten-foot tender tied off on the aft of a forty-five-foot powerboat bumping up against a pylon. An idea came to him. He raced down to it and saw it had a small outdrive engine. It wasn't a lot, but it was enough to carry him and Hannah across the channel. He climbed onto it and immediately examined the engine. He first checked the fuel reservoir and found it completely full. This was good, as it lessened the oxygenation of the fuel. He flipped the choke and pulled hard on the cord.

The engine sputtered.

The fact that it even made a sound gave him hope. "Come on, damn you," he barked. He pulled again.

Again a slight sputter.

He fiddled with the choke and pulled again. This time the engine came to life, only to die a second later.

"Damn it, work!" he growled. He adjusted the choke again and pulled as hard as he could.

The engine did the same, but before it died, he adjusted the choke and throttled it. Black smoke poured from the exhaust, but it was running, "Yes!" He couldn't believe it, as it seemed impossible, after all this time, this little engine was working. He looked up into the gray marine layer that hung above him and said, "I don't say thank you enough, but thank you."

Excited, he jumped out, sprinted down the dock, got Hannah, and wheeled her down. Using every ounce of care, he set her in the boat, but before he untied and set off, he looked to make sure he had paddles just in case, or for when the engine ran out of fuel. He found the paddles lying on the floor of the boat and rejoiced. He was set. He had a compass, a decent idea of the coordinates he'd need to travel, and untied the boat. He got in, pushed off, engaged the prop, and throttled it up. In seconds he was moving out of the marina and towards the sea channel.

The crisp, cool sea air hit his face as he sped along, leaving a foot-high wake behind him. He knew the trip would be rough in the boat he was in, but he didn't have a choice. Today was day seven. He had hours, if that, and still forty miles to go.

Yuma, Arizona

Brienne didn't know how to feel as she sat behind the wheel of the truck, staring at the Fort Yuma Road sign. Not a quarter of a mile down the road was her house. While everything looked familiar, it also looked strange, almost out of place. She had traveled thousands of miles and over years to get where she was, and now the moment of truth was upon her. Most people she thought would have kept driving, but she stopped only because she pondered if she truly wanted to know. She sat questioning her procrastination. Why, after all this time, would she just stop moving? What if she arrived only to find they had moved on to somewhere else unknown? Or what if she found them dead? How would she cope? She always thought of herself as someone strong, hell, she'd covered a ton of Earth and dealt with some of the worst people just so she could be where she was, but if they were dead, would she fall apart? Would that rough veneer simply melt away, exposing the little girl and vulnerable woman who hid behind it? And what about her purpose? This had been it for so long; she had done this longer than she had done anything else in her adult life. Where would she go if they were dead? Then again, if they were alive, then this pause was meaningless fear and she'd be rejoined with her family, and they could live out their years together. Then an odd almost comical thought came to mind: what if they were alive but Jake had taken a new wife? Of course it was possible. How would she handle that? Would she understand, or would she put a bullet in both of them?

"What's the matter?" Michael asked. His window was down and a cool breeze swept through the cab of the truck.

"I'm thinking," she replied. Never in her life had she been so confused and conflicted. She'd known fear, but now she was frozen by these questions that in the end were thoughts. Fear doesn't exist but in our heads, so why was she allowing her mind to paralyze her from the one thing she'd fought tooth and nail to get to?

"What are you thinking about?" Michael asked, a look of concern on his face.

"If I want to know what's really down there," she answered before taking a deep breath and hitting the accelerator.

The truck lurched forward, sputtered, and lurched again. The old truck had gotten them this far on old gas and prayers; it would be ironic for it to die now. It puttered down the road, black smoke billowing out of the tailpipe. She swung into the driveway and stared at the house. It looked the same, yet it looked different, much like the intersection she'd just been parked at.

"This is it?" Michael mused. "It's nice." He opened his door.

"Stay here," she ordered. She opened her door, stepped out onto the hard gravel, and walked off without muttering another word.

"Do you want your rifle?"

She didn't reply. She looked at the house then back to her rifle. Her senses were tingling, but she brushed it off as simple nerves and anxiety.

She made her way to the front door. Each step she took brought her back to the last time she was at the house. She could still see Jake walking her luggage down the sidewalk to the Uber she'd insisted on taking. He was against her taking a car for hire, but more importantly he was against the trip altogether, and now she could feel the weight of that decision, seeing the place. Near the front door she stopped again. In her thoughts, she could see Dustin, so young and sweet, standing with his hands in his pockets and a look of sadness that she was leaving. The flower bed to the right had been filled with snow-in-summer; the small white flowers had been in full bloom. Now the bed was dry and nothing remained.

She stepped up to the front door, looked to her right, and remembered when she and Jake had painted the house. Now that paint was flaking and faded. She shook her head and tears welled in her eyes. "So many lost years. I'm such a damn fool for leaving."

Deep down she could feel they weren't there. It was just the way the house looked. It wasn't that it appeared in disrepair, it was that it looked and, more importantly to her, felt dead. Houses become homes when people live in them; they breathe life into structures, giving them an air of vibrancy. Her home didn't have that, and she thought she knew why.

She turned the knob and found it unlocked. This made her heart jump, as it was another clue that they weren't there. She pushed it open and stared inside. Once more she was looking at something familiar yet alien. She crossed the threshold and took a deep breath, hoping to take in the old smell of the place, but it wasn't there. More tears filled her eyes and now streamed down her cheeks. She hadn't yet called out, and doing so now felt cliché. They weren't there; she knew it. She just prayed she wouldn't find their bodies. "No, please, no," she moaned as she made her way from the foyer into the dining room. Her head was turning from left to right, looking and hoping to see a clue that could give her a glimmer of hope. She transitioned into the living room, and there on the coffee table, she saw an empty can of fruit cocktail. What made it different than the other older packaging was she saw the juice on the side and lying on the table.

Her eyes grew wide. "Jake, Dustin!" she called out. She raced from the living room through the kitchen and to the master bedroom door. She turned the knob and called out, "Jake, Dustin, where are you?" She threw the door open and was jolted when she saw the one person she never imagined she'd see: Emily sitting on the edge of her bed.

"Hi, Brienne," Emily said, a devilish smile on her face. "Let me be the first person...oops, the only person to welcome you home."

"What? I, um, I," Brienne stuttered. The shock of seeing

Emily threw her, and she was mentally recoiling from it. "Why are you here? How did you find my house?"

"I'm disappointed that you're shocked that I'd be here. I did tell you when you left me for dead on the side of the road that I'd come for you."

"But how did you find me?"

Emily held up Brienne's diary. "You kept copious notes, thank you."

Brienne reached for her pistol but paused when Emily raised hers and pointed it directly at her chest. "If you just pull that gun out an inch, I'll put two bullets in you."

Brienne slowly moved her hands away from her sides and held them up. "What do you want?"

"You know, at first I came here with the intent to kill your family and—"

"If you hurt them, I'll—"

"Sssh, please stop talking. I didn't hurt them on account I can't," Emily replied. "Now let me get back to what I was saying. I came here to also kill you. In fact, at one time I wanted to rip your heart out and eat it, but I've changed my mind since arriving here yesterday. You could say I've had an epiphany of sorts."

"Do you have Jake and Dustin?" Brienne asked.

"Heavens no."

"Were they not here when you came?"

"Oh, they're here," she said, turning and throwing back the sheet to reveal Jake's mummified remains.

Brienne gasped, her hand covering her mouth. A faint sense of vertigo began to grip her. She sidestepped an inch then wobbled back.

"He seemed like a really nice guy," Emily said.

Brienne got her composure and thought about reaching for her pistol. Even if she was shot, she wanted nothing more now than to put a round in Emily's smug face.

"He wrote you a letter, a farewell letter you could call it, and it's what changed my mind. You see, I wanted to kill you, but it appears after reading your diary cover to cover, which I've done now, this letter is the silver bullet right to your heart. I don't need to kill you, Brienne, you killed yourself and very well might be responsible for your family's deaths."

Brienne trembled and her legs felt weak. Nausea and vertigo again began to grip her. She could feel a cool sweat build up on her brow.

"You don't look so good, Brienne," Emily mocked.

Brienne turned away and vomited.

"If you're wondering where little Dustin is, he's buried in the backyard next to his hamster, how cute."

Brienne continued to vomit.

Emily stood. In her right hand she held her pistol and in her left she had the letter. She walked up to Brienne and held the letter out. "It appears I wasn't the only person you left behind to die."

Brienne cocked her head and glared at Emily. "I fucking hate you."

"No, you don't, the hate you feel in your heart is just the buildup of shame and regret for abandoning your family so you could make a buck and pad your résumé. You see, Brienne, you hate yourself, not me. You think you're so high and righteous because I've eaten human flesh to stay alive, but you were consuming the lives of other people way before the virus came or the bombs dropped. And what makes it so much worse is you actually had a choice." Emily shoved the letter into Brienne's hands and walked out of the room.

Brienne stood and unfolded the paper. Again her eyes filled with tears as they cast down on Jake's handwriting. She carefully read the page, her sobs the only sounds. She stumbled to the bed and fell onto it. "Why, why?"

Emily watched her from the living room. She got what she came for but now felt like a perverted voyeur watching a sickening reality show of a person's life being destroyed and made meaningless. Unable to stay, she grabbed her pack, which she had hidden in the coat closet, and headed out the front door. She saw the truck then saw Michael.

In return, Michael saw her and sprang into action. He grabbed the Glock, brought it up, but was met by Emily with her pistol pointed directly at his head.

"I don't want to kill you, so please do me and you a favor and just get out of the truck," Emily threatened.

Michael gulped loudly, set his pistol on the seat, and said, "I'm going to open the door. Don't shoot me."

"Hurry up," Emily snapped.

"Where's Brienne?" Michael asked as he opened the door and swung it wide enough to step out.

"She's getting reacquainted with her family," Emily sneered.

Michael slid out of the cab and stepped several feet away, his arms held high.

Not wasting a moment, Emily ran around and got

behind the wheel. She turned the ignition; the truck fired up. "This really is my day!" She tossed her pack next to her, put the truck into gear, and backed out of the driveway. She cut the wheel hard, put it in drive, and sped off, leaving a cloud of dust behind her.

Inside, Brienne heard the truck drive off but didn't care. Her life was over as far as she was concerned. Emily had been right; she had abandoned her family for money they didn't need with hopes of expanding her career. She didn't need to go, but she did, and now she was confronted with the consequences of that act. She glanced back at Jake's body and sobbed uncontrollably. "I'm so sorry."

"Brienne!" Michael cried out from the foyer.

Brienne ignored him.

Michael made his way through the house and ended up at the master bedroom doorway. There he found Brienne exactly where Emily had left her. "That woman took the truck."

"I failed them. They're dead because of me," Brienne sobbed.

Michael hadn't noticed the body in the bed until then. At first he recoiled from the sight, then leaned closer to see who it might be. "Is that…"

"Dustin's buried out back," Brienne cried.

He went to her side, put his hand on her shoulder, and said, "I'm sorry, Brienne, I truly am."

She had no more words, only tears. She put her head in her hands and sobbed.

San Felipe, Baja California, Mexico

WHEN EMILY officially crossed the border, it marked the first time she'd ever traveled outside the United States, a designation that really meant nothing anymore. Now she was one hundred and twenty miles into Baja, with no issues or obstacles in her way. She'd seen an occasional person riding by on a bicycle or driving an old car or truck; she didn't see many people. Having never been to Baja, she chalked it up to it being a rural area, which it was.

She glanced at her fuel gauge and saw she had half a tank of gas, but in the bed were seven five-gallon cans, four of them full, with a syphon to get more if she needed it.

Ahead of her was a small fishing village, but just beyond that was the vast Sea of Cortez. It spanned the length of Baja California, which stretched seven hundred miles and at its widest point was one hundred and fifty miles. It was by no means a small body of water. She sat staring at the turquoise blue water, the sun's rays shimmering off it. Her life had been spent in Texas, from birth until the day she escaped the compound; never had she traveled outside its borders, never had she seen the ocean or any water like she was looking at now.

A tap on the driver's side window startled her. She snatched the pistol from her lap and pointed it at the glass.

On the other side was a young girl no older than six. She held up a box of what appeared to be chewing gum wrapped in clear plastic with the name Canel on the side and said, "*Chicle?*"

Emily looked all around to make sure no one else was there or that this wasn't some sort of ruse.

The girl's hair was jet black, filthy and hung down to her shoulders. Her small angelic face was smeared with grime and dirt. She again said, "*Chicle?*"

Feeling it was safe, Emily rolled down her window manually and asked, "What's a *chicle*?"

"*Chicle?*" the girl asked once more. She clearly didn't understand English.

Emily reached for the box, but the girl pulled away and said, "*Comida por chicle.*"

"*Comida*? I don't know what that means. I'm assuming *chicle* is whatever that candy stuff is," Emily said.

The girl motioned to her mouth and pretended to eat. "*Comida.*"

"Eat...oh, I know, you want food," Emily said. She grabbed her pack, threw it open, and reached inside. She pulled out the ziplock bag of human jerky, looked at it for a moment, and did consider giving it to the girl. She tossed it on the seat and reached back in, this time coming out with a can of fruit cocktail. She held it out to the girl and said, "*Comida.*"

The girl nodded and removed several packages of gum; she held them up in her open palm.

Emily took the gum and put the can in her small hand.

"*Gracias,*" the girl said with a big smile. She turned and ran off.

Emily watched her until she disappeared behind a berm. She looked at the gum and was curious, so she opened it and popped a piece in her mouth. She bit down, crunched the outer hard shell, and began to chew. The flavor was very sugary and tasted like stale lime. "So this is *chicle*. I suppose I'll have to learn Spanish if I'm going to be down here." She sat and chewed the gum for a few more minutes, then started the truck and drove off. She had no idea what Loreto would be like, but assumed that nothing could be as bad as where she had been living. She did have her regrets concerning the life she had lived, but she also felt that she could find redemption for her past actions, although she did feel that what she and her brother had done was done in the spirit of survival. When she and Emile had arrived with their friends at the compound, they were thirteen and tried to manage to eke out an existence but turned to cannibalism to prevent starvation. It was what it was, she wasn't proud of it, but she was still alive because of it.

A big smile stretched her face as she pondered the idea that Loreto might be filled with cannibals similar to the compound where she'd spent a large part of her life. If it were and she were to be eaten, she did find it to be a poetic way to go out. With the shimmering blue water to her left and the Sonoran desert ahead of her, she pressed down on the accelerator and sped off into the unknown.

San Clemente Island, Channel Islands (Off the Coast of Southern California)

Reid pulled the boat onto the shore and staked an anchor to hold it from drifting away if the tide came in.

Above him a series of buildings stood where there

weren't any in his memory of the island. He imagined these must have been where the government had located their laboratories. He scanned the beachhead and the rise above, looking for any signs of life, but didn't see any. "Where is everyone?"

He picked up Hannah out of the boat and cradled her tight in his arms, her small body tucked close to his chest. The hike up the wide beach to the mid-rise buildings appeared to be about a half mile. It wasn't a long way, but he was fatigued, and carrying her would no doubt add to his exhaustion.

"You ready to go, baby?" he asked Hannah.

She opened her eyes to reveal the whites were still blood red. She mumbled something unintelligible then closed her eyes and drifted off.

He made the climb up the slope and ended up along a road. Still he saw no one. If this was an active government facility, he would have made contact by now, he assumed. Determined to find what he'd come for, he carried on.

The gate in the chain-link fence that surrounded the buildings was open, and debris, garbage and an abandoned Humvee sat in the yard. On the gate a sign read *SAN CLEMENTE RESEARCH LABORATORIES, DEPARTMENT OF HOMELAND SECURITY.*

"Hello!" he cried out.

Nothing came back but his echo.

He walked past the Humvee and stopped in his tracks when he saw skeletal remains in a uniform. Reid was curious how the man had died but quickly pushed it out of his mind and pressed forward.

Hannah opened her eyes and mumbled, "Is it time for dinner?"

"No, sweetie, but if you're hungry, I can get you something to eat," he said.

"I...I," she said then closed her eyes.

He could tell things were getting close. It was day seven, and this was the day the vast majority of people died.

The first building he came upon had more skeletal remains out front; again they were in uniforms. One thing that was missing were any firearms. The doors and front of the building were riddled with bullet holes.

He now knew what had happened. They'd been attacked, and by the looks of it, the government had lost. Any hope he had melted away. There wasn't any established government operating and more than likely no cure to be found. "Is anyone here?" he called out.

Nothing, no reply but the ocean wind that barreled down through the empty street.

"Is anyone here? Please answer me. I need help!" he shouted. He stepped over rubble and a body that lay in front of the entrance of the first building, and crossed the threshold. "Hello?"

His eyes adjusted to the darkened hall, allowing him to see the debris and bodies continued inside. Each step he took, the hard soles of his boots crunched on glass and small chunks of plaster. There had been a battle there, but who attacked them? he wondered. He stopped at a desk in the entry and saw a security monitor was flickering. Was there power? he asked himself. No lights were on, but maybe they'd turned everything off due to the attack.

Scanning the space, he saw a light switch and flicked it on.

The hall lights came to life, their fluorescent tubes crackling and buzzing. "Power, hmm."

Carrying Hannah around as he searched the building wasn't optimal. He needed to lay her somewhere safe. In the first room he found, he hit the jackpot. It must have been a lounge due to the couches and television. He carefully laid her on the far couch, ensured her head was propped up, and exited the room. As he closed the door, he said, "I'll be back, sweetie, I promise."

With Hannah tucked away, he could navigate the first building and hopefully find what he had come so far for.

With his rifle now firmly in his hands, he slowly walked down the hall. As he passed the doors, he looked for signs that would simply say *LABORATORY*, but all he kept finding were offices marked senior staff. It finally came to him that this was an administration building. Getting an idea, he headed to the front desk. He dug through drawers and shifted through the contents on the desk. He then caught sight of what he was looking for, a map. Pinned on the wall behind a calendar was a map of the area. He pulled it down and examined it. On the lower right side was a key, and that was where he found what he was looking for. He was in the right place on the island, and building C was where the labs were. He identified the building he was in as A.

With the map shoved in his pocket, Reid grabbed Hannah and headed out. He meandered around a jersey wall and concertina wire to get to the entrance of building

C. Like the last building, the front of it was shot up, bullet holes everywhere, and on the ground, the remains of bodies. The doors were blasted open, telling the story that explosives had been used.

"Hello!" he called out. Like the other times, nothing.

Crossing the threshold, Hannah in his arms, he found a similar layout as building A. To the right was a front desk, and to the left was a lounge. Like before, he set Hannah down and locked her inside. Back in the hall, he went to turn on the lights, but for some unknown reason, they wouldn't turn on. He raised his rifle and marched down the hallway. As he went, he stepped over large chunks of ceiling and numerous bodies. These, however, were dressed in white lab coats.

From room to room he went on the first floor but only found destruction and death. All he could assume was they'd been attacked some time ago, and everyone was dead. At the far end of the hall, he found a diagram of the building and saw it had two levels down. Something told him that was where he'd find what he was looking for. He located the stairwell, but before he entered, he gazed down the hall. The only light came in from the outside front doors. He wondered if he should take Hannah with him, then came to the determination that if someone was alive and not welcoming, he'd have a better chance defending himself with both arms to wield a weapon.

He entered the stairwell. When the door closed, he was immersed in darkness. He dug in his back pocket and came out with a flashlight. He clicked it on and recoiled at the sight just a half floor below.

Piled four deep were bodies, and by the look of it, they'd been executed.

He didn't like the idea of climbing over them, but he didn't know another way to go. He cringed as he stepped on the bodies, his weight crushing the bones underneath, and the odor could only be described as musty death. After a grueling and unstable few minutes, he cleared the pile and made his way to the first floor below. He opened the door to find the lights were on here. He peeked his head out and looked in both directions. Like everywhere else, the hall appeared to have been the scene of a battle. This floor was different in that instead of walls and doors lining each side, there were large panels of windows, and beyond he spotted what he'd come all this way for, a laboratory.

He raced to the first door he came to and stepped through the shattered glass panel and into the space. From wall to wall were long stainless steel tables covered in an assortment of instruments. The damage that he'd found everywhere was also here, with much of everything broken and smashed. His heart began to melt as he now began to realize that there probably was no cure, and even if they had made one, there was a good chance it had been destroyed.

A loud beeping came from the far corner. He spied the location and saw it was a computer monitor. He went to it and found a corpse sitting in the chair, a pistol on the floor next to it. By the look of the person's skull, it appeared a single shot to the head had ended their life.

A Post-it note on the screen read *PLAY ME* with an

arrow pointing down to the keyboard. On the keyboard itself, another Post-it note with an arrow read *PRESS HERE*.

He assumed it was a message, a video more than likely. Excitement ran through him because now he'd get some type of answer to the question he'd been seeking.

Reid pressed the button.

The screen flickered and turned on. The monitor now showed a man in a lab coat.

Reid looked at the corpse in the chair and said, "That's you, huh?"

"My name is Dr. Chang. Today's date is February 3…"

Reid paused the video and looked at the time stamp. This video had been recorded four years ago, causing his sense of helplessness to expand. Needing to know more, he pressed the button to continue the video.

"I am the head virologist assigned to the team searching to create a vaccine for the H5N7 virus that has ravaged the world. Our team was relocated to San Nicolas Island three years ago, and we've been steadily and aggressively working. During these three years, we've not only been dealing with a lot of heartaches as the country we loved has disappeared, but have had to deal with team members' personal issues. With the United States government gone, we came to recognize that we now work for humanity. The shock of the devastating nuclear strikes and subsequent collapse of our government led many to question what we were doing and added stress to an already stressful and at times untenable situation. Over the months we've lost members. Some killed themselves, and others just left to go search for family members they hoped had survived. Even with all these issues, our team has continued to work hard, and we developed a vaccine strain that had proven to work in initial testing..."

Reid paused the video again. Hearing the words that they had developed a cure, he almost burst with joy. "So where is it?" he asked and hit the button to play.

"...but only appears to help with those that haven't yet contracted the virus or were in the initial symptoms of it. If a patient had gone into the latter stages of the virus' course, the vaccine appeared to do nothing. However, this hasn't stopped us from trying to find something that could help anyone infected. With the first vaccine testing complete, we were attempting to work on outreach with hopes of getting the vaccine distributed. This is where we found trouble, and that trouble came here. Last week the island suffered an attack. It appears our outreach informed the wrong people of our existence." Chang stopped and cleared his throat. He removed his glasses and rubbed the bridge of his nose.

"The attack on the island was overwhelming, resulting in the deaths of many on the team and support staff. The attackers fled without gaining what they wanted, and that was our large stores of supplies. However, the facility has been destroyed, as has the cold storage that held the vaccine and any data on how to create it."

Tears began to stream down Chang's face. "We worked

so hard to get where we are, only to have it destroyed by the very people we're hoping to help. It appears mankind cannot help themselves and that we were truly destined for everything that has happened to us. I sit here now the lone survivor. The others have left me and gone to the mainland, fearing the island would be attacked again. I, though, cannot leave. I have nowhere to go, as my family died in the bombing of San Francisco. I had hoped that my years of experience could be leveraged to help humanity, but I know now that isn't the case. I want whoever is watching this to know that we tried and had found success only to have it destroyed. I am sorry, deeply sorry that this vaccine couldn't have been distributed. If you've come looking for supplies, we have plenty in the basement of building D. There you'll find enough food to last ten or more years depending on the number that needs to be fed. I'll finish with a quote from Longfellow I put to memory while in grad school; it goes like this, 'Great is the art of beginning, but greater is the art of ending.'" Chang put a pistol to his temple and pulled the trigger.

Not wanting to watch anymore, Reid paused the video. So there it was, a vaccine had been developed then destroyed. It didn't matter though; nothing had been created to save Hannah from the point she was with the virus. She would die and soon.

———

LEFT HOPELESS, Reid carried Hannah down to the beach. He found a nice place clear of rocks and laid her down.

She had been going in and out of consciousness, and the last time he'd spoken to her, she was talking gibberish. This was no doubt the telltale sign that soon she'd convulse one last time then go into a catatonic state, with death not far behind.

Above his head, seagulls soared, and the rich briny smell of the ocean air filled his nostrils. He stared into the picture-perfect cloudless blue sky and said, "I wish you could see this."

He cradled her in his lap, his right hand locked in hers. He lowered his head and kissed the top of hers. "I failed you. I'm so sorry, baby." Tears welled in his eyes and streamed down his stubbled face. They gathered along his jawline and dripped onto her forehead and cheeks. "I'm so sorry I couldn't fix you."

Hannah began to convulse violently. Her body stopped for brief moments but remained rigid.

He held onto her more tightly each time she started a convulsion, and whispered to her his love. "I hope you can hear me, I really do. I want you to know that Daddy loves you so much and that soon you'll be in Mommy's arms. Tell her I'm sorry that I failed her too," he said, his salty tears hitting his lips.

Her convulsions stopped and her body went limp.

He'd never experienced this with Evelyn. The nurse had her taken away before this point. He placed two fingers against her neck and checked for a pulse and found a faint one. She was alive but barely. When he'd stood alongside Evelyn's bed, watching her die, he'd felt helpless. Now here he was witnessing the death of his only child, and again he was helpless to stop it. He wondered what purpose life would have now without Hannah in the world. Why go on living? Why even take another breath? There was no reason to wake each day; there wasn't a reason to live.

He reached into his coat and pulled out his pistol. He didn't need to confirm it was loaded; he knew it was and knew a round was in the chamber. All he needed to do was place it against his temple and pull the trigger. It was that simple, and then he could join Evelyn and Hannah.

He checked her pulse again and found it.

He then made up his mind. He would take his own life the second hers ended. The thought came of putting her out of her misery, but he couldn't bring himself to ponder the idea for more than a second.

Instead he decided to just wait and talk to her.

"It's beautiful here," he said, looking up and down the shoreline. "When I worked here, I never looked at the ocean and the beach like I'm doing now. I was blind, really, to the beauty of it all. I was too focused on the trivial details and meaningless things that I thought were so important to take notice of the breathtaking scenery and splendor of the world around me."

A fish jumped out of the water and came splashing down.

"Oh look, a fish just leapt from the water," he said excitedly. "God, how I wish you could see this. The seagulls are squawking to my right as they race around the sand, looking for anything to eat, while others are flying overhead. The fish are swimming and jumping, and the waves, they're crashing into the beach. The sound of it is so sooth-ing, I could lie here and listen until I fall asleep."

He lay back on the sand, Hannah in his arms. "Can you hear the waves, honey?" He closed his eyes and listened to the sounds of life around him, the warm sun hitting his face. Tears kept pouring from his eyes and down the sides of his face. His thoughts were of Hannah, some from when she was an infant, then a memory of her as a child. He could hear her first words, then pictured the first time she walked. His mind wandered through the years, her smiling face to her angry scowls. Oh, how he'd wanted to see her grow into adulthood and find love or become an adult to be proud of.

Unaware of how fatigued he was, he dozed off uninten-tionally.

———

THE COLD OCEAN water rushed up between his legs. He opened his eyes and saw that the morning sky had been replaced by an early afternoon one. He sat up and looked around.

The tide had come in, leaving his trousers soaked.

He looked down at Hannah, who was still cradled in his arms. Checking her pulse, he found she was still alive, but he noticed that it was stronger.

"Hannah, can you hear me?" he asked. "I'm going to move up on the beach or we'll be swimming soon." He set her down and got to his feet.

Gazing down on her, he paused before scooping her up.

"You look like an angel lying there."

Hannah stirred.

"Sweetheart?" he asked.

Her body jerked and her head twitched.

"Can you hear me?" he asked. "Are you with me?"

Again her body moved, this time both legs and an arm fluttered.

He dropped to his knees and held her head in his hands. "Hannah, sweetheart, can you hear me?"

A wave rushed up and washed over her.

She opened her eyes and looked around for a second before setting her gaze on him. "Daddy?"

The first thing he noticed was the whites of her eyes weren't blood red. "Yes, sweetheart."

Another wave crashed and coursed its way along the sand until it washed up on her.

She lifted her head and asked, "Where are we?"

"How do you feel?"

"Sore, tired."

Tears of joy now filled his eyes. "Your eyes, I don't understand," he said. He searched through his thoughts, trying to find a symptom such as what she was displaying, but couldn't come up with one. Was it possible? Had she just survived the dog flu, or was it the medicine that Hillary had given her?

"Daddy, are we at the beach?" she asked as she sat up slowly.

"We are. This is the beach and that's the ocean," he said, taking her hand in his and sitting next to her.

"Am I dead and this is heaven?" she asked, finding

everything very confusing. She had no recollection of the past day and a half.

"No, you're not dead, you're very much alive," he replied. "I can't believe it, to be honest, but I think the medicine Hillary gave you worked. She said the first sign that you've been cured is your eyes would return to normal, and they have." He peppered her face with countless kisses.

She giggled from the loving attention.

"I can't believe this, I can't, I thought you were…" he said, pausing before he said the word *dead*.

"It smells exactly as you said it would," she said, inhaling deeply.

"And the seagulls," he said, pointing at one flying by.

"They're beautiful."

He kissed her hand and said, "I love you, Hannah."

"You kept your promise."

Thinking of the promise he'd made to Evelyn, he replied, "I guess I did. I told your mother I'd do anything to protect you."

A weakened smile stretched across her face, she looked at him and said, "No, I'm talking about this." She motioned towards the water as another wave crashed and washed over them.

"It's beautiful, isn't it?" he asked.

"Can we go for a swim?"

"A swim? How about when you're a hundred percent?"

"Okay, but can we stay here and watch?" she asked sweetly.

"Of course, Hannah, anything for you."

EPILOGUE

Ten Miles West of Gila Bend, Arizona

"I KNEW we'd find a car, I knew it," Michael exclaimed happily. It had taken him and Brienne two weeks to find an old Dodge Ram truck that ran on old degraded gasoline.

While Michael was thrilled, Brienne kept her enthusiasm at bay, knowing that the engine could slow and gum up easily. "Let's just see how far we'll get before you get all excited."

"Well, it's made it forty miles so far. I'm feeling lucky," Michael chirped.

Brienne spotted something in the distance. She leaned over the steering wheel and looked carefully. "Is that what I think it is?"

Michael peered through the windshield and spotted the same thing. "Yeah, it looks like a man and a kid. Oh, wait, they just ran off the road."

The two people were Reid and Hannah.

Brienne pulled the truck up to where they'd last seen the people and pulled over.

"What are you doing?" Michael asked.

"I'm seeing if they need help," Brienne said. She taken a new tack in life and would help anyone if she could. "Roll the window down," she ordered Michael.

"Are you sure?"

"Yeah, they're just over in that brush," Brienne said and pointed to large brittlebushes fifty feet off the road. "Hey, are you all okay?"

No reply came from the two.

"My name is Brienne and this is Michael. If you need a lift somewhere, we can help," Brienne offered.

Reid poked his head out and said, "No, we're fine." Firmly in his grasp was his rifle.

Hannah clung to Reid's jacket and was just behind him. She peeked around his arm and asked, "Are they gonna hurt us, Daddy?"

"I don't know yet, but don't worry, I'll protect you," Reid said.

"I know you don't trust me, I probably wouldn't either, but we're headed to somewhere safe. You're welcome to join us," Brienne hollered.

"No, you just go ahead, we're fine," Reid shouted back.

"Are you sure?" Brienne asked.

"Yeah, you just keep moving," Reid said.

"Daddy, are they going to Deliverance?" Hannah asked.

"I doubt it," Reid said.

"Safe travels, I hope you make it wherever you're going," Brienne said. "Okay, roll up the window."

Michael cocked his head and shouted, "C'mon, we won't hurt you. We're headed to Deliverance, Oklahoma. It's a safe zone, they say."

Hearing the name, Reid lifted his head farther and asked, "Did you say Deliverance?"

"Yeah, we're headed there," Michael replied.

"Daddy, they're going to our home," Hannah said.

"Yeah, I heard," Reid said, perplexed by hearing the name.

"Are you sure you won't join us?" Brienne asked.

"They won't let you in," Reid shouted.

Brienne gave Michael an odd look and asked, "Why's that?"

"They don't let strangers in," Reid replied.

"And how would you know that?" Brienne asked.

Reid stood, his rifle at the ready. "On account that I'm from there."

"You're from Deliverance? If you are, then why are you in the middle of nowhere Arizona?" Brienne asked.

"That's a long story," Reid asked. "But you won't get in without us."

Michael got out of the truck, keeping his hands up high to show he wasn't armed. "Is it like they say? Is it safe?"

Reid paused for a second to think about his answer, then decided in an instant to be honest. "It is, it's safe, clean. It's a good place to be."

"It's home," Hannah said.

Michael turned back and gave Brienne a smile. "It's real."

"It sure sounds like it," Brienne replied and gave him a wink.

Facing Reid again, he asked, "Why don't you hop in?"

"Yeah, and you can tell us all about why you're out here and not there," Brienne said.

Reid gave Hannah a look and asked, "What do you think?"

Hannah stepped out from behind Reid, gave Brienne and Michael a long look, then glanced at Reid. "They seem nice, and it is a long walk back home."

"It sure is," Reid said.

"Do you think we can trust them?" Hannah asked.

"I never trust anyone completely, but they have a truck and we need to go a long way. I say we hop in."

Hannah nodded.

"I think we'll jump in," Reid said. He took Hannah by the hand and emerged from the bushes. He stopped a few feet from Michael and gave him a quick look up and down. "You're really headed to Deliverance?"

"Yes, sir," Michael replied.

"Say, is there any way we can stop in Santa Rosa, New Mexico?" Reid asked as he removed his backpack and put it in the bed of the truck.

Brienne had climbed out of the cab and was leaning against the edge of the bed. "What's in Santa Rosa?"

"It's a long story," Reid answered.

"You have a lot of long stories," Brienne quipped.

"I suppose I do," Reid said. He picked Hannah up and put her in the bed, then climbed in himself. "But if we want to get inside Deliverance, the key to that is there."

Brienne slapped the side of the truck and said, "Then I suppose Santa Rosa is our next stop." She turned to get back in the truck but stopped. "I'm rude, my name is Brienne and that's Michael."

"I'm Reid and…"

"I'm Hannah," Hannah said sweetly, a large smile stretched across her face.

Brienne returned Hannah's smile and said, "Nice to meet you, Reid and Hannah. How about we get you back home?"

THE END

EXCERPT FROM G. MICHAEL HOPF'S NOVEL

CRIES OF A DYING WORLD

———

PRESENT DAY

Traveling at 30,333 miles per hour and spanning over eleven kilometers in diameter, Asteroid Colossus made impact three hundred and thirteen miles northeast off the coast of the Hawaiian Islands.

The Earth shook. The seas heaved, and the planet groaned as massive chunks of itself were hurled into the lower atmosphere only to rain back down, causing further destruction. The torrid heat from Colossus' impact encircled the globe at a horrifying and inescapable speed of over nine thousand miles per hour. The inferno scorched and sterilized the planet, leaving nothing in its wake.

The impact crater covered an area over one hundred and ten miles in diameter. What lay in the miles-deep crater was nothing more than molten rock similar to the primordial soup that had been the planet six billion years before.

If one were to look back on Earth, they wouldn't recognize her. Gone were the vibrant colors of a once living planet. The deep blues and greens had been replaced by a searing red and charred black.

Hours after Colossus' arrival, over seven billion people were dead. Those who had found shelter deep in the bowels of Earth would eventually look upon those who died as the lucky ones, but theirs is another story entirely.

TWELVE DAYS BEFORE IMPACT

EIGHT MILES WEST OF OCOTILLO, CALIFORNIA

Her eyes were a radiating emerald warmed with inner sea grass. He often got lost in them. And when she'd look upon him, it would pierce his soul with cries of love and desire. Her whisper, soft and quiet enough to make him pay attention, worked, it always worked. Her touch, gentle and loving. Her lips and kisses felt like home. Her aroma, sweet and alluring like rose petals. Her body curved right where it needed, and from her beautiful face to the bottom of her feet, she was perfect, but she always lovingly reminded him that no one was perfect, and that she was simply perfectly imperfect. While he'd relent on those details, these he'd never surrender: she was an angel, his queen, his soulmate, and the love of his life.

"Ethan...I love you."

Those were her final words to him as her radiant eyes closed for the last time. It took them an hour and three men to remove him from the mangled debris of shattered glass, twisted steel, transmission fluid and blood: both his and hers. When she let out her last breath, she not only left this world, but the unborn child she was carrying went with her.

The truck had come out of nowhere, or that was what he remembered. It was the police report, though, that told a different story. His blood alcohol was just over the legal limit, but he had felt fine, and they were only a mile from home. She had normally driven since becoming pregnant, but that night she was tired. What had started with a jovial birthday party for a friend turned into tragedy, and he was to blame.

Out of body. Surreal. There was no other way to describe how he felt as he watched them put her body in a bag while he sat in the back of a police car, his hands cuffed behind his back. Repeatedly he pressed his eyes closed and prayed that he'd open them, and all would be back as it was. The two of them holding hands and laughing. Chatting about the future, baby names and the neutral color they should paint the nursery. Yet, no matter how many times he had played this game of make-believe, using his imagination with hopes of changing the past, it never worked. He'd always open them to the reality that eleven months before, he had killed his wife and unborn child.

Unable to sleep even though he needed to, Ethan lowered his window and looked out over the moonlit desert landscape. Coyotes howled in the distance; their cries always sounded eerie to him. Whenever he heard a coyote howl, he thought of the prey they were pursuing. The animal's heart thumping as it raced to escape the jaws of death. For billions of people around the world, they too were praying and hoping to find salvation or an escape from what was coming. Maybe it was best to not know. Be like the coyote. It wasn't living in fear right now. It was hungry and doing what coyotes do: hunt and kill. Theirs was a simple existence, blissfully ignorant that an asteroid larger than the one that had killed the dinosaurs was hurtling towards them. He sometimes wished he too was ignorant of Earth's fate, but that wasn't to be. Nope, he had the privilege, or that was what his older brother, Eric, had told him. He had a spot, two actually, in a bunker that had been built so some would survive the apocalypse, this extinction-level event that was being caused by a piece of rock called Colossus.

Who comes up with these names?, he thought. Sounded like the name a screenwriter would come up with, or maybe it was just some twisted astrophysicist's joke; nevertheless, that was the name of this monster left over from the dawn of the solar system, which was on a collision course with Earth.

It had been two days since the new president, not sworn in a day at the time, had gone on national television to inform Americans and the world of their fate. A fate the previous administration had known about for five years, but now admitted had been covered up to prevent societal collapse years before. The irony is the powers that be weren't really concerned about the chaos of this knowledge on the average person, they just wanted the time to build their bunkers, and they had gotten the time. Five years to plan, build, and coordinate in relative peace and prosperity while everyone else went about their lives thinking they'd have a future. However, the new president had thrown a curveball. Those who believed they had a spot in the bunker, dubbed Ark, up until days ago soon discovered that spot wasn't secure. With a new president comes new rules, new policies, and new political friends to help.

This was why Ethan was on the side of Interstate 8 outside of Ocotillo, California, with a destination of Tempe, Arizona. Eric worked for the new president and had secured two seats, one for Ethan and one for Ethan's estranged son, Chance. The plane was leaving in ten days from Hill Air Force Base in Utah. All Ethan needed to do was get there and do so in the bitter cold month of January. It seemed easy enough, but when you threw in the fact that millions of people were coming to grips with their fate, with some acting out violently, this road trip probably wasn't going to go as planned.

Living was one of the last things Ethan had been doing or even wanted to since the accident. However, if he could save Chance, he owed him that. He had called Chance minutes after Eric made his offer, and to his surprise Chance had answered on the first try. Upon giving him the news, Chance agreed to go and to set aside past grievances, but before they could work out the details, the phone went dead. He hadn't been able to reach Chance since except for an occasional text which told him Chance was okay and eagerly awaiting his arrival.

A cool breeze brushed across Ethan's face, bringing with it the unique odor of creosote. In his lap his Sig P239 semi-automatic 9 mm pistol sat; he stared at it and even picked it up to feel the grip. He'd had the Sig for years, having bought it when he lived in Florida, and like him, it had found a home in San Diego when he moved. He and his Sig now had an unhealthy relationship, one of master and servant; and for now, he was still the master although there had been times over the past eleven months he'd almost surrendered his role. Life without Jen had been just bearable enough up until a couple of days ago; then the call came at the right time. He had a purpose now, something to do and someone to help. So for right now, the Sig would remain the servant. He opened the center console and set the Sig inside.

The coyotes howled again, but now their song began to lull him to sleep. Like he had done since losing her, he thumbed his phone to his voicemail, found the message he wanted, and hit play.

"Hi, sweetie, I know I didn't get to say it, as I was in a hurry, but I love you so much. You're my life, my sun and stars. Have a great day."

He hit play again; her words soaked into his soul. Over and over, he repeated the message until he fell asleep.

———

Continue CRIES OF A DYING WORLD

ABOUT THE AUTHOR

G. Michael Hopf is a *USA Today* bestselling author of over forty books, including the international bestselling post-apocalyptic series, *THE NEW WORLD*. He is a prominent name in the post-apocalyptic, western and paranormal genres. To date he has sold well over one million copies of his books worldwide with many being translated into German, French and Spanish.

He is the Co-Founder and Managing Partner of Beyond The Fray Publishing and is a proud veteran of the United States Marine Corps.

facebook.com/gmichaelhopf
twitter.com/GMichaelHopf1
instagram.com/gmichaelhopf